The Arrangement

Also by Sylvia Day

Scandalous Liaisons
Ask for It
Passion for the Game
A Passion for Him
Don't Tempt Me
The Stranger I Married
Seven Years to Sin
Pride and Pleasure
In the Flesh

Also by Minerva Spencer

Dangerous
Barbarous
Scandalous

Also by Kristin Vayden

Gentlemen of Temptation series:

Falling from His Grace
Escaping His Grace
The Temptation of Grace

Elk Heights Ranch series:

Heart of a Cowboy
The Courage of a Cowboy
The Cowgirl Meets Her Match

The Arrangement

SYLVIA DAY

Minerva SPENCER

Kristin VAYDEN

ZEBRA BOOKS
KENSINGTON PUBLISHING CORP.

www.kensingtonbooks.com

CONTENTS

———◆———

MISCHIEF AND THE MARQUESS

———◆———

SYLVIA DAY

To Kate Duffy, who saw that I was lost
and showed me the way.
Thank you, Kate.

Acknowledgments

Thank you to my critique partner, Annette McCleave (www.AnnetteMcCleave.com), for her help, and to my friend Renee Luke for the much appreciated support.

CHAPTER 1

———✦———

Northamptonshire, 1817

For most men, spinsters were a breed of female to be avoided at all costs, and under any other circumstances the Marquess of Fontaine would be in hearty agreement with that sentiment. But not in this circumstance. And not in regard to this particular spinster.

"The years have been kind to her," the Dowager Lady Fontaine said, peering out the window beside him. "She is more beautiful than before, despite all that she has suffered."

"It pleases me to hear that," he murmured, his gaze locked on the willowy figure strolling through his rear garden.

He wished he could see her face, but it was shielded from the sun by a wide brim hat and the distance from the second floor window to where she stood made the cataloging of finer details impossible. Lady Sophie Milton-Riley had been barely a woman the last time they met, soft and sweet with a penchant for mischief that had once goaded him to say, *"Why can you never be serious?"* To which she had replied, *"Why can you never relax?"*

She seemed too serious now. She once traversed rooms with an elegant glide that forced him to stare and covet, but her present stride appeared to be confident, sure, and firmly grounded.

"How long will they be visiting?" he asked.

"Presently, a fortnight. But this is the first occasion Lady Sophie has ventured away from home since the scandal. I cannot be certain they will stay the duration."

Sophie had come with her grandmother, who was in collusion with his mother in this poorly veiled matchmaking scheme. The two women had been the best of friends for as long as he could remember. He was certain that in their minds the joining of their progeny in marriage was absolute perfection. Once, he had thought so, too. Back when he was a young lad hopelessly infatuated with the vivacious Sophie. Her feelings for him had been nowhere near as amorous, however, and when she had come of age, it was Lord Langley who had won her favor and her promise to wed.

"If you had not been so rude as to avoid their arrival," his mother said with undisguised chastisement, "you might have made her feel more welcome."

"You told me of their arrival only moments before the fact. It would have been far more appalling for me to greet them when I was mud-stained."

His mother could say nothing to that without admitting more than she wished to. The truth was, she had feared his refusal and so had hidden her actions. He understood why she had resorted to subterfuge, but the precaution was unnecessary. Sophie was welcome here. He held no ill will toward her and wished her nothing but happiness.

The marquess turned away from the velvet-framed window. "My presence is required in London, so I will be departing tomorrow."

"You will not."

He arched a brow. His blond hair was a maternal trait, as were his blue eyes. His mother's angelic features were hardly touched by time and she remained a lauded beauty, the liberal strands of gray in her tresses adding maturity to her youthful appearance. Today she had dressed in soft pink, and she looked not much older than his score and ten years.

"Why must you be so difficult?" she lamented, shaking her head.

"You had a spouse and two sons. How can you not understand the duress placed upon a male alone in the company of three females?"

The dowager mirrored his raised brow. "My dear boy, if you think I am unaware of how often you pay for the dubious privilege of spending time alone with multiple females, you are sadly mistaken."

"Lord save me," he said dryly, moving to sit in the nearby gilded chair with its elaborately carved arms and curved legs. "The horror of discussing my carnal proclivities with you is upsetting my sensibilities. The urge to flee is now overwhelming."

She snorted. "Nonsense."

"I am departing tomorrow, Mother." He lounged, stretching his long legs out and crossing one ankle over the other. "This evening will be sufficient enough time to renew our acquaintance."

"And if it is not sufficient," she asked with obvious hopefulness, "will you stay?"

Justin sighed inwardly. "I am not inventing the affairs

I am required to attend to. I was not expecting visitors, so I made no accommodations for any."

"But these affairs could be delayed, yes?"

"I refuse to speak any further on the matter," Fontaine muttered, "to avoid saying something I may later regret."

His mother joined him, sitting primly on the edge of the opposite cream and gold settee. Her gown was showcased to advantage in the setting of the family parlor, which had been spared the attentions of a decorator for many years.

The baroque style of the room with its elegant moldings and lavish abundance of gilt soothed him. His lineage was old and a source of great pride. This room reminded him of those who had preceded him and strengthened his desire to do justice to those who would follow.

"I was so hopeful when you were courting Lady Julienne," she said morosely. "A shame she is a bit touched."

"Oh?" Both brows rose. "Desiring a love match is a sign of insanity?"

She lifted her chin. "Wedding for love is all well and good, but the girl hadn't the sense to fall in love with you, instead of that Remington scoundrel. I still cannot collect it. What was she thinking?"

The marquess looked away to hide his smile. "That is your maternal pride talking."

"It's common sense," she retorted, "which she is obviously lacking. It is in a female's base nature to choose the strongest, handsomest, most established male in the herd."

"Ah, my day improves," he drawled. "What a relief it is to learn that I am the most impressive bovine in the marriageable lot." He refrained from pointing out that Sophie hadn't selected him either, choosing to betroth an earl of far lesser circumstance.

"You are incorrigible." His mother shook her head, setting the pale gold and silver curls at her nape to swaying.

"And you wish to marry me off to your dearest friend's granddaughter. What does that say about you?"

"I never said anything about marriage," she argued, but her blush betrayed her.

Justin knew when it was best to let a matter rest, so he said nothing, choosing instead to think about Sophie and the scandal that ruined her.

"You have no cause to be nervous," the Countess of Cardington reassured under her breath. "We are among friends."

Lady Sophie Milton-Riley managed a shaky smile against the lip of her sherry glass. "Nervous, *grand-mère*? Never."

She was very nearly terrified, but refused to say so aloud. Her memories of Lord Fontaine were clouded by years and the distorted memories of a child. What she had were mostly impressions, those of a tall youth whom she'd fancied as a golden prince, albeit a rather stern one.

The countess shook her head and shot her "the eye," the look filled with love that said she did not believe a word she was saying. Sophie leaned over and pressed her lips to a wrinkled cheek. "I intend to enjoy myself. I promise."

"Good. Oh!" The countess straightened and her voice lowered. "Here he comes."

Sophie glanced up as the Marquess of Fontaine entered

the lower parlor. Her breath caught, and when his gaze sought her out, she reached quickly for the pianoforte behind her for balance.

Dear God, had he always been so handsome?

He smiled, and she set her glass down before she spilled its contents.

How the devil could she have thought he was a prince? Princes were mortal. Fontaine was a golden *god*, with a body built for carnal sin, wrapped in the chilly infamous English hauteur she had never forgotten. How he used to intimidate her with that steely-eyed stare!

And how very different was her reaction to that same stare now.

Who knew aloofness and aristocratic arrogance could be such a potent lure when mixed with the body and face of Apollo?

There was a very substantial reason why the Marquess of Fontaine was not suitable husband material for her. Sophie was willing, however, to set aside such vital concerns for a moment so that she could admire him properly.

It was one of the few benefits to being a woman with a scandalous reputation. She did not have to lower her eyes and pretend that she wasn't struck nearly witless by his appeal. She could, instead, openly appreciate the male form approaching her with thoroughly masculine feline grace.

Sophie blew out her breath. Her childhood friend had grown into a man well worthy of the many hours Society dedicated to discussing him. He had always been an avid sportsman and his physique proved that he still was. His dark blue velvet jacket required no padding to enhance his broad shoulders, and his breeches were just tight enough to reveal powerful thighs, muscular calves, and . . .

She blinked.

Good heavens! She should not be staring *there*, scandalous past or not.

Jerking her gaze upward, Sophie focused on his lips instead. They were somewhat thin and given his inclination for . . . imperiousness . . . she had remembered them being rather stern. But they were nothing of the sort. Instead they were shamelessly sensual, curved in a way that teased a woman to make him smile. Or whisper shocking things.

Sophie's problem was that she enjoyed shocking things. They were much more fun than non-shocking things, hence the present state of her existence.

The moment he came to a halt before her it became extremely difficult to breathe properly. She bowed her head as she curtsied, hiding her confused frown. After all these years, he still unnerved her.

With a furtive gaze, Sophie watched as the marquess charmed her *grand-mère* into blushing, then he returned his attention to her. She hoped that she managed a semblance of a smile, but with her heart racing, she could not be sure.

"Lady Sophie," Fontaine murmured, lifting her gloved hand to his lips. "A pleasure to see you again."

She took note of his voice, which was deeper now and warm, so at odds with his rather formidable, icy exterior. How like him to be so starch-stiff and formal. And how like her to be so irritated by it. His composure had always goaded her to do rash things to break through it, and tonight was no exception. She set her hands on his chest for balance, lifted to her tiptoes, and pressed a quick kiss to his cheek.

"You look well, my lord," she returned, meeting his shocked gaze directly. Her lips tingled, forcing her to wrinkle her nose. She recalled suffering similar reactions to him when she was younger, which had prompted her to tell him that she was allergic to his arrogance. His reply, if she remembered correctly, had been a snort.

"Shall we?" the dowager marchioness asked, gesturing across the hall to the dining room.

For a moment longer, Fontaine stared at Sophie with a narrowed gaze, then he gave a curt nod and offered his arm to the countess.

The rest of the evening passed in a blur of casual discourse and more serious discussion regarding Lord Hastings and India. The meal was impressive and served over many courses. From the marquess's jest comparing the meal to the prince regent's now legendary banquet at the Brighton Pavilion back in January, Sophie collected that his lordship recognized the aim to keep them seated and talking as long as possible. She wondered how he felt about her visit and if he realized, as she did, that they were being paired. She needed to speak with him privately to know, and also to enlist his help. The dissuading of the countess and dowager was too great a task for one individual.

And so it was that Sophie found herself pacing outside Fontaine's private rooms after everyone retired. As apprehensive as she was about meeting with him alone, she forged ahead out of necessity. There was no other solution. She required his assistance in extricating them from this shameless matchmaking. They could not marry—a man of the marquess's station would never accept a woman in her circumstances, regardless of their past friendship— but neither could they simply point that out and be done with the business. The dowager and the countess knew everything, and it apparently had not swayed them. But if

Fontaine was willing to work with her to prove her point, they could prevail.

She sighed and came to an abrupt halt before the door.

Fontaine was known for his impeccable deportment and faultless manners. She could not predict how he would respond to the gross deviation of propriety she had committed so many years ago. He had been polite and dryly charming at dinner, but they had witnesses then. Now they would be alone and perhaps his true feelings would be aired. She had suffered and survived malicious gossip and been ostracized. But Justin . . .

Sophie swallowed hard. Dear God, how would she bear it if he was cruel?

Of course, there was only one way to find out.

Sophie lifted her chin, squared her shoulders, and knocked on the paneled door.

CHAPTER 2

⟡

The moments that passed after Sophie knocked seemed an eternity. She forced herself to breathe in and out with slow, deep breaths and wait, rather than scamper back to her room and find another way. Finally the door was opened by a manservant who was most likely Fontaine's valet. The smile she gave him was both a greeting and an expression of relief.

"Good evening," she said cheerfully. "I wish to speak with his lordship, if I may."

There was a pause as the man blinked wide eyes at her, then a large hand curled around the top of the door and pulled it open farther.

Fontaine came into view looking even better than he had at dinner. Then he had been fully, faultlessly dressed. Now he was sans coat, waistcoat, and cravat, the opening at his collar revealing honey-colored skin and a light dusting of pale blond hair. He looked relaxed and far less rigid than he had earlier, a softening her female sensibilities enjoyed far too much.

"Lady Sophie," he murmured, in the deep voice of a pure male. "An unexpected pleasure, to be sure."

"Might I come in, my lord?"

"This is my bedchamber," he pointed out.

She gave him a wry look. "Yes, I know."

His mouth twitched at the corners. "If you wish to compromise me, I must tell you that asking permission first is a rather odd way to go about it."

Sophie blew out her breath and tapped her foot impatiently. "Why must you always be so difficult? Have you any notion—"

He reached out and hauled her into the room.

Dismissing his valet, he then shut the door, enclosing them in a space that smelled strongly of him, a delicious blend of bergamot and tobacco that stirred her in ways she wasn't prepared for.

Needing distance between them, she stepped farther into his space. Her gaze drifted across the large, well-appointed chamber. Decorated in dark woods and shades of gold and brown, it reminded her of a lion's den and suited its master perfectly, as did the two matching, fully grown mastiffs who approached her.

You've no need to fear them," he assured her. "They are quite gentle."

"Well, hello," she greeted, extending both hands. The massive fawn-colored beasts pressed their great muzzles into her palms and sniffed. Apparently finding her acceptable, they welcomed her with copious amounts of viscous drool. She glanced over her shoulder at the marquess. "What do you call them?"

"George and Edward."

"Truly? How unusual."

"They share their names with the two gentlemen who were with me when I purchased them as pups. Since both men felt the need to jest at length about salivating animals, I deemed them appropriate monikers."

"Lovely!" Sophie laughed, pleasantly surprised by his sense of humor, which she did not remember ever seeing much of.

She watched him step behind the screen in the corner and when he returned, gratefully accepted the damp cloth he offered to wipe her hands. "They are beautiful dogs."

"I think so," he said easily, watching her with a stare that made her feel slightly breathless. His intensity had always frightened her a little, although she could not collect why. He would never hurt her; she knew that like she knew the sun would rise in the morn.

Moving to one of the two wingback chairs in front of the fire, Sophie sat and tugged a footstool closer so she could set her slippered feet upon it.

"Please, make yourself comfortable," he teased, taking a seat opposite her. The way he filled the chair caught her attention. He did not sit with any sort of straightness to his spine, as she would expect. Fontaine lounged like a king of the jungle, his long legs stretched out and his back angled into the groove between the chair back and the wing. George and Edward studied him a moment, then shuffled over to the footstool and set their giant heads atop each of her feet.

"They like you," he said.

"I like them."

"I thought you hated dogs, or were afraid of them. Some such. You could not tolerate Lady Cardington's pet. His name eludes me now . . ."

"Max, and he was a beast. I like dogs, truly. But Maximillian was not a dog; he was a demon. He chewed up my best shoes and lifted his leg on my bedpost at every opportunity." She smiled suddenly. "But I am grateful for him now, because he works in our favor."

"Oh? How so?"

"*Grand-mère* refused to see how horrid that animal was. I tried to tell her, but my complaints fell on deaf ears. He was wickedly clever and always on his best behavior for her."

"So you invented a fear of canines?" The chastising shaking of his head was tempered by obvious indulgence.

"The feigned phobia served its purpose," she said. "And now it will be one of the many points of contention between you and me."

He grinned, and she was riveted.

Tilting her head to the side, Sophie contemplated her old friend with new eyes. How dashing he looked in his inelegant sprawl with his throat revealed to her gaze. He had always been uncommonly handsome, but the intimate pose made him seem overwhelmingly so. Where once he had been lean and youthful, he was now large and mature. His features were more angular, his gaze more knowing. Sophie could not shake the feeling that she had just walked into a predator's lair.

"So we are to be contentious." His lips twisted wryly. "I am not certain how to feel about so much effort being expended to avoid marriage to me."

"Relieved?" she suggested blithely. "If I left the matter to you, you would most likely pronounce that you'd never marry a woman such as me, and that would goad them to dig in their heels. I am saving you endless trouble."

"You believe I would never wed you," he repeated, frowning.

Sophie drummed her fingers restlessly against the

end of the armrest. "Of course not. I would drive you to insanity."

"Perhaps I would like that."

"Stuff," she scoffed.

"Hmm . . ."

"Hmm?"

"Never mind. So tell me, how are you faring, Sophie?" The low, intimate timbre of his voice was slightly distracted, as if part of his mind was occupied with other thoughts.

She offered a small smile. "As well as can be expected, my lord."

"Justin," he corrected.

"Justin." Her gaze lowered to his throat, which she could not seem to resist looking at. "How are you? You look . . . well."

He tilted his head in acknowledgment. "Thank you. I am." There was a short pause, then, "How is your son?"

"Thomas is wonderful." Sophie smiled at the thought of him. "He's quite the loveliest thing in my life. But I shan't bore you with the details."

"If a topic interests you, it interests me. Does Thomas look like you?"

"No." Sophie frowned, startled by the marquess's words, which were delivered without inflection. "He looks like his father, thankfully. A blessing I appreciate immeasurably."

Lifting her hand, she rubbed at the space between her brows where an ache was building. She had been plagued with megrims in the months after Langley's passing, and the stress of her first outing and her unexpected reaction to Fontaine were bringing back echoes of that pain.

"I am sorry for your loss," he murmured.

"Thank you." Her hand dropped back into her lap. "But I have my son and I am tremendously grateful for him. He has been a brilliant light during a very dark time."

She had been faced with people who intimated that it would have been better had she lost the babe. The very suggestion angered her in a way nothing else could. To propose that the loss of her child would have been preferable to the loss of social standing was so heinous she could not credit it.

"Where is the boy now?"

"With Langley's younger brother—the current Lord Langley—and his family. Thomas visits with them often. He is a tangible piece of his father, and they cherish him."

"You are very brave, Sophie."

She studied Fontaine, attempting to discern if he was being facetious or not. She saw only sympathy. "No, I am not brave. Not at all. I have survived. That does not make me courageous; it is merely a testament of my stubbornness."

His mouth curved. "Call it what you like. I admire you a great deal. I doubt I would have weathered the storm near as well."

The combined effect of that smile and his praise left Sophie speechless. She was taken aback by how it affected her, warming her from the inside, loosening the tight knot of apprehension she had not known was there. When had his opinion become so important? Or . . . perhaps it had always been important.

"I would not have expected you to be supportive," she admitted, her damp palms wrapping around the end of the armrests.

"Why not?"

"Because you were forever chastising me when we were children."

The marquess's eyes widened. "I was not."

"Yes, you were. I remember the incidences quite clearly, especially that day in the garden when you shouted at me and I nearly fell. Scared me witless."

"Are you referring to the time you were attempting to climb to the top of the pagoda?" He snorted. "It was you who scared the wits from me! I rounded the corner in search of you and there you were, hanging some distance from the ground by only your fingertips. My heart stopped beating altogether. You could have killed yourself."

She snorted back. "As if you cared for my health. It simply offended your aristocratic sensibilities to see a female engaged in such sport."

Outwardly, Justin was fairly certain he maintained his composure. Inwardly, he was stunned. Sophie could not believe that. Not truly. "Are you daft?"

Sophie blinked her thickly lashed green eyes at him. "Beg your pardon?"

"If you believe I wished to hold you back due to your gender rather than out of concern for the safety of your person you are sorely mistaken."

As she continued to stare at him as if he had grown two heads, Justin in turn stared at the ravishing creature who sat across from him and felt a bit . . . addled. In his mind, he had held an image of her as she had looked the last time they met. She had been ten and nine months, slender yet lushly built, her hair a riot of dark chocolate curls shot with striking strips of burgundy. Full red lips and those lovely eyes had rounded out the picture of a beauty on the verge of blossoming. He had watched her grow from a child to a woman, accompanying his mother on every visit to Lady Cardington's just to witness the transformation. Biding his time. Waiting for the day when she would be his.

A day that had never come.

His mother had been the one to tell him that Sophie had accepted Lord Langley's addresses. After that, he never returned to the Cardington dower house again.

In the years since, his memories had not aged her. She had been arrested in that moment in time. Because of this, the vision who had greeted him in the parlor before dinner took him completely by surprise.

His mother was right. The years had been kind to Sophie, turning her youthful attractiveness into an intoxicating blend of innate sensuality and fully ripened curves. When she had kissed his cheek, the smell of her and the feel of her warm body so close to his had thrust home an undeniable truth—he still wanted her. This time with a man's desire, not a boy's infatuation.

And dear, sweet Sophie apparently had no notion of the hunger she had awakened. Otherwise she would not be visiting his private rooms and reclining in a way that bared her ankles. He was in a riot of lust over that view, such as many a naked woman had been unable to incite in him. The desire to press his lips to that tiny part of her rode him hard. He wanted to push up the hem of her skirts and follow the length of her lithe legs with his mouth. He wanted to spread her thighs wide and lick inside her, drink her in, hear the sounds she made when lost in climax.

"My lord . . . Justin."

She squirmed slightly, and he realized his lengthening silence was making her uncomfortable. He forced himself to look away. "Yes?"

He heard her sigh. "I feel as if we are strangers."

"Does that disturb you?"

"Yes, it does. Is it possible that you might stay a few more days?"

Justin refrained from smiling. That had been his intent ever since she kissed him in the parlor, but it was fortuitous that she asked. "Why?"

He could see that she was attuned to the growing sensual awareness he felt building between them. Her gaze roamed often from the top of his head to his polished Hessians and back up again, the green irises dark with female appreciation.

But the rapid lift and fall of her chest betrayed her unease. She had not expected to desire him, and therefore had no defenses in place to manage the attraction.

Which worked perfectly for him. He would ensure that she remained unsettled and unguarded so he could slip inside her . . . in every way possible.

"Because *grand-mère* will never believe we are ill-suited if she doesn't reach the conclusion on her own."

His gaze narrowed. "Are we ill-suited, Sophie?"

Again she looked at him as if he were an anomaly she could not classify. "Don't tease, Justin. You know my circumstances make me unacceptable for you. Besides which, I would never marry a man who did not love my son as much as I do."

"I am curious," he said softly. "What type of woman would you deem 'acceptable' for me?"

Sophie tucked a loose strand of hair behind her ear and waved her hand, both gestures betraying her nervousness. "Someone such as Lady Julienne Montrose, I suppose." A flush spread across her cheeks.

"Interesting." Pleasure filled him that she had kept apprised of his activities. "Perhaps it will surprise you to learn that the qualities I most enjoyed in Lady Julienne were ones that reminded me of you—her ability to disregard the opinions of the *ton*, her mischievous nature, and warm sensuality."

"My lord!" Her hand lifted to her throat.

He offered a wolfish smile, relishing the chance to shock her for a change. "I am quite serious."

Her cheeks flushed. "You are not."

"Who are you trying to convince? You can save your breath if you are attempting to sway me. I know a passionate woman when I see one."

"This conversation is ridiculous." Her arms crossed over her chest. "I am trying to extricate you from this mess, and you are making things difficult as usual."

"As usual? I have always been accommodating," he said smoothly.

She snorted. "You have been driving me mad for years."

On this particular occasion, Justin was fairly certain that the reason why she was maddened was for just the reason he'd like and if assisting her kept her within his grasp long enough to act upon it, he had no objections. "How can I help you?"

"If you could manage to delay your departure for a few days, we could contrive ways to demonstrate how we are completely inappropriate for one another—such as your love for dogs and my dislike of them. Not simply because we are contrary progeny who refuse to heed the wisdom of our elders, but because we are a disaster together."

"A disaster?" By the time all was said and done, he would know every reason why she had never considered him for marriage. He would know everything about her, including all the ways he could make her come.

"Well"—she shrugged—"something similar to that, if we have any luck at all. Imagine the fun! Eventually, they will retreat from their plans, hopefully before we cause any permanent damage."

Justin laughed.

And Sophie was captivated.

Merriment transformed him, thawed him. Fine lines spread out from the corners of his eyes, revealing how often he found amusement in his life. Suddenly, Sophie wished she knew the man who had earned those laugh lines, the private one. Someone he had recently become. Or perhaps he'd always had a hidden side? One she had failed to see?

The prickle of sexual awareness she had felt all evening intensified to the point where she was forced to rub her arms. She stared at him, unable to look away. His smile slowly faded, his expression altering to become fiercely intent. It made her shiver, that look. And he had been giving it to her ever since she'd entered his bedchamber.

"Have you been alone since Langley passed?" he asked in an intimate murmur.

"I have my son."

"That is not what I meant, and well you know it."

Sophie tugged her feet out from under George's and Edward's great heads and stood. "Heavens, it's late."

Fontaine rose as well, and followed her to the door. She reached for the knob and was startled when he came up behind her, his palm pressed to the panel over her head, preventing her from leaving. Caged by his big body, there was no way to avoid breathing in the scent of his skin. It was delicious, as was the warmth that radiated from him. He moved closer, pressing his front to her back. She began to pant. The knowledge that he was fully, impressively aroused was inescapable.

She was tormented by her confusion. Reconciling the seductive male behind her with the aloof boy she knew from the past was beyond difficult. There had been a measure of safety in the distance inherent in friendship. Now, the imaginings in her mind of the two of them as lovers bridged that gap.

"Your heart is racing," he whispered, his breath hot against her skin. His tongue swept across the vein that fluttered madly at her throat. Her back arched and a startled cry escaped her.

"A portion of your response is desire." His open mouth brushed behind her ear and she shuddered violently. "But a portion of it is fear. Why? You must know that I would never hurt you."

Unable to speak, Sophie agreed with a jerky nod. His teeth bit gently into the tender flesh where her shoulder met her neck. Her knees weakened and his free arm came around her, banding at her waist to support her. Taking further liberties, his thumb stroked the side of her breast in a soothing rhythm that did nothing to calm her.

Sophie's eyes closed and her damp forehead rested against the door. His chest labored against her back; the heat of his body set hers on fire. Her nipples peaked hard and tight, aching. As if he knew, he cupped her breast and kneaded it. Her sex clenched in rhythm with his grasp and she grew wet, slippery, and hot.

"Oh dear God," she moaned, quaking. How did a woman manage a desire such as this? She had lusted for Langley and relished his lovemaking, but those emotions had not reached this depth. She hadn't the experience required to control her responses. "You overwhelm me. I cannot think or breathe."

"And I am undone." His mouth was moving over her bared skin. Nipping, licking, biting. "This is passion, Sophie. Need and hunger."

"It is insanity, my l–lord." Her voice broke as he continued to fondle her intimately. "With a small ch–child dependent upon me, I cannot afford to go in–insane."

"There is only one cure," he murmured. "Shall we administer it?"

She shook her head, but lack of energy gave the movement no strength. "I do not understand . . . what is happening."

Justin breathed deeply. "We are becoming lovers, sweet Sophie. *Finally.*"

He tilted his head and took her mouth. She gasped at the contact, the tingling of her lips urging her to press them hard against his. Her angle was awkward, but she did not care. The kiss was perfect, his lips so soft, yet firm, the taste of him dark and delectable. She could not temper the ardent way she answered him. Her response was instinctual and greedy.

The groan that left his throat made her shiver, so filled with rough longing and ravenous need. He licked deep inside her, his tongue gliding back and forth against hers, the measured tempo blatantly erotic. She whimpered softly as tension coiled in her womb. He pulled back at the sound, breathing harshly. "Stay with me tonight."

Her lower lip quivered, her thoughts scattered and unable to settle. Justin licked the soft curve of her mouth, his touch so reverent it coaxed a tear to blur her vision, then slip down her cheek. He wrenched himself away. She felt his loss keenly; the lack of his warmth left her cold, the lack of his support left her shaky.

"Damn you." The look he gave her scorched. "I can make you stay. I can make you beg me to allow you to stay. But that is not what I want. You will give yourself to me. I will have you no other way."

Sophie turned to face him, lifting her fingers to press against her kiss-swollen lips. "You have always . . ." She reached behind her and gripped the knob.

"Always what?" he asked gruffly, the lust within him a palpable thing, barely leashed.

"Always been too much." With a quick pivot, she opened the door. "Good night, my lord."

She fled, leaving him standing there staring after her.

George whined softly. Edward paced at the threshold.

Justin knew just how they felt.

CHAPTER 3

―――――◆―――――

"Lady Sophie said something to me last evening that perplexes me," the marquess murmured to his mother the next morning as they descended the stairs to the lower floor for breakfast.

"Oh?"

"Yes, she said I have always been 'too much.' I've no notion of what that is supposed to mean."

Her mouth curved innocently, an affectation reinforced by her pale ringlets and light blue gown. "Interesting."

He glanced aside at her. "Do you know what she is referring to?"

"Hmm . . . Perhaps she means to say you are over-whelming."

"Yes." Justin scowled. "She said that, too."

"Truly? How did I miss this discussion? I recall you two sat quite some distance from each other in the parlor after dinner."

"Never mind that," he muttered. "Can you explain what the devil she is talking about?"

She linked her slender arm with his. "When you both

were children, she used to make up stories about you. You were a 'prince' most often, though sometimes when you were surly, you were cast as a toad or an ass."

He choked.

"I noted something in her stories. You were usually set atop an intimidating pedestal. A character who ruled over all with an iron fist and nary a smile. She would speak of you with awe."

Justin shook his head, frowning. "I was a boy."

"A very serious boy," she corrected. "You changed a great deal after your father passed on."

"I have a great deal of history to live up to."

"Yes, you do."

"She has a bastard child."

"Yes, she does." The dowager patted his arm. "Your father and I didn't wait either."

His eyes turned heavenward. "I could have lived my entire life without that knowledge, Mother, and been quite content."

"Stuff. Don't be prudish."

Heaving out his breath, the marquess prayed for the rest of his day to improve upon his morning. He had spent restless hours the night before contemplating Lady Sophie and her circumstances, and how he could have her.

Had she stayed the night with him, it would have been something he would have regretted as much as she. A man of his station could not marry a woman in her circumstances; she was absolutely correct about that. Which left him with only one option—to take her as his mistress. It was an offer he could not make to her, not to Sophie. He respected her too much to suggest such an arrangement; the mere thought sickened him.

But not having her at all was impossible. He *would* have her. He only needed to discern *how*.

His mother shot him a narrowed side-glance as they reached the parquet floor of the foyer. "I should like to see a man retain his virginity until marriage."

"How progressive of you," he murmured.

"With all your rumored excesses with females of unsavory reputation, I would think you'd appreciate a woman with a healthy appetite for sexual congress."

"I will not discuss anyone's sexual appetite with you, not mine and most definitely not yours." He steered her toward the dining room.

"Why not?"

"I would rather go to the tooth-drawer's," Justin muttered, "or wear a hair shirt."

He assisted her into her chair at the end of the table. "I have decided to remain in residence for a few more days, but that does not mean you should send for the parson. Do I make myself clear?"

The startled, yet hopeful glance the dowager bestowed on him over her shoulder made him smile and bend to kiss her cheek. God help him, he adored her, daft as she was.

That same kiss—when witnessed by Sophie as she entered the dining room—inspired tender feelings of a different sort. Her stomach fluttered madly in response. She came to an abrupt halt in the doorway, her *grand-mère*'s arm wrapped around hers.

"See?" Lady Cardington whispered. "A good man. Do not let that stiff-as-pudding exterior fool you."

Sophie could say that she wasn't fooled, not after visiting his rooms last night, but she held her tongue and shivered when he straightened and caught sight of her. The look he gave her flared instantly from innocuous to indecent.

"Good morning, my lord," she greeted, in a voice remarkably composed.

He approached them with that animal grace that made her breathing shallow. All the incongruities about him intrigued her so much. The unflappable deportment mixed with latent sensuality. The dry wit mixed with the wicked gleam in his eyes. Arrogantly arched brows over glances filled with pure male appreciation.

Such as the glance he was heating her with right at this very moment.

Sophie took a deep breath. She had chosen her day gown of soft green trimmed in darker green ribbon because it was her best. The long sleepless night had been spent wondering if the marquess's attraction to her had been spurred by the late hour or if he would still desire her in the light of day. Now that she knew the answer, she had even more to consider.

She held no illusions. Nothing could ever come of this attraction. A man of Justin's station could not marry a woman in her position and mothers did not become mistresses, at least not *this* mother. Despite this, she worried that she would succumb to his seduction if she remained under his roof. He had awakened a hunger in her that had gnawed at her all night. She could not take the chance that feeding it would not appease it.

"Lady Sophie," he murmured in that warm, rich-as-honey voice. "Lady Cardington."

Fontaine took her *grand-mère*'s arm and led her to the table. Sophie followed. Once the countess was seated, he turned to her. "Shall we?"

He gestured toward the covered salvers on the buffet. She nodded and joined him, taking in his fine form so elegantly displayed in brown breeches and coat, with a multicolored embroidered waistcoat to counter the austerity. It suited the man he had become, somber yet possessed of a more colorful side that he showed only rarely.

"You steal my breath," he whispered.

She looked away, afraid her expressive face would reveal too much. "Thank you."

"Thank *you*. Already my day is complete, now that I have seen you."

As Fontaine reached for a plate, Sophie reached for the pepper with a shaking hand. As she sprinkled the spice into her palm, she glanced at the two women at the table and noted that they were engrossed in a discussion. She exhaled sharply.

"Do you remember the time we picked flowers and I had a reaction to one of them? The pollen or some such?"

He stared at her quizzically. "Of course I remember. You sneezed for hours."

"Do you recall the treatment?"

"It was long ago."

"I changed my garments, blew my nose, and applied a cold compress."

"Are we reminiscing?" His mouth curved fondly and she was struck by guilt. "If so, I remember more pleasant memories."

"Forgive me," she whispered. Then she lifted her hand and blew him a kiss, which also served to blow pepper—

—right up his lordship's aquiline nose.

"Good God!" he shouted, staring at her in wide-eyed horror. Then he sneezed.

And sneezed.

And sneezed.

"Dear heavens!" the dowager cried, pushing back from the table in a rush. "What is the matter with you, Fontaine?"

His reply was a sneeze. Then another. And another. He doubled over, sneezing like a madman.

Patting his back sympathetically and ignoring the fulminating glare his reddened eyes shot in her direction, Sophie said, "I cannot be certain, my lady, but it appears he is having an olfactory fit of some sort." She leaned over and stared at him, then leapt back when he sneezed violently.

"Heinous!" he gasped at her, covering his mouth in a vain attempt to curb his pulmonary spasms.

"What could it be?" the dowager asked, as she hurried over to them. "I have never seen him like this."

"He is having a paroxysm, obviously," the countess pronounced, joining them at the buffet. "A violent reaction to something that does not agree with his constitution."

"If he has never been this way before, perhaps it is my presence that distresses?" Sophie suggested.

"Ridiculous!" the countess and dowager negated in unison.

Sophie shrugged. "Of course you both would know better than I, but it seems that the offending smell would have to be recently introduced, and I just thought—"

She was cut off by more sneezing and offered a sympathetic glance that was met with a scowl. "It would probably be best for me to break the fast in my room. If his lordship improves, then we shall know it's me. Perhaps my perfume? He told me yesterday evening that it was"—she winced—"not to his liking."

"My lord!" the two women chastised, sounding every bit like offended mother hens.

"Vixen," Justin hissed.

"Fontaine!" the dowager protested. "It is not Lady Sophie's fault that your olfactory sense is overly sensitive. Personally, I think she smells lovely."

"He could be allergic to me," Sophie continued, raising her voice to be heard over the noise the marquess was making. "The removal of my person should rectify the problem. If he worsens, then we will have to search for another culprit."

Stepping gingerly away, Sophie noted the watery eyes and reddened nose of the Marquess of Fontaine, and felt odious. But an hour or so of discomfort could spare them a lifetime of regret. When considered in that light, her actions were somewhat less reprehensible.

"I do hope you feel better soon," she said to Justin, meaning every word.

His lordship replied with a galvanic sneeze.

"Has Lord Fontaine's condition improved?" Sophie asked her *grand-mère* as they sat in the private sitting room that bisected their two chambers. Decorated in pale blue and white with delicately carved furniture, it was a relaxing retreat, yet Sophie was anything but soothed.

"Yes." The countess sighed. "He felt better soon after you retired."

"Oh, good."

"It is not good. Not at all."

Sophie looked down at the book in her hands and felt awful to have caused the disappointment she heard in the beloved voice. "You can still enjoy your visit with Lady Fontaine. I can keep myself occupied."

"That is not the point. Fontaine is a powerful man who

occupies the highest strata of society. His friendship is extremely valuable, and he has a *tendré* for you."

"He does not!" Sophie felt the blush sweep up her cheeks and into her hairline. How obvious was the attraction between them?

The countess shook her head. "Child, he may have grown past it now, but he was once quite smitten with you. Affection for first loves lingers for a lifetime."

"He was not smitten!" she denied vehemently, even as her heart leapt at the thought. "I would have known if he was."

"I wondered if you were blind to it." Her *grand-mère* sighed.

"Why do you think he accompanied his mother so often? A man of his station had more important matters to attend to."

Sophie snapped her book closed and rose to her feet, agitated. "You are mistaken. He . . . he . . ."

"Do not think to say that he came because of his mother. Fontaine is not the type of man to be tied to any woman's apron strings." The countess abandoned her needlepoint on the small walnut table beside her, and linked her fingers in her lap. "Did you never wonder why he ceased to visit after your betrothal was announced?"

Sweat misted Sophie's forehead. "He was always so critical . . . so chastising . . . he—"

"Critical? Or concerned? You were forever involved in some scrape or another. You were angry and unruly, most likely due to the premature death of your parents. You took unnecessary risks and defied convention. I was worried about you, but knew that the more I intervened, the more you would resist. I expected you would outgrow such behavior, which you did. However, Fontaine was less patient."

"He wanted me to be someone I am not!"

"He wanted you safe. Did he ever ask you to curb your mischief? How often did he depart with ruined attire from following you into another mess?"

Spinning away, Sophie found herself breathing with difficulty, images from the past rushing forward in a deluge. "I don't know . . ." Her hand lifted to her chest and rubbed ineffectually at the ache there. She wondered if she had hurt him in her ignorance. It pained her dreadfully to think of it.

"He appears to hold no ill will toward you, and his support could do much to improve your circumstance. It is unfortunate that he has acquired intolerance for your person." Her *grandmère* studied her a moment and then offered a smile. "Perhaps you could refrain from wearing your perfume?"

Sophie rubbed the back of her neck. "That will change nothing. We are completely unsuitable. He prefers blondes, such as Lady Julienne—"

"And you prefer brunettes such as Langley."

"Yes, well . . ." She had adored Langley, loved him madly, had thought him the most charming man in the world. But she lusted for the golden marquess. Hungered for him. Ached for him in unmentionable places. When he entered the room, her body hummed with energy that wanted spending in a bed.

But she was also frightened by that need for him. How could she, a woman of so many faults, live up to the expectations of a man who seemed to have no faults at all?

"Regardless"—Sophie cleared her clenched throat— "I have Thomas, and Lord Fontaine requires a woman as different from me as night is to day. Even Rothschild washed his hands of me."

"Your brother is a self-centered idiot." The countess patted the vacant seat next to her on the gilded settee. "He will have his comeuppance one day. That is the way fate works."

Sinking into the proffered space, Sophie leaned into her *grand-mère* and set her head on the frail shoulder. The scent of jasmine made her eyes water, the memories of a less complicated time bringing sadness. Now she was looking at the past with new eyes, remembering earlier conversations with new ears, feeling new emotions.

Wondering what she would have done then, if she had known what she knew now.

CHAPTER 4

———◆———

When the knock came to Justin's bedchamber door after dinner, the smile that curved his mouth was mirrored inside him. George and Edward immediately rolled to their bellies from their previous positions on their sides, then they padded over to the door at the same time Sophie's husky voice drifted to his ears.

Justin rose from the chair before the fire. "Show her in," he said to his valet, "then you may go."

Inside him, something wild coiled tight, prepared to spring. But when Sophie came into view with sad eyes and her lower lip caught nervously between straight white teeth, it quieted abruptly. She was wound up as well, but not for the same reasons he was.

"Who knew such mischief could hide beneath the exterior of an angel?" he murmured, attempting to calm her with gentle teasing.

She was dressed in deep blue this evening, the cut of the bodice and sleeves so painfully simple that on a lesser woman, it would have been plain. On Sophie, however, it allowed her lush figure to take the stage. She had kept herself sequestered all day, tormenting him with the knowledge that she was under his roof, yet unreachable.

With her head bowed, she said, "I meant no harm."

Her palpable unhappiness disturbed him. "Why do I feel that you are upset about more than my inability to smell a blasted thing all day?"

"I am sorry about that, too," she said contritely, startling him by stepping closer and running the tip of her index finger down the bridge of his nose. The innocent touch nearly undid him. It was the first intimate connection she had ever initiated. "I thought only of escape."

"Escape?" he asked gruffly, his body reacting to her proximity and the scent of her skin.

She stepped back and clasped her hands. "Did I misunderstand our previous relationship?"

Justin arched a brow.

Sophie looked deep into his eyes, searching. "Have you ever contemplated walking on the surface of the moon?"

The other brow rose to meet the first.

"I never have," she continued, her tongue flickering out to wet her lips. "Not until this afternoon when *grand-mère* suggested that perhaps you once cared for me beyond mere friendship and I attempted to conceive of something more impossible."

"Sophie—"

Holding up a hand, she halted his speech. "If I wounded you, I never meant to. I was simply unaware. It never occurred to me that a man such as you would ever find me . . . would ever find anything—"

"Sophie—"

"You were always so damn perfect, so poised, so rigid . . . so . . . so . . . so *arrogant*!" She pointed an agitated and accusing finger at him. "Always ordering me about and correcting me and . . . and . . . and—"

Justin glanced heavenward, then snatched her to him and kissed her full on her indignant mouth.

"Mmpf . . . !" A weak protest died before it was born. She melted into him, all soft warm passionate woman.

Heat flared instantly, burning across his skin and setting his blood on fire. Cupping her nape, he held her still, fitting his mouth to hers. Taking it. Possessing it. As he should have done years ago.

Her hands pushed at his shoulders, then slid up and over them, thrusting into his hair. He growled, maddened by the simple contact, aroused to bursting, his cock hard and throbbing. Cupping her hip, he urged her closer, grinding his erection into the soft flesh of her lower belly. She surged into him in response, feverish and ardent, her body writhing in his grasp. Her grip on his scalp began to hurt and he welcomed the pain. It grounded him. Otherwise, he feared he would pull her to the floor, push up her skirts, and show her how far beyond friendship his feelings went.

Sophie yanked her head to the side, panting. "I cannot breathe." His mouth moved to her throat, then to her shoulder. "Justin." Her hands roamed over the length of his back, caressing through the fine linen of his shirt. "You entice me to give what I shouldn't."

The sob in her voice struck him with the force of a blow to the gut and pained him as deeply.

With a growl, he pushed her away.

They stood apart, breathing harshly, flushed and disheveled. He ran his hands through his hair, feeling the sweat that dampened the roots. His entire frame was tight, tense, hard, his jaw clenched.

"I am at a loss," he said, his hands fisting. "I cannot have you, and yet I cannot conceive of not having you. Not when this"—he gestured between them—"is all I can think about."

"I am so confused." Her green eyes were dark and fathomless. "I feel . . . for you . . ."

"Say no more. I am a man, not a saint."

"I loved him. He made me happy."

"It pleases me to know that you were content."

"I know it does." Her hand lifted and came over her heart. "I would not change my past because it gave me both beautiful memories and my son, and yet all day I have been haunted by imaginings of what could have been. Where would we be in our lives if I had known?"

"All this time, I thought you were aware and chose differently regardless."

"No." She held her hand out to him, but he did not take it, afraid of what he would do if they touched again. Her arm lowered slowly. "I have no wish to hurt you."

"This is not your fault, Sophie. Any guilt you might feel is unwarranted."

"There is no way for us to be together, is there?"

"No way that we could both live with," he said gruffly.

Cursing, he turned from her and crossed to the grate. He rested his arm on the mantel and stared into the fire, willing his burning blood to cool. He could taste her on his lips, smell her on his clothing. She was in the palm of his hand, yet he could not hold on to her. "I will leave in the morning."

"I cannot run you from your own home."

"I prefer it." His eyes closed. "I would smell you here. See you here. Want you here."

"Why? Why me? I make every misstep and you walk true."

Justin looked over his shoulder. She stood where he had left her, watching him, so heartrendingly beautiful in her yearning. "Who can explain the attraction between opposites?"

Her lower lip quivered, yet she stood tall and proud, undaunted by the unkind turns in her life. He wished he could shelter her from more pain and tragedy, but fate was cruel to him as well, mocking him for his youthful caution. He should have made clear how he felt years ago, and left no room for doubt or misunderstanding. All this time, he had thought she was never meant to be his, that she was not capable of deeper affection for him. Now he realized that he might have had his heart's desire, if only he had disregarded his pride and opened himself to her.

"You should return to your room," he murmured, looking away, resigned.

Silence filled the space between them. Only the sounds of the crackling fire and his rapid breathing offered relief.

"Justin . . . ?"

He heard the soft plea in her voice and his back tensed.

She cleared her throat, causing his mouth to twitch. He knew that sound well. It was the sound of her gathering courage.

It was also the herald to mischief.

"I cannot be your wife or mistress," she said in a low, husky voice that warmed his blood like strong wine. "But for tonight . . . I can be your l–lover."

Justin spun to face her, flushing with avid lust and soul-deep longing. "Bloody hell."

Her lovely face took on that obstinate cast he adored. The tapers around the room burnished her, their golden glow gleaming off her creamy skin and glossy curls. "I want . . . I want . . ."

"Christ," he muttered, lacing his fingers at the back of his neck, "I know what you want. Do not give voice to it, or I may not have the strength to resist giving it to you."

Sophie stared at the marquess displayed in the alluring pose, his throat bared to her, his shoulders so broad, his arms flexing powerfully. She licked her lips, and moved toward him. "Why resist?"

"You owe me nothing."

"This is not about the past. This is about now, this moment, when I feel as if something in me is dying. I came to you tonight knowing this visit would lead to farewell, and yet now that we are agreed, I mourn. I haven't the strength to sleep alone tonight, aware that in the morning you will leave and I will not see you again."

His gaze narrowed. "You ask too much from me, Sophie. Better to wonder how it would be, than to know."

"Is it? Would it not be better to live on real memories, than it would be to live on fantasy?" She rounded the wingback.

"And what of tomorrow?"

"We can worry then."

He snorted and dropped his hands to his lean hips. "It is exactly that sort of thinking that lands you into trouble so often."

Lowering her voice, she moved with what she prayed was a seductive sway to her hips. "This time, I hope it lands me into your bed."

The groan that rumbled in his throat made her breasts swell further until they ached.

"I have a confession, my lord."

He waited. Alert. A predator crouched for the pounce.

Sophie shivered, then embraced the driving urge she had to touch him, hold him, clasp him deep within her. Here, in his lair, with its earthy colors and dark, masculine appeal.

Dressed only in his shirtsleeves and trousers, he revealed a glimpse of the man he was in his private hours. A man she could have had. She regretted the loss, although she would not alter her past decisions.

"You see, my lord"—she stepped up to him, coming to a halt a mere inch away—"your supreme self-possession is an irresistible lure. I want to crawl beneath it, see inside you, slip under your skin."

Lifting her hand, she set it over his heart and felt its frantic tempo. She was in much the same state; short of breath with raging blood. "When we were younger, I would sometimes shock you deliberately just to see beneath your exterior."

"You have always been under my skin," he murmured, pulling her into his embrace, where she wanted to be. He seemed to consider her carefully, then he cupped her cheek, staring down at her with a starkly intense gaze. "Be certain, love. Once we walk down this path, there is no turning back."

Sophie soaked in the warmth of his hard body and the rich, spicy scent that clung to him. Just days ago, the thought of him had set her insides aflutter. She felt the same now, but for an entirely different reason. It was no longer the anxiety of reacquainting oneself with someone who had once been dear. It was anticipation and pure, heady desire.

"I have always admired you," she confessed, nuzzling into his palm. "My life has been in such disarray since the death of my parents, but you were so solid and immutable. Even as I provoked you, you strengthened and motivated me. Over the years, I often found myself imagining what you would do and considered that carefully before acting. I would not be the woman I am today had you not been in my life."

Heat flared in his eyes, and he pressed warm, firm lips to her forehead. "I am glad you thought of me."

"I never forgot you. And now . . . how easily you have turned my childhood awe into a woman's fascination. I was told you had the appearance of a god amongst men, but the tales failed to convey how seductive you are."

He snorted.

"Scoff all you like," she said. "It's true. Your voice makes me shiver and your presence inspires shockingly carnal musings."

"Do you imagine my mouth on you?" he asked roughly. "Everywhere? Do you imagine being taken on your hands and knees? Or bound and restrained for my pleasure?"

Her exhale was shaky and she clung to him for balance. Dear God, he sounded so primitive, blatantly defying his civilized exterior and reputation.

"I will *know* you, Sophie," he warned darkly. "I will know every inch of you, every curve and crevice. I will know you as no one else has ever known you. I will own you. Are you prepared to accept that?"

Sophie wondered at the change in him, the sudden seriousness of his bearing. "I want to be with you. However you would have me."

She turned her head and pressed her lips into his palm. The flutters in her stomach were riotous, causing her to quiver against him, but she was not afraid.

"My love," he murmured, his gaze bright with fierce adoration.

Following her heart, she surged into him, her lips bumping awkwardly into his.

A low, delighted chuckle rumbled in his chest at her eagerness. Then he cupped her nape and fitted his mouth over hers. Perfectly.

Sophie stopped breathing, arrested by the kiss. Her lips tingled and her ears rang, her skin flushed and her toes curled. As the world spun behind her closed lids, she leaned heavily into him. He paused, his lips moving along her cheekbone to her ear.

"Breathe, love," he admonished in a deepened tone that made her breasts swell.

His hand came up and squeezed the full, aching flesh. She inhaled sharply as he kneaded her, and then he took her mouth again, teasing her with gentle flicks of his tongue. Dizzy and unbearably aroused, she opened wider with a moan, shivering as he accepted the invitation with lush, deep licks.

The smell of his skin intoxicated her. She was beginning to love that unique combination of bergamot and tobacco. She already loved the feel of his body, so big and powerful. He dwarfed her, made her feel as if she was enveloped in warm, tangible safety. He was not pulling her under or drowning her. He was revealing the depth of his desire, and she was empowered by his admission.

With his hand on the curve of her hip and a low sound of encouragement, Justin urged her closer. Unresisting, Sophie slipped her fingers into the silky strands of his golden hair. The simple touch seemed to affect him strongly, made him shudder, and crush her slender body roughly to his hardness.

Their mouths sealed together, so that each labored breath was shared.

Heat swept across her skin in a prickling wave. Perspiration dampened her forehead. She began to writhe against him, goaded by a physical sense of urgency she had never felt before. He hummed soothingly and attempted to calm her, but there was no help for it. She wanted his bare skin pressed to hers, his body straining over and inside hers.

Her arms fell to his hips, then her hands slid up the length of his spine. The muscles of his back tensed to rock-hardness beneath her fingertips, despite the linen that separated her touch from his flesh. Her returning kiss became more feverish, the rushing of blood in her ears near deafening.

All the while his mouth drank from hers, the frantic movements of her body in stark contrast to the deep, luxurious pace of his kiss. He cupped her buttocks and rocked her into him, the lewd, blatant carnality of the gesture shocking her and inciting her further. Tension coiled tightly in her womb, becoming a deep hunger that fueled her growing desperation.

"Easy," he rasped, gentling her with calming strokes of his large hands. "Or we won't make it to the bed."

Part of Sophie's mind comprehended that he was threatening to make love to her in this very spot. Her body, however, clearly felt the venue was not an issue, blindly seeking to appease the insane need she felt to eat the man up like a tasty dessert. To nibble on all the hard lengths of muscle she felt beneath her palms, and to lick across what she imagined was rough satin skin. She nipped at his jaw and he groaned, the provocative sound filled with lustful longing. Tugging at his clothing, Sophie attempted to work her way to the man within.

"Sophie." Emotion thickened the normally clipped accents of his voice. He continued to fondle her breast and she whimpered as she grew wet with desire.

His thumb stroked across her thrusting nipple, and she released a throaty cry. Her knees gave out and his arm at her waist tightened, locking her against him. His erection strained into her lower belly, goading her to rock into it. His responding growl excited her unbearably. The expert manipulation of her breast became more aggressive as one thickly muscled thigh intruded between her legs.

"Justin," she breathed.

"Tell me what you want."

"You."

Lifting her feet from the floor, he carried her to the bed.

CHAPTER 5

———◆———

Justin found his hands shaking as he worked to release the buttons that held the sapphire gown to Sophie's lush body. She was fidgeting with impatience, as she was often wont to do, and he smiled, his chest filling with a deep, tender ache.

"Hurry," she urged, glancing over her shoulder at him, her green eyes heavy-lidded with passion.

"You still have no notion how to wait for the things you want." He softened his statement with a quick, hard kiss to the top of her shoulder.

"Would you prefer me to have patience when I want you?"

"I have waited a lifetime." Sliding his hands into the gaping back of her gown, he cupped her shoulders, then pushed the garment off and onto the floor. "Perhaps you should know a little of what it feels like to want something and be denied."

She turned into his embrace, clad only in a sheer chemise and silk stockings. He inhaled harshly at the feel of her pressed against him. "I never denied you," she murmured, nipping at his chin with her teeth.

Crushing her soft curves into his painfully aroused body, Justin buried his face in her short-cropped curls and breathed her in. The smell of her was delicious and he laughed softly.

Sophie pulled back slightly to look up at him.

"The way you smell appeals to me," he replied to her silent query.

She blushed, but her eyes sparkled with mischief. "What would you do if you were truly allergic?"

"Make love to you in a bath. Or pin my nose."

"You would not!"

"You doubt me?" Cupping her buttocks he tugged her into him, pressing the throbbing length of his cock against her.

Her gaze lowered to his throat and her hands lifted to pluck at his collar. "Would you . . . undress for me?"

"Of course." Justin smiled. "Will you assist me?"

Nodding, she reached for the placket of his trousers.

"Ah, love," he murmured, exquisitely tormented by her proximity and the knowledge that in moments she would be naked and arching beneath him. "You always did move directly to the point."

"I want to see you." She was nervous. He could see it in the way she worried her lower lip between her teeth. But she was eager, too. Open. Curious. He cupped her face in his hands.

"I am yours," he promised, his thumbs brushing over her cheekbones. "You have no need to be uncertain with me."

He tensed as the backs of her fingers brushed tantalizingly over the bulge of his erection. He was so hard for her it was painful and he groaned in relief when his cock sprang free of its confinement, coming to rest heavily within her palms.

"Is this mine, too?" she whispered, tracing the veins that pulsed along the length of him.

"Does it please you?" He grit his teeth as she stroked him with both hands.

"Yes. It suits you."

Justin managed a choked laugh. "How so?"

"It is large, proud, and arrogant."

"How the devil can a penis be arrogant?"

Sophie looked up at him from beneath long, dark lashes. Her thumb slid over the head of his cock, the journey eased by the drop of semen that collected there. "Look how ready he is. I am not certain he will wait for me."

"Continue fondling me like that and he might not."

He began to disrobe, but she did not release him, her fingers caressing him with such gentleness he was amazed he didn't come. By the time he was bared to her, perspiration covered his skin in a fine sheen and his seed leaked copiously, coating her hands.

"Undress," he said urgently, tugging his aching ballocks down to stave off an imminent release. He watched in an agony of lust as she removed her stockings, then frowned as she crawled on top of the bed. "The chemise, as well."

She shook her head. "I would rather wear it."

"No." Justin did not intend for the word to come out so harshly, but damn it all, he wanted her naked beneath him. Her skin to his.

Sophie arranged herself like a sensual feast, her lithe body sprawled across the many pillows that piled against his headboard. The last remaining vestige of her attire was so sheer, he could see the shadow of her areolas and the impatient thrust of erect nipples. Between her legs a dark triangle lured him, enticed him. But it was not enough.

"You deny me?" He frowned, hating the material that separated him from his deepest desire.

The fingers of her right hand fidgeted with the lace that framed the neckline. "I am not young. And I have had a child. In this instance, I believe wondering is better than knowing."

Sophie knew the moment understanding dawned. Fontaine's eyes widened and he stilled, taking stock before acting, as was his way. She leapt before looking. He looked before leaping. It was one of the many things she appreciated about him.

She watched him move to the bed, eyeing his powerful masculine beauty with hunger and infatuation. He was so lean, yet muscular. Perfect. Everything about him was perfect. And she was so imperfect.

He took a seat on the edge of the bed, and cradled one of her hands within his own. "I am grateful for your beauty," he murmured. "It arouses and amazes me." His mouth curved in a slow smile. "But I adored you when you were gangly."

"I was never gangly!"

"You were." His smile widened into a grin. "No breasts or hips. Just tall and reed-thin. And I adored you. I adored you with mud on your face and food on your chin and twigs in your hair."

"I never had food on my chin!"

"You did." He crawled over her, his knees resting on either side of her hips, his cock right where she wanted it . . . if only he would lower his body six inches or so. "It is *you* who captivates me, love. Your impulsiveness, your vitality, your lust for life. You have no fear. You see what you desire and grab it with both hands. I admire those qualities about you because I lack them myself. I am overly cautious and sometimes take too long to act, a fault that has cost me dearly."

Her hand lifted to cover her mouth and hide the trembling of her lips. She knew he referred to losing her to Langley and her heart ached. She made it a point to regret nothing in her life. If she proceeded with an action, it was because she was decided. But she regretted having caused him pain, even though she had done so unwittingly.

"So you see," he continued, collecting the hem of her chemise and tugging it upward, "while I am thoroughly smitten with your exterior, it is your interior that won my deeper regard."

Sophie arrested his movements with her hands over his. He met her gaze squarely, his brows lifted in silent challenge. She knew that look well, and it made her smile. She took a moment to marvel over how comfortable she felt with him, as if they had been lovers forever, then said, "Allow me."

With her heart full, she sat up and pulled her chemise over her head. It was not as easy as she would hope, her insecurity around the marquess a lifetime habit. The change in position put their torsos in close proximity, and she shivered slightly as she felt the heat of his skin. Releasing a deep breath, she settled back against the pillows and lifted her chin.

His gaze was so hot it made her perspire. Her eyes closed as Justin touched her stomach just above her pelvic bone. She did not have to look to know he followed the mark left by her pregnancy. The mattress dipped and swayed as he moved away from her, and her eyes burned at the unbearable intimacy. A moment later she jerked in surprise when his open mouth pressed to the spot, then moved upward, his tongue slipping into her navel. One hair-dusted leg hooked over hers and tugged it aside, opening her thighs to his avid touch.

"Justin!" she gasped, arching as he parted her and stroked her with his fingertips.

His mouth moved to her breast, brushing along the side, kissing the faint marks that marred the under curve. "Christ, you are so beautiful."

Her arms lifted, embracing him, as he found her nipple and engulfed it, suckling strongly. A callused fingertip circled her clitoris, then dipped lower to slip inside her. She cried out and bowed upward, straining, her body echoing the contractions of his mouth around his plunging finger. Aroused by his praise and gentle ministrations, Sophie felt herself softening, opening, becoming slick with welcome so that every thrust of his hand sounded wetly in the room.

Lifting his head, Justin watched her, giving her no room to hide. His skin was flushed, his eyes fever-bright, his lips parted with harsh, panting breaths.

"I used to imagine you like this," he confessed in a husky whisper, withdrawing from her depths, only to return with two fingers. Stroking along her inner walls, rubbing, caressing, making her writhe. Her nails dug into his forearms, her nipples peaked hard and painfully tight.

He kissed her, absorbing her cries into the heat of his mouth. "If you open your legs wider," he whispered, "I can fuck you deeper."

His crude wording first startled her, then inflamed her. Squeezing her eyes shut, she spread her thighs shamelessly, hungrily accepting the deluge of sensation after the last few years of numbness.

"No, look at me," he murmured, his throbbing erection a hard pressure against her leg. "Let me watch you."

Sophie relented, unable and unwilling to deny him, feeling safe with him in a way that made such sharing possible. Her eyes locked onto his, her body quivered against his, her gasps mingled with his, until she cried out. Falling into orgasm with a hot rush of tears. Clinging to his big, hard body with all her strength. Grateful he was with her, just as she had always been grateful when he was at her side.

"Justin," she whimpered, rubbing her tearstained cheek against his. "Darling Justin."

He came over her, the ripples of his abdomen glistening in the candlelight, the muscles in his arms flexing as he held his weight aloft. "Put me inside you," he rasped, his chest heaving as if he had run a great distance.

Touching his lips with the fingertips of one hand, she reached down with the other and positioned him. His breath blew hot against her skin as he rolled his hips and eased into her.

She tensed as he breached her, her lungs seizing as the first thick inches spread her wide.

"Hush," he murmured, freeing one hand to stroke down her side. Reaching beneath her thigh, he pulled it up, anchoring it on his hip so that the pressure lessened. "You were made to hold me."

He settled more of his weight on top of her, pinning her down, forcing her to accept his leisurely pace.

Senses that had been dazed by her recent climax, flared to renewed life. "Please," she begged, squirming. "Please hurry."

"You never had any patience, love."

She moaned as he sank deeper. And deeper. So slowly. Taking his time. Finally, with a breathtaking lunge, he filled her to the hilt, his thighs shaking violently against hers.

"Christ, you feel good." His forehead pressed to hers. "Perfect. No! Don't move . . . be still . . . allow me a moment . . ."

Near mindless with lust, she rocked her hips restlessly, pushing him deeper into her, but it wasn't enough. Not nearly.

Justin brushed her damp curls away from her forehead. She stilled, staring up at him, arrested by the sight of the deep hunger and longing in his eyes. He made no effort to disguise it. Here, in this moment, Sophie saw inside him such as she never had before, finding the man beneath the collected exterior.

"Kiss me," she whispered. "Please, kiss me."

"Yes," he murmured, his lips lowering to hover over hers. "Yes."

As their open mouths met in a passionate mating, he withdrew from her drenched sex and then slid home, the thick head of his shaft rubbing inside her just as his fingers had. Her kiss grew frantic, her desire near maddening. Her nostrils filled with the scent of his skin and their joint arousal, urging her to action. She pressed her heels into the mattress and lifted to meet his next downward thrust.

He growled when he hit the end of her. "I want this to last."

"No! Dear God, no." Sophie grabbed his buttocks and urged him to pump faster. His firm ass clenched within her palms on every downstroke, the feel of him propelling his cock into her so erotic she began to plead softly.

"Whatever you want," she promised in a rush, desperate to give him pleasure, desperate to break through his iron control. "Anything you want . . . *please* . . . faster . . ."

Justin pulled back and lunged hard, pounding deep. "Is this what you want?"

"Yes! Yes." She writhed upward, straining with him, her body moving as a thing separate from her mind, driven by an animal greed that should have shocked her. Instead, she was empowered by it.

Embracing her need for him with all the passion she possessed, Sophie took him as hard as he took her, accepting the fierce driving thrusts of his cock with no restraint. Relishing the sounds of his guttural cries of pleasure.

Then he plunged into the root, swiveling his hips to grind against her. Her neck arched, her eyes flew wide. "Justin?" she gasped, taut as a bow, suspended on the edge of something wonderful.

"Come, Sophie," he crooned breathlessly, stroking in measured rhythm. "Come, and I will come with you."

Arms around his neck, she pressed her cheek to his and shivered into orgasm with his name on her lips. As he promised, he followed, holding her, loving her, supporting her.

Just as he always had.

CHAPTER 6

———◆———

Justin sprawled naked atop the counterpane, one arm tucked behind his head, the other holding Sophie close to his side. The fire in the grate burned low, the tapers extinguished. Her fingers wandered idly across his chest, and her leg was tossed over his. As far as heaven went, he was fairly certain this was it.

"What is your life like with your son?" he asked.

"It's wonderful." Her tone held a soft breathy quality of happiness. "Every day is an adventure. You never know when you will find a toad in your bed or a grasshopper loose in your dining room. Some nights there are monsters in the armoire and on others, there are faeries in the air."

"I would enjoy that, I think."

He felt her smile against his skin. "You will be a wonderful father, I'm sure. I realize now that it was only my own insecurities that made me feel as if you looked unfavorably upon me. You were merely trying to protect me from myself. I think you will be somewhat of a mother hen, fussing after your progeny and taking great pains to ensure their safety."

He snorted.

"And that snort," she commented. "I used to think it was arrogant and dismissive. Now I collect that you make that noise when you are embarrassed by praise."

"Provoking wench. Is the only way to keep you from teasing me to make love to you? You are much more agreeable then. Tractable even."

She hugged him tightly. "You are quite good at the business, you know. I did not know that I could . . . feel like *that* . . ."—she exhaled in a rush—"while you are inside me."

He looked down at her. "An orgasm?"

"I have had them before," she amended quickly, lifting her head to look at him. With her face framed in a riot of short, dark curls, and her eyes bright, she looked younger and happier than when she had arrived. Pushing his fingers into her hair, he massaged her scalp, finding deep joy in his right to touch her as he wished.

"But not during intercourse?" He smiled. "I hope you enjoyed it. I intend to repeat the experience as often as possible."

She sighed forlornly. "I would love to stay, but time draws short. The sun will rise soon."

He cupped her cheek. "Only hours separate my body from yours."

Sophie pushed up, baring her curves to his gaze. In the faint orange glow from the banked fire, she looked like a pagan sexual goddess. His cock twitched in appreciation of the view.

"What are you saying?" she asked with a frown.

"I am saying that I will have you again tonight, if not before then. Do not be startled to find yourself in a secluded corner with your skirts around your waist."

"You said you were leaving!"

Justin arched a brow. "That was before you asked me to bed you."

She gasped. "I will not be your mistress! I have a child who shares my life."

"You insult me," he said, swinging his legs off the edge of the mattress and standing. "I would never ask that of you." Collecting his black silk robe from the armoire, he shrugged into it, then moved to the grate. "Do you truly believe that I would think you were sufficient for fucking, but not for wedding?"

"I cannot marry you!" she protested.

He blew out his breath and kept his face averted to the fire. It would not do for her to see him wounded. Though it was ridiculous to feel that way, he knew. He had known from the moment he acknowledged what he must do, that she would fight him tooth and nail. "That sounded like a refusal."

"Oh, do not be daft!" she muttered. "Marriage to me would ruin you."

"Allow me to worry about that."

"What is the matter with you?"

He finished stoking the new coals and rose from his crouch. "Sophie—" His voice fell to silence as he faced her. She had pulled on her discarded chemise and knelt on the bed with her hands cupping both knees. He thought her the most glorious creature in the world.

His gaze moved away from the flashing green eyes and came to rest on the Fontaine crest carved into his headboard. Immutable resolution filled him. Sophie was where she belonged and he would fight to keep her with every breath in his body.

"You are a model of respectability," she continued,

warming into a full-blown heated debate, "and an admired member of the aristocracy, and I am an example of how far one can fall from grace."

Justin crossed the distance between them, caught up her hands, and pulled her from the bed. "Lady Sophie Milton-Riley," he said with all due seriousness, "would you do me the great honor of becoming my wife?"

She stomped her foot. "No, no, no, you mad fool. You said there was no way for us to be together that we could both live with, and you were of sound mind then. Obviously sexual congress disturbs your brain functions in some way. You need sleep," she pronounced. "Once you wake, you will see how insane your proposal is."

"I love you."

"Dear God." She gasped and bent over slightly, as if struck.

"I have always loved you."

Sophie shook her head violently. "You are mistaking the remnants of orgasm with elevated feelings. You did not feel that way before sex."

"My love." He pulled her into his embrace. "We would not have had sex, if I did not intend to marry you. I asked you, quite clearly, if you were prepared to be owned by me. You agreed."

"That is not what you meant!"

"It was. Kindly remember that *you* are the impulsive one in this pairing. I am the one who considers all aspects in great detail."

Sophie pushed at his chest in a bid for freedom and he released her, knowing that she would pace in her agitation. It was quite comforting to know her so well.

"You might grow to love me," he said, watching her.

"I already love you," she snapped.

He grinned.

She glared. "But that is the worst of all reasons to wed!"

"I *will* marry you, sweetheart, so you should accustom yourself to that fate posthaste. I lost you once. I refuse to lose you again."

"Justin." She heaved out her frustration, striding back and forth in front of the fire, oblivious to the way the back-lighting revealed every inch of her delectable form. "Why must you always be so difficult? I will not allow you to sacrifice yourself for me."

"Yet you intend to sacrifice our love for me?" He shrugged out of his robe and went to her, tossing it about her shoulders to keep her warm. "Where is the fairness in that?"

She stopped, her gaze dropping between his legs. He saw her swallow hard. "You would resent me after awhile. Society will never accept me, and that would reflect upon you. I would become a great hindrance. That would be unbearable for a socially active man such as you."

He lifted her chin so that their gazes met. "Not having you would make me more wretched."

"You've no notion." Her eyes were luminous with unshed tears. "It is not pleasant to be relegated to the fringes."

His hands settled on her shoulders, then slid down to her elbows. "Do you trust me?"

"You know I do."

"Then trust me to manage this."

"How?"

"I will find a way," he promised, sliding his hands beneath his robe to circle her waist and lift her off her feet. The feel of their bodies touching made his heart leap and then race madly. His cock swelled between them, and her breathing quickened. The instant, intoxicating, wildly uncontrollable hunger that flared between them was delicious.

To feel so alive, to be loved by the one woman whose affection he had needed for so long, to have the opportunity to correct the greatest error of his life . . . it was all together nearly enough to make him shout with joy.

But the weight of their dilemma hung over them like a dark cloud. They were both highly aware of the imminent thundercrack and the downpour of censure that would follow. The only certainty was this moment, these last hours before dawn.

So he determined to relish them. He stepped toward the bed with his precious Sophie in his arms. She clung to him, her mouth at his throat, kissing and nibbling in a way that drove him to madness.

Laying her on the chocolate velvet counterpane, he followed her down, brushing the edges of the robe aside so that he could cup her breasts. His open mouth lowered, surrounding her nipple through her chemise, his tongue flickering across the tightened peak. He rested on his side, freeing his hand to slide down between her thighs. She opened without reservation, baring her cunt to his reverent caresses. A deep sound of praise rumbled up in his chest, vibrating against her skin as he continued to suck deeply at her breast. He parted her and stroked through the slickness he found, both hers and his. With two fingers he pushed into her, feeling the soft-as-satin walls tighten and release as he pumped in and out.

The sounds she made as he pleasured her were music. Her breathless pleas were aphrodisiacs. The feel of her hands in his hair and on his shoulders made his heart clench with longing. Wrapping his leg around hers, Justin ground his cock into the soft flesh of her outer thigh in a vain effort to relieve the desperate ache.

Then he gave up and levered over her. Kneeling, he draped her legs over his thighs and pushed her chemise up over her breasts. "My God," he breathed, undone at the sight of her dishevelment. The wanton pose was the realization of his deepest carnal fantasies. "You are so beautiful."

His fingers caressed her from breast to cunt in featherlight adoration.

"Please," she cried, wiggling delightfully.

"Shh," he soothed, gripping his cock and angling it down to the tiny slitted entrance to her body. "You should watch, love. It will excite you."

Sophie pushed up onto her elbows and stared at where they almost joined. Rolling his hips, he eased into her, sinking into hot, slick silk. The sight of his penetration moved them both. He hardened and grew thicker; she began to pant and flooded with moisture so plentiful it bathed his cock. As he had before, he took his time, memorizing every moment. The final surge to the root made him groan and grind against her, shoving himself as deep into her as he could go. She was stuffed full of him, a fit so perfect it made him want to howl with pleasure.

Her cunt fluttered rhythmically, betraying how close she was to coming. His thumb to her clitoris, he pushed her over, gritting his teeth as she milked his tortured cock with strong pulses. "Yes," he growled, watching the orgasm move through her, watching her fall helpless to the passion that had gripped him alone for so long.

Only when she settled limply into the pillows did Justin begin to fuck her. Holding her hips, he withdrew to the tip, then thrust hard and deep. Out. In. Powerful, driving strokes straight into the heart of her. Hearing the sounds of flesh slapping against flesh, feeling the heavy weight of his balls striking the firm curve of her ass, listening rapturously to Sophie's sobbing pleas for more. Always more. He made no effort to coddle her sensibilities. She had to know how it would be between them, had to understand that while he loved her with a gentleman's heart he would fuck her with a man's primitive desire.

And she loved it. Loved him.

Justin's skin misted with sweat, then dripped with it, and still it went on, his fingertips bruising her flesh as he held her down. Pumping her to orgasm again so he could see the startled pleasure drift across her features and the way her green eyes dazed in the throes. As she convulsed around him, he released his control, tossing his head back with a guttural cry. The climax shook him, making him shudder and jerk violently with every hard, thick spurt of his seed inside her.

His jaw ached with the force with which he clenched it and he lowered into her open arms with gratitude. Nestled against her breast, he listened to her heart's desperate beating.

"I love you," she whispered, stroking the perspiration-slick length of his back. "Whatever happens, know that I return the depth of your affection."

"I will marry you," he returned, kissing the nipple closest to his mouth. "And I will know how you feel, because you shall tell me every day."

She said nothing, but her silence spoke a sad farewell.

Justin closed his eyes, and began to plan.

CHAPTER 7

———◆———

Freshly bathed with his hair still damp, the marquess paced in his study with his hands clasped at the small of his back. The hour was early; Sophie was still abed in her own chamber, having left his rooms just before dawn. He had hated that parting, temporary though it was. Hated that they could not be lazy and lie abed all day, wrapped up in each other.

"My lord, you summoned?"

He paused, turning to face the countess and his mother as they entered. He greeted them, gestured for them to sit on the settee, and then leaned back against the front of his desk.

With his arms crossed, he asked, "When you both conceived of this matchmaking scheme, did you consider all of the many impediments to marital bliss?"

The women shot furtive glances at one another.

"We've no notion of what you are talking about," his mother said finally.

Narrowing his gaze, the marquess studied his mother's gown, a near garish mix of flowery profusion that she somehow managed to make attractive. "Lady Sophie has declined my proposal of marriage."

Twin smiles spread across the two faces before him. "Bright girl," the countess said with laughter in her voice. "I would not wish to be sneezed upon for the rest of my life either."

His mother grinned. "And this will spare your dogs from certain separation from you."

"I've no notion," he said dryly, "how I have retained even a modicum of sanity after spending most of my life around you three troublesome females."

"Forgive us, my lord," Lady Cardington said, blinking in an exaggerated show of innocence. "You must collect that we were under the impression that you and Lady Sophie did not suit."

His mouth curved. "If you think I am too proud to admit that you were correct, you shall be disappointed." Justin knew the effort his mother must be exerting to contain a crow of delight.

"So you wish to wed her?" she asked.

"Yes."

"And what of the boy?" the countess asked.

"He is a part of Sophie. His position in my life will equal hers."

"Oh, this is wonderful!" his mother said, clapping her hands gleefully.

"Yes, yes!" agreed the countess.

Affording the two a moment to relish their near success, Justin's gaze drifted around the room. Decorated in various shades of gray and blue and filled with stained walnut furnishings, it reminded him of a stormy day. He found himself contemplating what Sophie would think of such a somber setting. He wondered what shades she might have chosen. A lighter palette, he imagined. One more cheerful to suit her carefree personality.

He was madly in love, obviously. When a man spent his quiet moments reflecting on a woman's taste in decor, there was no denying it.

His mother's spine straightened and her face took on a suitably serious mien. "Does she display a similar interest in you?"

"Yes." He rubbed his jaw, remembering the feel of Sophie's mouth moving across it with ardent kisses. "But she refuses to wed me with her tattered reputation. Somehow, we must make her acceptable. I assume you both would have considered this before pairing us."

The countess sighed. "She requires a great deal of support and something that would make her irresistible."

"You must first begin with Lord Rothschild," his mother instructed. "Restoring her brother's favor to her would be of immense help."

Justin nodded. "Yes, of course." He had considered that this morning while bathing, and believed he knew how he might convince the earl to bend in this.

"Then we must find something sensational, something that will make it much more advantageous to accept her than it is to snub her. Truly, if that Princess Caraboo creature can manage the task, our darling Sophie can do the same."

"Dear God." He cringed. "We want her to be acceptable, not a blasted curiosity!"

"No, no, of course not," Lady Cardington agreed. "We are simply pointing out that nearly anyone can become a welcome and celebrated personage under the right circumstances."

"I will leave those machinations up to you," he said,

shaking his head. "That part of the affair sounds as if it needs a female mind to concoct it. But whatever mischief you conceive of, I want to hear of it before you act. Do I make myself clear?"

Two heads nodded in unison.

"I am departing shortly to attend to the matter of Rothschild." He pointed a chastising finger at both of them. "Keep Sophie out of trouble until I return."

"Yes, my lord."

He moved toward the door, pausing to kiss his mother and the countess on their cheeks. "Thank you," he murmured. "I owe you both a great deal for your meddling."

"We do not meddle!" the dowager protested, affronted.

Shaking his head, Justin departed.

A sennight later, impatience was riding the marquess hard as he vaulted down from his carriage in front of the impressive three-story columned entrance to Remington's Gentlemen's Club in London. Taking the steps two at a time, Justin strode swiftly through the watered glass double doors held open by black and silver liveried footmen. As he handed his hat and gloves to the waiting attendant, he took stock of his surroundings. Lucien Remington was acknowledged as a man of impeccable taste, and he ensured his establishment's position as the most exclusive in England by continuously updating the decor. Remington did not follow prevailing inclinations in design. He set the standard for them.

Justin noted the multitude of improvements with a suitably appreciative eye. The lay of the rooms remained the same. Straight ahead was the gaming area, which was the center of all business. From there, one could access the stairs to the fencing studio, courtesans, and private rooms above. The pugilist rings were on the lower floor. To the left, the bar and kitchen. Justin's destination—Lucien Remington's office—was to the right and he turned in that direction without further delay.

"Good afternoon, Lord Fontaine," the secretary greeted, leaping to his feet from his position behind a desk. He reached for the knob of the nearby door and opened it, ushering Justin in with due haste.

Remington glanced up at the intrusion and stood upon recognizing his expected visitor. "My lord." He bowed slightly in welcome.

"Remington."

The marquess's gaze swept across the room. The first thing one noticed upon entering was the carved mahogany desk that directly faced the door. The second was the massive painting that hung above the fireplace. From there, the lovely Lady Julienne smiled, her dark eyes bright with happiness and love. Two strapping lads with the dark hair of their father stood behind either shoulder, and a young girl with the golden hair of their mother sat at her feet.

"Your wife grows lovelier by the day."

"I couldn't agree more." The softening of Remington's features as he glanced at the portrait revealed how deeply he loved his wife, a gently bred earl's daughter who had rejected Society in favor of a love match with a bastard. Once Remington had been a gazetted rake; his black-as-pitch hair and irises a unique shade of near purple had been irresistible to most women. Now he was known as a man unfashionably devoted to his spouse.

"You are a fortunate man," Justin said, feeling no ill will. Julienne had made the best choice for her happiness.

Yes, marriage to him would have afforded her the social status due a woman of her breeding, but he knew that he would not have made her as content as Remington did.

"Yes," Remington agreed, "fairly impressive for a mongrel, some say."

Justin returned his attention to his host, finding Remington's lauded eyes filled with laughter as he alluded to the time when they had been rivals for Julienne's affections and Justin had disparaged Remington for his common breeding.

"You have not yet forgotten?" Justin asked, taking a seat before Remington's desk. The surface was littered with piles of paperwork, betraying the breadth of Remington's empire. The product of a long-standing romance between a demimondaine and a duke, his obscene wealth had been hard-won and was a source of great envy.

"I will never forget it, my lord." Remington moved to the row of decanters on the nearby console. "The moment those words were spoken, it was an uphill battle for you to win Julienne. I am not usually grateful for aristocratic arrogance, but in this case, I have made an exception."

Accepting the proffered libation, Justin smiled. "You will be surprised to learn the reason why I am here today, Remington. I do wish I could preserve the look on your face when I tell you."

"Hmm . . ." Remington resumed his seat, held his snifter in both hands, and arched both brows expectantly.

"Lord Rothschild is a member of your club, is he not?"

"Yes. Of course."

"Excellent. Perhaps you have extended credit to him in the past?"

Remington's gaze narrowed. "Where is this leading, my lord?"

"To a file of information, I hope," Justin said blithely. "You see, I wish to marry his sister, who is quite ruined. I would wed her regardless, but the obstinate woman refuses out of concern for me. She was disowned by Rothschild when the scandal broke and I am certain that adds to her reticence. Therefore, I must persuade him to accept her back into the fold. Publicly and dramatically."

His smile turned into a grin as Remington's face took on a noticeably shocked cast.

"For clarification, Fontaine: Are you asking me to disclose private information about a peer so that you may extort his cooperation in order to marry his scandalous, ostracized sibling?"

"Exactly! Extraordinary, is it not? Who would have guessed that I would one day do something so dastardly? And with such glee?"

"Not I," Remington said wryly. "I begin to think I was lucky that you conceded Julienne so easily."

Justin considered the man across from him carefully. "Oh?"

"You said you would fight for her, yet you never truly did. You could have been a grave threat to me, had you chosen to be."

"She was in love with you and you made it clear that you reciprocated her feelings. You both had my reluctant sympathy. I did think she was daft to choose you, however. Gads, to think of the social heights she could have achieved as my wife!"

"Ah, now I recognize you, my lord," Remington said, laughing. Setting down his snifter he pushed to his feet and moved to the shelves on the wall to the left of the grate. Some action on his part exposed a hidden doorway, which in turn led to a hidden gallery. Remington disappeared into the opening, and a moment or two later he emerged with a thick file. He whistled low. "For your first effort at extortion, you selected a fat bird."

"Truly?" Justin stood, startled to realize how relieved he was. "Is there information I would find useful?"

Remington's mouth curled slightly at the corners. "Plenty."

The marquess crossed the room, set his glass down on the small table near the settee, and accepted the file. As he skimmed the contents, his mouth fell open. He shot a glance at Remington. "Damnation, how do you acquire such knowledge?"

"I have my ways," Remington said evasively.

"Have you such detailed observations about others?"

"When necessary."

"Bloody hell."

"The information I hold is quite safe, I assure you. Aside from my man-of-affairs, you are the only person I have ever allowed to see a personal file."

Justin nodded gravely. "I owe you a debt of gratitude."

Remington waved the comment away with a careless gesture.

"Consider it my debt paid for doing your least to win Julienne."

"I should like to take some notes, if I could."

"Certainly."

A few moments later, after an attendant was summoned with fresh parchment and quill, Justin sat on the settee before the grate. A brief flash of light caught his eye, and he bent to investigate. When he straightened, he held aloft a lone tin soldier. The mental image of Remington's children here with Lady Julienne made him smile.

"Remington?"

"Yes, my lord?" Remington glanced up from his paper-work.

"Would you be so kind as to compile a small list of merchants I might visit to purchase amusements for a small boy?"

Remington's gaze moved to the toy and he grinned. "Certainly."

Justin nodded his gratitude, then returned his attention to his most pressing task and began to write.

First, to his mother:

> *. . . plan a dinner party. Make certain Lady*
> *Cardington and Lady Sophie are in attendance.*
> *Also invite the following . . .*

Then, to Lord Rothschild:

> *. . . requires a discussion regarding a matter of*
> *grave importance to both of us . . .*

And finally, he began to transcribe the most grievous, valuable, and intriguing information of that held in the file. All the while he thought of Sophie, wondering what she would think of the man he had become—one willing to go to any length for love.

CHAPTER 8

Fontaine pulled his mount to a halt before the Earl of Rothschild's London townhouse. He imagined he should feel out of sorts or ill-at-ease at the very least. Instead he was determined and sure of his intent. In an hour or so, his life would be firmly set upon the path of his choosing. There was no way to avoid feeling triumphant about that.

Passing the reins to the waiting groomsman, the marquess climbed the short stairs with a decided spring to his step. Within moments, he was announced and shown into a large sitting room that boasted walls of pale gray woodwork inset with panels of grayish-green damask and a ceiling that was the canvas for an impressive mural featuring fat cherubs frolicking amongst fatter clouds. The overall impression was one of affluence, but Justin was well aware that, in this instance, appearances were deceiving.

"Lord Fontaine."

Turning his attention to the man who approached him, Justin noted the assured stride and uplifted chin of Sophie's brother. They were very much alike, the two Milton-Riley siblings. Physically similar in coloring and bearing, both tall and slender, yet there was a gulf between the two so wide they were nearly strangers to one another. Justin suspected it was due to the fact that they had been raised apart. Rothschild had been sent away to school, while Sophie resided with her *grand-mère*.

"Lord Rothschild," he greeted.

"An unexpected call," Rothschild said, returning the avid scrutiny with narrowed green eyes.

"Though not unwelcome, I hope."

"That remains to be seen, does it not? Grave matters are rarely pleasant."

Fontaine smiled and sank into the nearest chair, a narrow settee covered in soft green fabric and backed with intricately carved wood. "I have come bearing honorable intentions toward Lady Sophie."

The earl's eyes widened. A brief shocked silence filled the room, and then he threw his head back and laughed.

Bending down, Justin reached into the leather satchel he had set on the floor at his feet. He carefully withdrew the documents his solicitor had drawn up at his behest and passed them over. Rothschild's amused gaze turned to one of bewilderment as he accepted the proffered packet and settled into the seat opposite.

For a time, the only sounds in the room where those of pages turning and the ticking of the clock. Justin waited out the earl's reaction to his demands by studying the contents of the room, looking for any item that might match the articles mentioned in Remington's file.

"Dear God. Who arranged this farce?" Rothschild asked finally.

"I beg your pardon?"

Lifting his head, the earl blinked in obvious confusion.

"I would not have thought you likely to be involved in a mockery of this magnitude. What wager did you lose to be pressed into this?"

"I am entirely sincere," Justin assured. "I wish to wed your sister and you shall make that possible."

"Are you serious?"

"Quite."

"Bloody hell." An incredulous silence filled the room for a long moment, then the earl snorted. "Have her, if you so desire, but the stipulations you make in this agreement are the ravings of a madman. I am free of her as it stands. I've no need to part with anything of value in order to accomplish that."

"True. I appeal to your gentleman's honor."

"You waste both of our afternoons with this nonsense." Rothschild stood, tossing the packet onto the small table between them.

"I ask only for the items that belong to Lady Sophie. I've no desire for anything beyond that."

"I will not simply hand them over to you, Fontaine, which will necessitate a lengthy courtroom drama while you attempt to prove ownership. You may have lost your head over Sophie, but I think there are limits to the amount of scandal you are capable of tolerating."

Justin's mouth curved grimly as he reached back into his satchel. He watched as the earl crossed the room to stand before the window. Rothschild appeared irritated, yes, but his frame also vibrated with a barely perceptible anxiousness that betrayed his concern. The earl was not ignorant. He would know that leverage of some sort was involved. The man was bluffing, as all gamblers were wont to do.

"I had hoped to keep this exchange on pleasant footing," Fontaine said easily, leaning forward to set a sealed document atop the table. Although he was completely focused on the nuances of the earl's physical reactions to his increasingly aggressive salvos, he kept his own exterior relaxed and innocuous.

Rothschild glanced over, his verdant gaze dropping to the tabletop. His hands were clasped at his back, stretching the dark broadcloth of his coat across his shoulders. Unlike many who found that addiction to gambling and the drinking of strong spirits went hand-in-hand, the earl was trim, fit, and known only as one who liked to wager on just about anything. Sadly, he wasn't very good at it.

Sighing, Sophie's brother returned to his previous seat to inspect the new offering and Justin turned his attention to a small statue that graced one of several artfully arranged bookcases. The many volumes that lined the shelves were displayed in every possible fashion—on their sides, spine outward, and front-facing. In between, various antiquities waited to be admired and coveted. It was not long before the earl made some hideous noise that was something between a strangled gasp and a sob.

"By God!" Rothschild sputtered. "Where did you get this information?"

The marquess shrugged. "I have my ways."

"You cannot prove any of this!"

"Do I need to?" Looking at the earl, Fontaine raised both brows in silent query. "What a deucedly nasty business that would be. Of course, it might be worth it. Your scandal might take some of the attention away from mine. Yours is decidedly more lurid, I think you will agree."

Rothschild's face flushed with anger and embarrassment. "You do not understand my position."

"Oh, I think I do. You and Sophie were bequeathed a modest collection of Egyptian antiquities by a French relative, and you are presently using them to guarantee your markers."

"So, you see, I must retain them."

"No, *you* must see that I do not care about your predicament. I might have been more accommodating had you shown even a modicum of support for your sister when she needed it most, but you did not, so I shall not." The marquess rocked back on his heels. "Instead I shall drag you unwillingly up to my estate in Northamptonshire where you will dine with your sister and several highly esteemed members of the peerage who happen to have a fascination with antiquities. You will support her now, as you did not previously."

A cold, hard edge entered Rothschild's eyes. "You think you can make her suitable? You are delusional."

"I think I can make her an Eccentric, and that, Rothschild, will make her acceptable to other Eccentrics. It is a beginning."

What followed was a tedious hour of complaining, cajoling, and conniving that resulted nevertheless in Rothschild ordering his valet to prepare for a journey north. With such a disagreeable companion in tow, Justin anticipated a miserable trip, but as he watched the loading of the earl's trunks onto the rear of his coach, he was grinning from ear to ear regardless.

"Dear heavens, he's done it!" the dowager Lady Fontaine cried.

She lifted her gaze from the boldly slashed penmanship of her son, and smiled at her dearest friend. She had gratefully accepted the invitation to join the countess and Sophie on their return to their residence, despite her concern that her removal from Northamptonshire would delay word. She should not have worried. Fontaine had written directly to the Cardington dower property, having anticipated her inability to wait out news alone. "He has convinced Lord Rothschild to assist us."

Lady Cardington clapped her hands, the tension that had gripped her slight frame upon the arrival of the post dissipating with a relieved smile. "His lordship has hidden depths. Of course, we both knew that."

"Yes, we did." The dowager refolded the short missive carefully. "But now we have work to do, Caroline."

Blowing out her breath, Lady Cardington set her shoulders back. "What is required of us?"

"We are to arrange a gathering." Leaning forward, the dowager passed the letter over. "I have no notion how we shall manage the guest list he has demanded."

Caroline rose from her floral slipper chair and moved to the walnut escritoire in the corner where her spectacles waited. "We shall lie and elaborate." She gazed out the window to where Sophie walked beside Thomas in the rear garden. "We need only to entice them to come. The rest we leave to Fontaine and Sophie."

"Did you truly attempt to climb to the top of the pagoda?"

Sophie glanced down at her son with a sheepish smile. "I did."

"I am glad I was not here to see it," Thomas said, gazing

up at her with Langley's dark eyes. "I would have been frightened for you."

"Then perhaps you can understand why I was so frightened when I found you attempting the feat yourself."

"I thought you were angry."

She set her hand atop his unruly chocolate brown waves. "No, not angry, darling. Terrified."

Looking at the structure, she remembered fragments of the day when Fontaine had caught her hanging from the roof's edge.

"By God, you mad creature!" he'd cried, just before he wrapped his arms around her waist and pulled her free, spilling them both to the grass in a tangle of limbs.

He had been shaking with fury, or so she had believed at the time. Now she realized how he must have felt and her heart hurt. How could she have been so blind to his feelings for her?

She sighed. She suspected she knew why. Confusion at the loss of her parents and the lack of connection to her only sibling had made it difficult for her to perceive affection. She had been angry at the world, and therefore saw only anger returned to her.

"I have been invited to visit the Fontaine estate again," Sophie said, dropping her hand to link fingers with Thomas's grubby ones. They rounded the corner and she gestured to a crescent-shaped marble bench beneath a tree.

"I like Lady Fontaine."

"So do I." Although it was Justin who had requested her return in a short but sweet note that offered a chance at happiness. However, there was more at stake than her feelings. "Would you be upset if I went?"

Thomas appeared to consider the question carefully. "You have been sad since you returned."

Sophie blinked, startled that he had been perceptive enough to notice. "I miss a friend."

"Will you see your friend again when you go?"

"Yes."

"Then I will not be upset, though I will miss you."

With watering eyes, Sophie pulled Thomas into her lap and hugged him tightly to her. He wriggled and squirmed, protesting indignantly. And then he settled into her arms with an exasperated sigh.

"Thank you," she said, when she had collected herself.

He squeezed her back and then climbed off her lap. "Since I cannot climb, can we catch insects?"

"I suppose."

With a whoop of joy, Thomas led the way to the nearest bush. And for the first time in a very long time, Sophie felt hope.

CHAPTER 9

Sophie jumped when the knock came to the door of her guest chamber in the Fontaine manse. She was not high-strung by nature—energetic, yes, but prone to nerves, no—but on this occasion she could not help it. When she had arrived that afternoon she'd taken note of the Roth-schild crest on the travel coach in the drive. For the first time in many years she was sharing the same roof as her brother. In fact, she was fairly certain it was the first time they had been in the same province since their parents had passed on.

She rushed to the door and pulled it open. "Lady Fontaine," she greeted as she saw who called on her.

The dowager was already dressed for dinner, her slender figure encased in cream-colored satin skirts capped with a forest green bodice. Her blonde hair was artfully curled and her wrists, ears, and throat were adorned with brilliant emeralds rimmed with diamonds. Altogether, she presented a picture of elegant, affluent, mature beauty, and the care she displayed in her choice of attire was a vivid reminder of how important tonight would be.

"Lady Sophie."

Dipping into a swift curtsy, Sophie hoped she hid her disappointment. As focused as she was on Rothschild, she was equally focused on Fontaine. To know that he was so close . . . to imagine him relaxed in his den, the place where he had loved her so ardently and so skillfully . . .

Her body thrummed in response to her yearning, and she released her breath in a rush. She had hoped to find him on the opposite side of the door, although she had known it would be far too risky an action for him to take with so many guests about. Her silly heart did not care about the reasonableness of its expectations. It cared only about its infatuation with Justin.

"Do not tax yourself worrying," the dowager said with a reassuring curve to her lips, misunderstanding. "I am duly impressed with Fontaine's arrangements and feel comfortable advising you to leave everything within his capable hands."

Sophie nodded. "I trust him."

"Of course you do. He is a most trustworthy man. He does nothing in half-measure. You can be certain that he has no doubts regarding the outcome of this evening. He would not risk your unhappiness."

Sophie lifted her chin and smiled. The thought of her love for Justin straightened her spine and strengthened her determination to make the night a success, whatever he had planned. "I will make him happy."

"I know you will." The dowager gestured down the hall. "I offer you the use of my abigail and my rooms for dressing. Everything you need awaits you there."

It was odd that the dowager would see to such a task herself, rather than sending her maid to Sophie, but Sophie didn't question the offer, or how it was presented. She simply expressed her gratitude and followed Lady Fontaine down the gallery until they reached their destination.

Stepping into the lovely suite of rooms decorated in varying shades of gold, wine, and pink, Sophie was immediately arrested by the profusion of boxes set atop the chaise. Big and small, it appeared that every size and shape imaginable was represented.

"I took the liberty of peeking," the countess confessed. "Fontaine has excellent taste. I hope you agree."

The thought of wearing garments selected by the marquess caused a low quiver of excitement in Sophie's belly.

"He also spent much of this afternoon upstairs in the nursery," Lady Fontaine continued, "finding and setting aside his favorite toys from childhood for Master Thomas."

Sophie's eyes stung at the mental image those words evoked. The countess seemed to understand. After a gentle squeeze of Sophie's shoulder, she departed the room in silence.

Riveted in place, Sophie allowed the tears to fall. She could not have foreseen that she would fall in love again, but there was no doubt. She was giddy with it.

The door reopened and then closed behind her. The sudden flare of awareness across her skin revealed the identity of her visitor.

She inhaled deeply, then turned to face him. Justin lounged against the closed portal in a sultry pose so rakish it aroused a hot, carnal longing. He had loved her body long and well, and she craved more of the same.

"My lord," she breathed, dipping into a slow curtsy. She could not move any faster. The sight of him made her heart race until she felt dizzy. She stared, drinking him in, unable to do otherwise. He was different now than he had ever been. The infamous, chilly hauteur was nowhere to be found. He was warm and vibrant, the air around him charged with energy.

"My lady," he returned, the corner of his mouth lifting as he straightened and came toward her. Dressed in tight breeches, white waistcoat, and artfully tied cravat, he was devastatingly handsome. The effect he had on her was so powerful that despite the gloves he wore, when he lifted her hand to his lips, her skin tingled.

"You mustn't look at me in that manner in front of the others," she whispered.

"In what manner?"

"As if you are besotted."

The slow curving of his sensual mouth made her heart race. "I have always looked at you this way. After all these years, I cannot change it now."

"Justin . . ."

"You must be unaware of how you look at me. I may look besotted, but your returning perusal is indecent."

"Indecent?"

"As if you wish to lick me from head to toe, and nibble on everything in between."

The scent of starch and bergamot teased her nostrils. He was so close, she could feel the warmth that radiated from him.

"I do wish to do that," she admitted.

Her confession elicited a groan from deep in his throat, followed immediately by the banding of his arms around her and the lifting of her feet from the floor. Tilting his head, he took her mouth with a passion that stole her wits. Sophie could only cling to his broad shoulders and kiss him back with like desperation.

He pulled back with a deep timbral laugh, turning his head when she pursued him for more. "I did not come here for this, love."

Sophie stuck her lower lip out in a pout, and he nipped it playfully with his teeth. "Did you miss me?" he purred.

"Sometimes." He arched an arrogant brow and she wrinkled her nose. "Most of the time."

Fontaine grinned.

"All of the time," she amended, blushing.

"How lovely you are when you blush," he murmured in an intimate, possessive tone that made her toes curl. He pressed his lips to the tip of her nose and then set her down.

"What have you planned?" she asked, studying him for signs of unease. She found none.

"In the family parlor, you will find Lady Cardington entertaining an elderly gentleman who is endlessly fascinated by a small statue, which I collected along with Rothschild from his London residence. In return for promised access to study the thing, he has agreed to school you on its finer points."

"A statue?"

"Yes. A small part of a larger collection of valuable antiquities that belongs to you."

"To me?"

"Yes." His blue eyes laughed at her. "My darling, I adore you."

Sophie shook her head with a smile. "You must."

"Once you feel comfortable enough discussing the subject, the three of you will join us in the lower drawing room where your brother will greet you as if you are both fond of one another. Can you follow along with the ruse?"

"I can do anything if it means you will be mine."

Justin reached for her again. In the decidedly feminine surroundings of his mother's suite, his blatant masculinity was even more compelling. "I have waited a lifetime for you to want me."

"I will want you for a lifetime." She cupped his cheek, her thumb drifting across the cleanly shaven skin. "Will that make up for the delay?"

"Hmmm . . ."

"Something else, then?" Her hand slid around to cup his nape. There, the silky smooth ends of his hair curled around his collar and tickled her knuckles. She pressed her lips to his ear and whispered, "Some licking and nibbling, perhaps?"

"Yes," he said hoarsely, his body hard and tense against hers. "That might do it."

"So . . . I am to greet Rothschild as if we are the closest of siblings," she repeated, "and discuss my heretofore unknown antiquity with feigned knowledge, and then?"

"Then we will spend the evening listening to Rothschild enlighten us about your collection while pretending that we knew everything he is saying prior to him saying it. The other esteemed gentlemen will weigh in with their thoughts and eventually one of them will have the poor manners to yawn, freeing us to retire."

Sophie wriggled seductively. "And then?"

"Minx."

"Will you be mine then?"

"I have always been yours."

"You will make me cry," she sniffled.

"No." His smile was wicked. "I will make you limp with pleasure. Then I will make you my wife."

CHAPTER 10

Justin slouched before the fire in his bedchamber with a brandy-filled goblet in one hand and George's head nuzzled in the other. He watched the blue flames in the grate and thought of Sophie, so dazzlingly beautiful in the gown he had wheedled out of the modiste. It had cost him a bloody fortune to convince the woman that the garment would receive more attention on Sophie than it would on the woman for whom it was originally made. But he would gladly pay the amount a hundred times over to have the same result.

The countess and his mother had wanted something sensational, and he would like to think he had managed to accomplish that.

The soft knock he waited for finally came. Leaping to his feet, he startled the dogs and spilled his libation as he set it hastily on a table as he rushed past. Justin threw open the door and his heart clenched.

"Sophie."

She said nothing, but words weren't necessary. Her dazzling smile was enough. He looked quickly to the left and right, to be certain she was not seen, then he caught her hand and pulled her into his bedchamber.

He locked the door and shooed the dogs into the sitting room. When he turned back, he found her waiting where he had left her. With great, joyful strides Justin caught her up and lifted her high. She set her hands on his shoulders and threw her head back, laughing as he spun them about.

"I began to despair," he said, setting her on her feet so that he could pull her into his embrace. "I thought perhaps I would not see you until morning, a delay I would find unbearable."

Sophie's eyes gazed luminously up into his. "As if I could stay away," she whispered. "I was near desperate to be alone with you all evening."

"Well then, I forgive you for making me wait," he said magnanimously, making her smile.

"I love you, you arrogant man." Cupping his nape, she pulled his head down to steal a kiss.

For a moment, he allowed her the lead, then the scent of her skin and the feel of her body inflamed him. Her soft mouth was parted and moving feverishly against his.

Breathing hard, he somehow managed to wrench his head away. "Will you consent to marry me now?"

"How can you ask questions at a time such as this?" she complained. "We have been apart for weeks on end."

"I've learned extortion has its uses. My title, which usually lures women in droves, is a deterrent to you. But you seem to enjoy my body well enough. If I have to withhold it from you to gain your acceptance, I will do it. Much as it will pain me."

The soft glaze of lust in her eyes turned to rich amusement. "I still cannot collect how you extorted that performance out of Rothschild this evening."

He grinned. "What do you think of that?"

"I think my influence is already corrupting you." She cupped his cheek in the palm of her hand. "Was he telling the truth?"

"About the value of the antiquities bequeathed to you? Yes. Rothschild has been using them to guarantee his markers, which are not inconsiderable."

"All that excitement displayed over that little statue . . . Incredible!"

"Quite. Adventurers such as Belzoni have fueled the great interest in such things, fortunately for us. Your collection, while small, is priceless." It took some clever maneuvering on his mother's part to lure both lauded experts in the field and members of the peerage who were avidly engaged in the topic to his estate in Northamptonshire on such short notice. But somehow the task was managed, resulting in a dinner party that would not be forgotten for some time. "You are now an eccentric collector of some means, which grants you a bit more license."

"And my once barren social calendar has become filled with numerous invitations to display the rest of my private collection."

"Once word spreads, you will scarcely be able to keep up. As long as those items can be seen only through you and not a museum, you shall be in some demand."

She shook her head. "How did you learn of Rothschild's deception?"

"I have my ways."

"My darling." Sophie lifted to her tiptoes and pressed a kiss to his chin. "How will I ever do you justice?"

"Never mind that nonsense. Simply say yes." He rocked his hips suggestively against her. "I have something you want and I am quite desperate to give it to you."

Her laughter was music to his ears. "Yes, you wicked man. Yes!"

Sophie rubbed her breasts into his chest, brushing his lapels open so that only the material of her bodice and chemise separated her nipples from his skin. The brazen advance undid him, bringing to life fantasies he had cherished in his youth and again as a man. She gazed up at him seductively beneath long, thick lashes. "Now, will you take me to your bed?"

He growled and lifted her, taking the few steps necessary to reach the nearest wall so he could pin her roughly against it. She gasped softly at the impact, her arms at her sides, her hands pressed palms down against the damask.

"The bed is too far away," he said gruffly, shrugging out of his robe.

"Dear God," she breathed when he stood naked before her. He stroked himself, lengthening and thickening his cock, watching her pupils dilate with a similar desire to the one that raged within him.

Impassioned, he caged her between his arms, his mouth at her throat, his teeth nipping the sensitive skin. "Pull up your gown."

He felt her swallow hard beneath his lips. *"Here?"*

"Yes, here. I want to lick you, Sophie love," he purred, his hands moving all over her, rediscovering all the curves and valleys of her body. "I want to put my mouth on you, eat at you, kiss you between your legs"—he took her mouth with lush, deep flicks of his tongue—"just like this."

"Yes." Her head fell to the side, baring her throat to him. He felt her hands between them, pulling up her skirts. Her movements brushed against his cock, and his jaw tensed. His gut cramped tight, lust warring with deeper, more powerful emotions.

He reached down and cupped her, parted her, finding her cunt slick and hot and soft as satin. He tested her with a gently probing finger, the feel of her grasping tissues pushing him beyond any hope of restraint.

"Bloody hell." Sinking to his knees, he lunged for the pulsing flesh between her legs and covered it with his open mouth.

Sophie jerked violently at the shocking sensation of a lover's kiss in her most intimate place. Her senses were overwhelmed with the sight and smell of him, her heart racing at the boldness of his actions. The growling sounds he made as his tongue flickered desperately over the clenching opening of her sex made her knees weak. He held her upright and draped her leg over his shoulder, giving her the support she needed to bear the exquisite torment while opening her farther to his relentless demands.

Her fingers dug into the wall. The sounds of the ticking clock and her labored exhales were muted by the blood roaring in her ears. She looked down, watching the way the fire reflected in the golden strands of Justin's hair. He held her open with his fingers, nuzzling his parted lips against her, worshiping her with reverent kisses. The sight of her gown held to her waist and the beautifully built man on his knees before her was deeply, searingly erotic.

"I need you." Her eyes slid closed and her hot cheek pressed against the cool damask. "Please . . ."

Justin tilted his head and pushed his tongue deep, the slight roughness of early stubble on his chin rasping against the sensitive skin of her inner thighs. She keened softly at the shallow, teasing plunges, nowhere near satisfying, but wonderful nevertheless. In and out. Piercing her hard and fast. He ate at her with near ravenous hunger, groaning in a way that made her cup her breasts and squeeze, fighting the aching swelling.

"Please," she begged, twisting and arching, rocking into his mouth. "Please . . ."

He altered position, moving higher, his agile tongue fluttering rapidly over the tight bundle of nerves that begged for his attention.

The surge of release hit her hard.

She cried out and clung to his perspiration-slick shoulders as the climax stole her wits. He continued to torment her, to lick her on the outside and the inside, pushing her to orgasm again. This time she could only whimper as her sex spasmed madly.

"Beautiful," he praised, his voice husky and low. "I believe I shall do that every day."

Flushed and panting for air, Sophie was still quivering violently when Fontaine pushed to his feet and carried her to the bed.

Laying her on her side, he exposed the back of her gown and began to free the long row of buttons. The task was a lengthy one, giving her the time she needed to return to herself. When she was finally nude and he was levering over her, she was ready, her arms and legs opening wide in welcome. His lean hips settled against her, and his arms—so strong and warm—embraced her in a cocoon of bergamot and tobacco-scented male that she never wanted to leave.

How quickly her need had reached this level. And yet she did not doubt her feelings. Or his. They were simply there, inside her, feelings of connection that had made separation a misery. Talking with him and being with him were gifts she had always enjoyed. Now lusting for him was a state she had come to crave in her life. Waking in the morning and knowing that the new day would have him in it brought her a kind of joy she had thought never to feel again. It was not the same sensation as she had felt for Langley, but it was every bit as wonderful. She knew Justin so well, and more important, he knew her so well. Better than anyone, she thought. And he loved her in spite of her faults, or maybe even because of them.

"Share your thoughts," he murmured, as the broad head of his cock lodged at the entrance to her body.

She set her hands on his shoulders. "I want to make love to you in the sunshine so I can see every inch of you without shadow. I so love to look at you when you are inside me."

The smile he gave her was warm and wicked. It made her breath catch and her heart leap. "Ah, love. Promise me you will always be wild."

"Because of you," she breathed. "You make it safe for me to take risks. You always have."

He pushed the first thick inches of his beautiful cock into her and she gasped, her back arching upward as her body attempted to contain such pleasure.

"Sophie . . ." A violent shudder coursed the length of his frame.

She panted, writhing beneath him. "Th–that feels delicious."

It was more than Justin could take, that throaty praise. He held her hips down, and plunged deep.

Sophie's broken cry as he hilted had him groaning in near pain. She was tight as a fist around him, and swollen from his previous ministrations.

"Hold still," he ordered hoarsely, sucking in air like a man too long under water. Her cunt was rippling along his cock, sucking him deeper, luring him to forgo courtesy and fuck her until neither of them had the energy required to go on.

"I can't bear it," she sobbed, scratching him, struggling in her impatience, urging him to ride her to the finish.

Christ, but he loved it. Loved her. Had always loved her. He relished having her, owning her, and the way everything in his world had altered irrevocably because of her. His future, so orderly and well planned just weeks ago, was now an adventure waiting to happen.

His thighs flexed against hers as he kept her pinned, and fucked her slow and deep. Rolling his hips. Making her beg for more, because it drove his lust higher to hear how desperately she craved his body inside hers.

"Justin," she moaned, arching her breasts upward to press against his chest, their skin sticking together with the sweat of their exertions. His head lowered, his lips fastening on a tightened nipple, his cheeks hallowing as he drew on her in long pulls that mimicked the stroking of his cock inside her.

He rode her at length, thrusting between her spread thighs in a lazy, sensual rhythm, feeling her climax again. And again. Such a passionate woman. Her body quaking beneath his, stirring his ardor further until the sheets were fisted in his white-knuckled grip and he was driving powerfully into her. The tension coiled in his shoulders, slid down his spine, and gathered at the base of his aching cock. He was so hard, so ferociously aroused, he almost feared the impending orgasm.

When it came, it tore guttural cries from his throat. Killing him. He shuddered violently and she clung to him, his darling Sophie. She whispered to him, anchored him, so that the violent spewing of his seed inside her was not the loss of his soul, but the merging of hers to his.

He pumped hard and fast into her, taking her over the edge with him.

Fitted to him, the other half of a whole.

With her cheek on Fontaine's chest and her legs intertwined with his, Sophie spoke of her son. Countless moments of joy and discovery.

He listened quietly, his hands stroking down the length of her spine. "I wish I could alleviate your concerns."

"You will," she said, her mouth curving against his skin. "I adore you. I fail to see how anyone could not."

She felt his cock twitch against her thigh and raised her head to meet his gaze. Sprawled against a pile of pillows and lying amid monogrammed white sheets, the marquess was unbearably handsome. He looked disheveled and thoroughly sated, an appearance that flattered him so well she found her passions rising along with his. His big, hard body was a finely wrought instrument of pleasure, and the golden skin that covered the lean lengths of muscle was so sensitive to her attentions. She could make him groan with the slightest of touches. "Will I always be able to rouse you with a compliment?"

"You rouse me by breathing, love." He winked and scratched at the center of his chest. "And I adore you, too."

Sophie stared at him a moment, comparing the warm man whose bed she shared with the cooler, more reserved boy she remembered.

"We should depart as soon as possible," he said. "I would like to meet your son."

"How soon?"

"As soon as we can urge our guests to depart."

She kissed his jaw in silent gratitude. "Good. I miss him."

"I know." He hugged her tightly. "You will be together again as quickly as I can manage it."

She heard the faintest trace of worry in his tone, and understood how hard this must be for him. How would she feel, were he to have a child to win over? Knowing how deep the bond between parent and child was, and wondering if she would ever be even a small part of that connection, or if she would forever be an unwanted intrusion. It made her love him all the more that he was willing to make so many changes to his life and take so many risks just to be with her.

Pinching the sheet with two fingers, Sophie tugged it downward until the edge reached his upper thighs and his cock was bared to her gaze. A quick glance upward found him watching her with eyes that glittered in the near darkness.

"I want to kiss you here," she said, circling his cock with gentle fingers. "Such as you did to me."

"Feel free." A hint of laughter had replaced the apprehension in his voice.

The sound made her smile.

"I've come to be wary when you wear that mischievous look," he said.

Sophie fluttered her lashes innocently. "Mischief? Me?"

"Ha!"

She crawled over him and settled between his spread legs. The pattern of his breathing changed, became faster as the muscles in his thighs tensed. Her breasts brushed against his skin and his breath hissed out between his teeth. The power she held to give him pleasure was heady, as was the sight of his body, which aroused her to a fever pitch. Her hand closed around him and angled his throbbing cock to meet her eager mouth.

"Christ!" Justin arched off the bed as Sophie's soft, wet lips surrounded him.

He had been serviced this way countless times, yet it had never felt like this. He was ready to blow. After his recent galvanic orgasm, he should be able to enjoy a lazy climb to the peak. Instead, he was gritting his teeth to prevent toppling over.

"Umm . . ." she purred, lifting her head. "I like this. I believe I shall do this every day."

He choked. The sight of her mouth poised just above his cock was a fantasy he had cherished for years. To think of such pleasure daily . . . "You'll kill me."

"You'll bear it." Sophie pumped her hand and his hips jerked.

"Bloody hell!"

Cum beaded the tip of his cock. He watched in an agony of lust as her tongue came out and licked up the drop. The sound she made, one of deep pleasure, made his balls draw up.

"Suck it," he groaned, reaching for her, cupping her cheeks so that he could feel her mouth open. He felt his hardness through the softness of her cheek, and gasped as her tongue lifted and stroked the sensitive underside of his shaft.

The next he knew he was writhing atop the linens, his jaw aching with the force with which he clenched it, his arms tense and fingers cramped as he forced himself to hold her gently.

Sweet Sophie was driving him insane, her hungry

mouth sucking and sucking, her cheeks hollowing with every drawing pull, her head bobbing in a wild, unrestrained rhythm as if loving him this way was for her pleasure alone.

Dear God, he was going to die. He was muttering and cursing and begging, wanting her to stop. Wanting her never to stop.

Her gentle fingers cupped his tight sac and squeezed gently, rolling his balls, heating them with the warmth of her palm. His eyes widened with the knowledge that he was about to come, his throat working to warn her, but no sound came out.

With the last of his strength he pushed her away. Her response was a growl and hard, deep suction.

He came like a geyser, groaning, blasting deep into the welcoming depths of her mouth. Her hand urgently stroked the length of him that would not fit inside her, pumping his cum up the shaft to spill over her working tongue. She wouldn't stop, the demented female, taking him to heights of pleasure he'd never reached, then carrying him back down with long, savoring licks.

The mattress cradled him as he sank into it, devastated. Then it was Sophie who cradled him, her lush body coming to rest over his, her cheek settling over his madly beating heart.

"I love you," he whispered, his damp face nestled in her fragrant hair, his arms hugging her close. "Christ, I love you so much."

He felt her press a kiss into his chest. He gazed up at the canopy above them and basked in his contentment. The days ahead would bring challenges, but if the nights ended thusly, he would bear them all with nary a complaint.

"I will make you happy," he promised. "I will do my best to make Thomas happy."

"I know, my love," she crooned.

"But"—his tone was a warning—"if you ever blow pepper up my nose again, I will take my hand to your arse."

"Perhaps I shall like that," she teased mischievously.

His cock twitched wearily, insanely interested despite being spent. "Bloody hell."

CHAPTER 11

———❖———

The day promised to be bright and beautiful the morning Justin began his campaign to win over the young Master Thomas. His mind was occupied with possible things to say, suggestions for activities they could share, answers to questions that may be asked of him. It was a dreadfully taxing business, this. The happiness of his fiancée rested on his ability to bond with her child. It therefore meant a great deal to him.

He intended to give the boy an active and prominent role in the wedding, but that plan would only succeed if the child was willing. To that aim he intended to make a nuisance of himself until they were friends. Of course, the emotions behind the plan were nowise near as simple as that.

He was nervous such as he had never been. Standing before the mirror that morning, he had rejected several cravats and coats, trying to picture himself through a five-year-old child's eyes. Would Sophie's son find him distant and hard to approach, as some adults did? Would Thomas resent him for winning some of his mother's affection?

Filled with concerns and doubts, Justin took a deep, fortifying breath as the golden-bricked manor house came into view. Despite his mental preparations, he felt in need of a stiff drink by the time he reached the end of the front drive.

He dismounted and handed the reins to the waiting groomsman. Then he took the steps to the front door two at a time. Before he could knock, the portal swung open and Sophie was launching herself into his arms. His heart stuttered at the feel of her and he crushed her close.

"My lord," she greeted, lifting to her toes and kissing him full on the mouth.

"Stop that," he admonished, glancing nervously over her head. "What if he sees you?"

"My darling." Her eyes sparkled. "How I love you. Thomas is in the nursery and cannot witness my affection."

"You might be surprised. When I was his age, I was never where anyone would expect."

Common courtesy dictated that they share tea with the countess first and so they did, both of them enjoying the obvious happiness Lady Cardington felt over their union.

And then it was time.

With her fingers linked with his, Sophie led him up to the nursery on the upper floor.

"Ready?" she asked when they reached the closed door.

"Yes." As he would ever be.

She pushed the portal open and entered. "Tommy," she called, her voice pitched sweetly.

"Hmm?"

The distracted-sounding reply made Justin smile. He

stepped into the sunshine-filled room and found the source of his anxiousness seated innocuously on an English rug surrounded by a legion of tin soldiers. Nearby, on the window bench, a governess knitted quietly.

"I would like you to meet someone," Sophie said, sinking to a crouch.

The small, dark head lifted, revealing handsome features and big brown eyes. Justin tensed as Thomas turned his head and found him, steeling himself for an unknown reaction.

Sophie made the introductions.

"Hello, Master Thomas," Justin said carefully.

"Hello, my lord." The boy's inquisitive gaze dropped to the marquess's riding boots. He frowned, then looked back at his toys.

Justin thought he had been summarily dismissed, which tied his stomach in knots, then Thomas picked up a soldier and held it out to him. "This one has boots like yours."

"Oh?" Bending at the knees, Justin accepted the offering and remarked, "So he does. How lucky I am to have such boots."

Thomas smiled. The gesture was Sophie's in miniature, and Justin's chest tightened. He sank the rest of the way to the floor.

"You can play with the red ones," Thomas said magnanimously. "I shall be blue."

"Thank you. I should like that very much." Justin glanced at Sophie. She blew him a kiss that went straight to his heart, then rose and moved to the bookcase.

"Shall I read you both a story?" she asked, in a voice huskier than usual.

"Yes! The fables." Thomas glanced at him. "You do enjoy fables, don't you, my lord?"

"I do."

The child beamed. "Excellent."

And so it was a beginning. Auspicious, to be sure.

EPILOGUE

$\longrightarrow\!\!\!\Longleftarrow\!\!\!\longleftarrow$

Tiptoeing carefully through the maze in the rear garden, Sophie shivered slightly at the thrill of being hunted. Somewhere, her husband was searching for her. She knew that the longer she kept him waiting, the hotter his blood would run. Just a sennight ago, she had managed to evade him for almost a half hour, and when he'd caught her . . .

She stifled a moan as sudden lewd images filled her mind and made her lustful. She would never look at the alcove near the music room in quite the same way again.

A twig snapped, and Sophie dropped to a crouch. She waited with bated breath, then, when she felt certain the way was clear, she crawled through a small gap and emerged in the neighboring row.

"Caught you!"

Screeching, Sophie flailed slightly as she was hauled to her feet, then the maze fell silent as Justin smothered her protest with a deep, possessive, toe-curling kiss.

"Umm . . ." she moaned, rubbing against his big, hard body. "You, my lord, give perfect kisses."

He pulled back far enough to reveal his silently chastising arched brow. "Do not attempt to distract me from your mischief, Lady Fontaine. A woman in your condition should not be crawling through bushes."

"Nonsense!" she protested.

"It is not nonsense. Shall we ask Thomas how he feels about your activities?"

Sophie pouted. "You have me at an unfair advantage. The two of you are always joining forces."

"Because we love you. He is desperate for a sibling, as you well know since he has plagued us for one since the day we wed." Justin pressed a lingering kiss to her forehead. "You mustn't overtax yourself, love."

Wrapping her arms around his lean waist, she rested her cheek against his heart and sighed. "I am only a few months along. Besides, I feel the need to point out that sharing your bed can be far more strenuous."

That comment earned her a gentle swat to the derriere. "Insatiable wench." He linked his fingers with hers and led them out of the maze. "I beg to service you with my mouth and have you plead for my cock until I can either do as you ask or never manage a moment's rest."

"You have a divine mouth," she murmured, hugging his arm. "I love it, as I love all of you. But that other part you mention is . . ." Sophie purred softly. "Well, it is quite irreplaceable."

He shot her a scorching side-glance, and she grinned impishly in reply. They approached the manse with rapid strides, their eagerness to be alone and as close as two people can be goading them to haste.

"My lord! Come swiftly!"

They paused at the sound of Thomas's cry. Turning their heads, they found him standing at the edge of the garden.

Just beyond him was the stream and by the looks of his

wet pants, muddy sleeves, and beleaguered-looking tutor he had been enjoying himself immensely there. George and Edward sat on their haunches to the left and right of him, guarding him as they'd been doing since the first night the three had slept under the same roof. They shared his room now, which suited everyone perfectly.

Justin lifted his hand and waved.

Thomas rimmed his mouth with both hands to amplify his voice and shouted, "I found a five-legged frog!"

The deep pride revealed on her husband's face brought tears to Sophie's eyes. Being *enceinte*, she was more emotional than usual, but the depth of affection Fontaine bore for her son had moved her from the beginning. It was one of the many reasons she loved him as she did—with every breath in her body.

"We must go see this wonder of nature," he murmured.

"Yes, my love." She lifted their linked hands and pressed a kiss to his knuckles. "We must."

"Pregnancy suits her," the dowager marchioness said to her dearest friend as they admired the handsome family from their vantage on the rear terrace.

"Most decidedly," Lady Cardington agreed, stirring sugar into her tea.

The gentle summer breeze pressed Sophie's golden muslin skirts to her body, revealing a softly swelling belly. "I cannot tell you how it affects me to see her so happy. She was deeply grieving when she carried Thomas. It was difficult to see such a happy event marred by such despair."

The dowager offered a sympathetic smile. "She is an admirable woman, Caroline."

"And your son is an admirable man, strong enough to make decisions with his heart and disregard those who have smaller minds. I knew they would be perfect together." Shaking her head, Lady Cardington rearranged the cashmere blanket that warmed her legs. "Those two. You do realize that I have never looked at pepper the same way again?"

"Oh, dear heavens, neither have I! But you did warn me."

"Yes. She was a fanciful child. Always concocting some mischief or tall tale. I had thought that light within her had died with Langley, but Fontaine's affection has restored it."

"And Sophie has shown him a different view of the world that has altered him for the better. They are well-met. Of course, you and I knew that from the beginning."

The two women leaned back in their wrought-iron chairs and shared a secret smile.

"Beautifully done," one said to the other.

The laud was apropos of both of them.

Don't miss the book that inspired *Bared to You*.
Read *Seven Years to Sin*, available now!

CHAPTER 2

———◈———

"And this," the captain said, turning slightly to gesture at the gentleman, "is Mr. Alistair Caulfield, owner of this fine vessel and brilliant violinist, as you 'eard."

Jess swore her heart ceased beating for a moment. Certainly, she stopped breathing. Caulfield faced her and sketched a perfectly executed, elegant bow. Yet his head never lowered and his gaze never left hers.

Dear God . . .

What were the odds that they would cross paths this way?

There was very little of the young man Jess had once known left in the man who faced her. Alistair Caulfield was no longer pretty. The planes of his face had sharpened, etching his features into a thoroughly masculine countenance. Darkly winged brows and thick lashes framed those infamous eyes of rich, deep blue. In the fading light of the setting sun and the flickering flames of the turpentine lamps, his coal black hair gleamed with health and vitality. Previously his beauty had been striking, but now he was larger. More worldly and mature. Undeniably formidable.

Breathtakingly male.

"Lady Tarley," he greeted her, straightening. "It is a great pleasure to see you again."

His voice was lower and deeper in pitch than she remembered. It had a soft, rumbling quality to it. Almost a purr. He walked with equal feline grace, his step light and surefooted despite his powerful build. His gaze was sharp and intense, assessing. Challenging. As before, it felt as if he looked right into the very heart of her and dared her to deny that he could.

She sucked in a shaky breath and met him halfway, offering her hand. "Mr. Caulfield. It has been some time since we last crossed paths."

"Years."

His look was so intimate she couldn't help but think of that night in the Pennington woods. A rush of heat swept up her arm from where their skin connected.

He went on, "Please accept my condolences on your recent loss. Tarley was a good man. I admired him, and liked him quite well."

"Your thoughts are appreciated," she managed, in spite of a suddenly dry mouth. "I offer the same to you. I was deeply sorry to hear that your brother had passed."

His jaw tightened and he released her, sliding his hand away so that his fingertips stroked over the center of her palm. "Two of them," he replied grimly.

Jess caught her hand back and rubbed it discreetly against her thigh to no avail. The tingle left by his touch was inerasable.

"Shall we?" the captain said, tilting his head toward the table. He pulled a chair out for Jess, then the men sat.

Caulfield took a seat directly across from her. She was

discomfited at first, but he seemed to forget her the moment the food was brought in. To ensure the steady flow of conversation, she took pains to direct the discussion to topics addressing the ship and seafaring, and they easily followed. No doubt they were relieved not to have to focus on her life of limited scope, which was of little interest to men. What followed was a rather fantastic hour of food and conversation the likes of which she'd never been exposed to before. Gentlemen did not often discuss matters of business around her.

It quickly became clear that Alistair Caulfield was enjoying laudable financial success. He didn't comment on it personally, but he participated in the discussion about the trade, making it clear he was very involved in the minutiae of his business endeavors. He was also expertly dressed. His coat was made with a gray-green velvet she thought was quite lovely and the stylishly short cut of the shoulders emphasized how fit he was.

"Did you make the trip to Jamaica often, Captain?" Jess asked.

"Not as often as some of Mr. Caulfield's other ships do." He set his elbows on the table and toyed with his beard. "London is where we berth most often. The others dock in Liverpool or Bristol."

"How many ships are there?"

The captain looked at Caulfield. "'Ow many are there now? Five?"

"Six," Caulfield said, looking directly at Jess.

She met his gaze with difficulty. She couldn't explain why she felt as she did, but it was almost as if the intimacies she had witnessed that night in the woods had been between Caulfield and herself, not another woman.

Something profound had transpired in the moment they'd first become aware of each other in the darkness. A connecting thread had been sewn between them, and she had no notion how to sever it. She knew things about the man she should not know, and there was no way for her to return to blissful ignorance. . . .

THE DUKE'S TREASURE

MINERVA SPENCER

Dedicated to Jeffe and George

Acknowledgments

I'd like to thank Alicia Condon for bringing me into this project, Pam Hopkins for her calm and thoughtful advice (especially when I'm impatient), Jeffe Kennedy for offering stellar input and fantastic insights that have earned her drinks for life, George M. who made the time to read my work (over and over) and give me priceless, line-by-line critiques, even on short notice and in the midst of his hectic schedule, and last, but never least, to my husband, Brantly, who continues to love and support me in everything I do and really is my greatest treasure.

CHAPTER 1

———◆———

London, 1816

There were few things Beaumont Halliwell, Sixth Duke of Wroxton, loathed more than unpunctual behavior—especially on his wedding day.

Beau took out his watch; it was four minutes after the last time he'd checked. His bride-to-be was officially late.

He slipped the watch into his pocket and drummed his fingers on the carved altar rail, staring at the stained-glass window on the east wall. It cast a colorful, but sullen, glow over the dark flagstone floor and battered pews, but it did little to shed light in the ancient church.

The window was a depiction of Queen Elizabeth with two massive bells at her feet. He assumed they were a reference to the church bells alleged to have rung so joyously the day Princess Elizabeth was released from the Tower prison.

Prison.

The word clanged in his head like the slamming of a

cell door. Yes, prison was a good thought to keep in mind just now. Of course, as a duke and counselor to the regent, Beau could not actually be *thrown* into debtors' prison— as much a relief as that thought might be at this particular moment.

No. There would be no prison for Beau. Instead, there would be marriage. Although there would not even be *that* if his betrothed did not arrive.

Beau felt no relief at that thought: if he didn't marry Josephine Loman, he'd have to marry somebody similar— and this time Beau would have to find a rich wife rather than having one tossed into his lap.

He snorted. Good God, what a blur these past months had been.

Beau had known the moment he'd learned of his brother's death that he couldn't hide from his responsibilities indefinitely. But a series of momentous events conspired to keep him from assuming his ducal duties.

First it had been Napoleon keeping Beau—and hundreds of thousands of other soldiers—lethally occupied in Belgium.

After Waterloo, it had been unavoidable diplomatic duties with Ambassador Stuart's staff in Paris. But then, by the beginning of the New Year, after almost a decade at war, all plausible excuses for staying away had disappeared and he'd returned home, not to visit, but to stay.

Whether he liked it or not, Beau was the new head of a large, demanding, and impoverished family. And whether he liked it or not, he'd *had* to accept Edward Loman's offer to marry his daughter.

Josephine Loman was a woman Beau had never met before today, although—thanks to her father's persistence—

he'd been betrothed to her since last August, less than a month after Jason's death.

It had been Beau's engagement to one of the richest women in Britain that had placated his dead brother's— and now his—creditors and allowed him to remain away as long as he had.

"Pssst."

Beau turned to the only person in the dim, dank church besides himself and the vicar.

"What is it, Moreton?" he asked, deliberately repressive.

Lucas Powell, the Earl of Moreton and Beau's best friend, grinned up at him, unrepressed. "I think she's done a runner on you, Wroxton. Maybe I'll take a whack at her next."

Beau ignored his friend's levity.

Behind him, the vicar said, "Er, Your Grace, is it pos—"

A noise from the narthex cut off whatever he was about to say and all three men turned as two people entered the church.

"Ah." The vicar sounded so relieved, you'd have thought it was *his* bloody wedding.

Beau strode toward the newcomers, propelled by irritation and anger, his eyes riveted to the slight, veiled figure in pale blue: his wife-to-be.

"I'm terribly sorry, Your Grace," the companion said, a woman whose name Beau had forgotten, if he'd ever known it.

She wittered and flapped and came toward him. "I'm afraid there was a—"

Beau raised a staying hand that instantly stopped her chatter.

"Is aught amiss, Miss Loman?" he asked the woman

who *should* have been his wife by now—had she arrived promptly.

Her shoulders stiffened at his sharp tone. *Good.* Beau *wanted* her to know he didn't appreciate being badgered toward a hasty wedding by her father and then kept waiting by *her*.

The older woman opened her mouth, but Beau shook his head. "Give us a moment in private." It was not a request.

He led Miss Loman a few feet away. "What is going on? Where is your father?" he demanded, unable to see her face through the almost opaque veil.

"Don't bark at me as if I'm one of your servants."

Beau winced at the flat, nasal vowels. *Good God, how bloody atrocious!* He knew her father spoke with an even more appalling accent, but Loman was a product of the stews—why the hell hadn't the man sent his daughter to a proper school?

Beau shuddered; just wait until his family met the woman the newspapers unflatteringly referred to as the Potted Meat Princess.

Later. He'd have ample time to deal with that later.

But for now, he took a deep breath and leashed both his revulsion and his temper. "Are we to wait for your father, or not, Miss Loman?"

"He is not coming."

She sniffed and Beau stared at her thickly veiled person with mounting horror. *Damnation! Was she—?*

She raised a gloved hand that held a handkerchief beneath her veil.

An unfamiliar emotion—shame—heated his face. *Bloody hell!* What a beast he was. The woman had been crying—

perhaps was *still* crying—and he'd been entertaining uncharitable thoughts about her person.

He grimaced. Regardless of her background and accent, Josephine Loman was his, and his family's, savior and she deserved respect.

"I am sorry to hear Mr. Loman is doing so poorly." Lord, he'd just seen the man eight days ago; he'd looked ill, but not—

"He tried to get out of bed and fell," she said in a vaguely accusatory tone—as if this unseemly haste to marry were *Beau's* notion rather than her father's.

"Do you wish to postpone the ceremony?" he asked, hoping the answer was *no*, hoping they could get this farce—or at least *this* part of it—over already.

Her head snapped up. "No, Your Grace," she said coldly, her answer the turning of a key in the cell door he'd heard close earlier. "It is my father's wish that we go through with the wedding. Today."

And what is yours? Beau wanted to ask, but of course he didn't.

Jo was grateful for the veil. The last thing she wanted the beautiful, arrogant, and proud aristocrat to see right now was her homely, tear-stained face—which was doubtless even less attractive than usual.

Not that her face—homely or otherwise—would make a speck of difference to the Duke of Wroxton; he was marrying her for one thing only: her money.

Even with the advantages that her father's wealth had purchased for her, the glorious creature across from her might as well be a separate species from Jo. She had no doubt that *he* believed he was a separate, superior, and more cultured species.

Of course Jo wasn't helping matters by adopting a false accent and speaking to him like a fishwife, but what did he expect when he addressed her in such a peremptory tone, as if she were his serf?

Besides, Jo had seen from his expression that he'd been revolted by her accent, but not particularly surprised. Indeed, he'd likely expected a coarse, pushing Cit—a wife who'd be a constant reminder of just how low he'd stooped for the sake of her father's money.

Not that he'd need a reminder; the Duke of Wroxton would never let either of them forget the vast gulf between them.

And what about you, Jo? Will you ever forget—or forgive—Wroxton for something he doesn't even know he did? Will you forgive him for not wanting you five years ago? Or will you take this chance to make his life a misery?

Jo flinched away from the thought. *Good Lord—could that really be true?* Was that why she was so furious? So quick to see a slight in his expression, his tone? His actions?

Hell hath no fury like a woman scorned.

Jo closed her eyes, as if that might somehow transport her away from the muddle she'd made of her life.

But when she opened them again, the dark little chapel was still waiting for her.

St. Olav's, with its terrifying gargoyles, and crooked grave markers that looked as though the very earth were trying to expel them, seemed a grim choice for a wedding.

Jo wondered if Wroxton had purposely chosen the bleakest church in all of London for their nuptials.

After all, she thought, cutting a quick glance from beneath her veil, her groom was looking more than a little bleak, himself.

And all thanks to you, Jo.

Jo kicked and shoved the taunting voice into a cupboard in her mind and latched the door shut. *There*, that was the last time she needed to listen to such drivel today.

But just when she'd banished one voice, another took its place: this one her father's.

"This is what I've always wanted for you, Josie, but do you want it for yourself?" Edward Loman had asked her, just last night. "It's not too late to change your mind." His deep-set green-gray eyes were shadowed by unease, as well as the pain that always plagued him now.

"What? Second thoughts, Papa?" Jo had teased, not because she'd felt lighthearted but because she'd asked herself that same question at least a hundred times: Was she mad to want a man whose only communication to her—a brief, businesslike letter—proved he'd not remembered her, and wouldn't want her if he did?

Had she been mad, or just desperate, to have snatched at her father's scheme so quickly when he'd raised it all those months ago?

"I got you a duke, Josie!" He'd been gleeful, like a little boy who'd discovered a shiny penny, when he'd told her the news last August.

Jo knew whom her father had *gotten* for her even before he told her: Beaumont Halliwell, the newly minted Duke of Wroxton, a man she'd not seen for over five years but hadn't been able to forget. And not for lack of trying.

Now, looking up over half a foot at her betrothed's cold, hardened face, Jo wondered if she shouldn't have rejected her father's seductive offer and worked harder on scouring her brain of the duke's memory.

While he was every bit as gorgeous and golden as the last time she'd seen him—a dashing soldier on leave who'd been engaged to marry the diamond of the Season, Lady Victoria Beamish—his angelic face was now that of a haughty, remote, and weary angel.

What had made him so grim? Had it happened when Victoria broke off their engagement to marry his brother, the former duke? Or was it the inevitable effect of a decade's worth of war on a man's soul?

Or perhaps it is his impending marriage to you, Jo?

Jo sighed.

"Hello again, Miss Loman."

She looked up from her unpleasant musings to find the Earl of Moreton had come to stand beside the duke. Jo's lips curved in response to his grin, even though he wouldn't be able to see her expression through the heavy lace veil.

"Good day, my lord," Jo said.

"It's been a long time, Miss Loman. What—five years?"

Jo was flattered Moreton remembered. "You have a good memory, my lord. It was indeed the spring and summer of 1811."

Wroxton turned to her, arrested, his lips parted in surprise, a flush darkening his cheekbones.

Any pleasure Jo felt at taunting him was crushed beneath humiliation. She had only *suspected* he had no memory of her; now he'd confirmed it.

The vicar cleared his throat. "Your Grace? Shall we proceed?"

"I am ready," Wroxton said, his expression that of a condemned man on his walk to the gallows.

He will never love you, Jo, never! Run! Run!

Jo ignored the shrill warning and stared up into blue eyes that were as beautiful as the sky, and just as unreachable.

Even his cold, obvious disregard couldn't quench her burning desire to possess him. Jo didn't care that he would never love her, or even like her. All that mattered was that he would finally be *hers*.

"Yes," she said, "I am ready."

I've been ready for five years.

CHAPTER 2

"Sorry to receive you this way, Your Grace," Edward Loman said in a wheezy voice, his claw-like hand gesturing at his nightcap and wild Chinese silk banyan. "Won't you sit?"

Beau lowered himself into the chair beside the massive four-poster bed, trying not to stare. He'd only met Loman once—when he'd arrived in England—and the changes those few days had wrought on the older man were shocking.

"I regret not making it to the ceremony."

"Your presence was missed, sir. Your daughter is waiting below, most eager to see you."

Loman coughed, his face spasming in pain, the pulpy rattle in his chest sounding like overripe fruit falling from a tree. His eyes, when he opened them, were red rimmed but as sharp as a saber blade. "You can send her up after we have one last word."

"Of course, sir."

"I have vaults full of money and mansions stuffed with costly frippery, but my daughter is my priceless treasure,

Wroxton. And now she is yours to cherish." The look he gave Beau must have been the one he'd used to intimidate business opponents in the course of accumulating one of the biggest fortunes in Britain.

Beau was not threatened, but he respected the sentiment behind the look.

"Everything is yours now, Wroxton. *Everything,*" Loman hissed, his eyes burning. "And I swear this, Your Grace: if you don't do right by my daughter, I will come back from the grave and haunt you the rest of your days."

Although Beau knew Loman's words were nothing more than the hollow threat of a dying man, he felt a chill.

But the chill was nothing compared to the molten anger simmering in his belly: anger at his brother for dying and leaving this mess for Beau to clean up; anger at his family for expecting him to save them all; and anger at this crude, upstart Cit who'd wrapped Beau up in a marriage contract with his daughter as quickly and effortlessly as a butcher wrapped up a leg of mutton.

And now this—this *unlettered oaf* had the audacity to impugn Beau's honor?

How dare Loman believe that he needed to threaten a Duke of Wroxton to live up to his part of a bargain?

"I am a gentleman, Mr. Loman," Beau reminded him coolly. "I would never treat your daughter as anything less than a lady." His brief discussion with the woman in question came back to him and he gritted his teeth against it. "As my duchess she will be received everywhere and treated with the utmost respect." She would never be welcomed by the *ton*, of course, but then that was not something Beau had promised. "All that said, I do hope I've never given you—"

"I know you ain't marrying my Josey for love." Loman

snorted rudely, the action sending him into another fit of coughing. "I might be an ignorant upstart Cit," he said, grinning at whatever expression he saw on Beau's face. "But I ain't stupid. Nor is my girl—she's been groomed for such a marriage." Beau barely held his tongue at the old man's outrageous claim. "She don't expect love from you, so don't fret about that. But she deserves your protection and respect. We struck our bargain fair and square: my girl and my money for your title and a grandson." His bluish lips twisted into a mocking smile. "Don't you forget that after I'm gone, Wroxton: my fortune for a few spurts from you."

Beau's mouth twisted with distaste at the vulgar allusion. "If it is within my power, you shall have grandchildren."

To his surprise, the old man gave a gurgle of a laugh. "Aye, I know that, lad, I know." His voice was weary, his sunken eyes lined with pain. "I know you're a man of your word—unlike your brother. And I'm—"

The next round of coughing wracked his body so badly that Beau laid his hand on the bellpull. But Loman shook his head, lifting his hand in a staying gesture as he fought for breath.

So Beau waited, wishing he were anywhere else.

When Loman could speak again his voice was a frayed whisper. "I need your word on something."

What now, for God's sake?

Beau sighed. "Yes, sir?"

Loman swallowed, the sound so labored it made Beaumont's own throat ache. "Don't tell her about five years ago. She don't know about it."

Beau's eyebrows shot up. "Are you trying to tell me

that you never told your daughter you were negotiating a marriage contract—*her* marriage contract—with my brother?" he demanded, not bothering to keep the disbelief out of his voice.

"Aye, that's what I'm tellin' ye!" Loman's pale, papery skin flushed with—Beau surmised—well-deserved shame. "I didn't want to get 'er hopes up. I was just about to tell 'er after 'ee signed it. I was just waitin' for the right moment."

Beau snorted.

The old man shot him a venomous look. "Turned out to be a damned good thing I didn't tell 'er, eh, my lad? Since your brother broke 'is word?"

Beau scowled, more furious at his dead brother than this wily old git.

"But that ain't your fault," Loman said soothingly. "You're makin' it right now, savin' your family's honor by takin' on 'is obligation."

Beau had no bloody intention of discussing his brother's dishonorable behavior.

"Promise you won't tell 'er."

"I'm hardly eager to tell my new wife that my brother shabbed off on his contract with her to marry another woman, now am I?" Beau asked, allowing his fury to show: fury at the man's audacity, fury at being made to remember that dreadful summer, and fury at his brother for his refusal to do his duty so now it was *Beau* who was stuck having to marry the girl.

"Thank 'ee," Loman said with unconvincing meekness. "And there is one last thing."

You mean another last last thing?

"And what would that be, Mr. Loman?"

"I don't want her coming back after today. I want you

to take her off to that pile of stone in the country—
Wroxton Court." He said the words with relish, his dulled
eyes briefly glinting with acquisitive pleasure. "Immediately."

Beau blinked. "Come again?"

"You heard me," he wheezed. "She watched 'er ma die
a slow, painful death; she don't need to see me do the same
thing."

Beau couldn't believe his bloody ears. "She will *hate*
me for taking her away from you."

Loman flashed him a crooked, roguish smile that gave
Beau an idea of the charm this man must have once
wielded. "It's a dyin' man's last wish—and I know you're
a gentleman, so you'll see it's done."

"My family is due in London in five days, Mr. Loman.
Would you have me leave before they get here?" Beau
demanded. "And I've already accepted a dinner invitation
from Uxbridge when he passes through London. I am *not*
leaving before then."

Loman's lips curled up at the corners and Beau knew
the shameless old mushroom was smirking at the thought
of his daughter rubbing shoulders with the one-legged hero
of Waterloo.

"You got time to send word to your family an' tell 'em
to stay put. You didn't want 'em in London, anyway—
did ye?"

That was certainly true, not that Beau felt compelled
to admit as much to his new father-in-law. These first few
days—at least—with his new wife would be difficult
enough without his meddling mother and ungovernable
siblings adding to the chaos. And then there was his devious sister-in-law, Victoria; Beau's head ached at the mere

thought of her name. Yes, it would actually be a relief to tell his family to remain in Yorkshire.

"But you should stay for dinner with 'Is Lordship. With Uxbridge," Loman added smugly—as if *he* were the one dining with the marquess.

"Why, *thank* you, sir."

Loman ignored Beau's sarcasm. "When's the dinner?"

Beau rounded up. "A week."

Loman grimaced but nodded. "All right. Get her out of here after that."

Beau shook his head. "How the devil do you expect me to keep a woman away from her dying father? I shall have to tie her up to get her into the bloody carriage."

"You're her husband, ain'tcha?" Loman demanded, anger flaring in his rheumy eyes. "Didn't you command thousands of soldiers? You bloody *tell* Josey when and where to go and she'll do it. I raised 'er to 'ave 'er own mind, but she knows every house has only one master." He sneered up at Beau. "Who's that to be in your household, *Your Grace*?"

Beau opened his mouth to say something brutal and quelling to the obnoxious upstart when he noticed Loman's eyes—which had been blazing only seconds earlier—had dulled with alarming speed.

Bloody hell. It would be just Beau's luck if the old bastard went off while they were bickering.

"Well?" Loman persisted, dogged even though his face was lined with pain.

Beau glared down, not bothering to hide his intense dislike. "Fine. I shall do as you ask."

Loman gave him a faint—but triumphant—smile. "Yer a good lad. Now open that top drawer." He jerked his chin toward the nightstand and then winced from the effort.

"Give 'er that letter when I'm gone. It will explain why you kept 'er from me."

"Perhaps you might explain to *me* why I am taking her away, sir?"

Loman's jaw worked angrily and Beau thought he was going to tell him to go to the devil. But instead he said, "I've not got long—maybe not even a few days—and *right bloody now* I'm in so much damned pain that I've *soiled* meself from it." His eyes glowed with misery, rage, and shame. "Can you even imagine that kind of pain?"

Beau forbore to point out he'd been at Waterloo and a dozen other battles before that. Of course he knew about pain.

"As soon as you're both gone today I'll take as much of that"—he pointed to the green bottle that sat on a table beyond his reach—"as that quack will give me and I'll go to sleep, and 'opefully never wake up. If my Josey knew any of that she'd want me to fight—to stay with 'er as long as possible. If she knew I was givin' up, wild 'orses couldn't keep her away. So, my lord *duke*, is that good enough reason for you?"

Beau yanked open the drawer, snatched up the letter, and shoved it into his coat pocket.

"Don't give it to 'er on 'er wedding day, Yer Grace. Wait 'til tomorrow."

"Anything else, sir?"

The pain in Loman's eyes overshadowed any satisfaction he might have felt at ordering Beau about like a bloody servant. "I'll extort no more promises from you, lad. Now, go on—" He made a weak shooing motion with his hand. "Send up my Josie."

* * *

Jo paced a circuit around the horrifically gaudy room her father liked to call the Gold Salon—because he'd stuffed it with more gilt furniture than Versailles.

"Please, Your Grace," Lady Constance said, flapping behind her like a lone duckling after its mother. "Won't you—"

"It helps me to pace," Jo snapped, and then immediately felt bad for snapping.

Lord. How quickly could she reasonably dispense with the other woman's services? The countess wasn't cruel or condescending, but she was an annoying fusser, and if there was one thing Jo abhorred, it was fussing.

"Perhaps if I rang for—"

The door opened and Jo whipped around; it was the duke.

Your husband, a gloating voice reminded her.

The thought left burning shame in its wake: What kind of selfish monster was gleeful about such a marriage when her father lay dying overhead?

Jo strode toward him, palms sweating and heart pounding. "Is he—?"

"No." The full, beautiful lips she'd dreamed of kissing a thousand times compressed into a harsh pink line. His expression held none of the open dislike it had during their wedding ceremony but was a blend of pity, reserve, and— yes—disdain.

You've married a man who despises you.

Jo's body went weak at the enormity of what she'd done and she swayed.

"Steady on." His strong, warm hand gripped her elbow.

Even a small, impersonal gesture such as that sent a crippling wave of want through her body.

Jo snatched away her arm and the skin over Wroxton's

lovely, sculpted cheekbones darkened at her reaction: he believed she disliked his touch.

Good. Better that than his knowing the humiliating truth.

"I need to see him." Jo forced the words between clenched jaws.

"And he wishes to see you," Wroxton said coolly. "But he doesn't need to see you *this* way." He gestured to one of the many gilt mirrors that festooned the walls and Jo saw her plain, tear-stained face and mussed hair reflected. Right beside her was her beautiful, immaculate husband, who was regarding her with open censure.

But his expression gentled when he met her gaze. "Take a moment to dry your face and—"

"How dare you?" she hissed, glaring up at him, her body throbbing with rage toward this cold, unyielding god of a man who would *never* love—or even like—her and made no effort to hide it.

Jo shoved past him, not waiting for an answer. She vaguely registered Lady Constance's voice calling for her to come back. By the time she reached the doors to her father's room, her tears were streaming.

She stopped to look in the hall mirror and winced. Yes, there was the Duchess of Wroxton, a red-faced, tear-stained, splotchy little squab of a woman. No wonder her new husband had regarded her with such contempt. Even on her best days, Jo wasn't much to look at. And today was far from her best.

He'd been right—at least about not arriving in her father's room looking like a hysterical wreck.

So Jo yanked the handkerchief she'd tucked up the sleeve of her wedding dress and dried her cheeks. Her hair, which she wore in a short crop, had been flattened by her hat and she ran her fingers through it until it was its usual mass of springy brown curls.

Jo snorted at her reflection; now she resembled a curly-headed, tear-streaked *boy*.

So be it.

She fixed a smile on her face and wrenched open his door.

And her resolve dissolved like sugar in tea when she was confronted by his pale, shrunken form dwarfed by the huge bed.

"Oh, Papa!" Jo ran toward him, barely recalling herself and stopping from leaping up onto his bed and taking his fragile form into her arms.

Why was this happening? Why was he becoming so much worse, so fast? He was a shadow of her strapping father—worse even than this morning.

"Ah, Your Grace—why are you crying, Josie-girl? I'm not dead yet." He gave a laugh that was supposed to reassure her but was so breathy and weak it left her terrified. "Don't cry. It's yer wedding day." His mouth pulled into a shadow of his old smug, arrogant grin. "Yer a duchess, Jo—are you happy?"

Jo heard the worry in his voice and forced a smile. "Yes, Papa, it's all I've ever dreamed of," she lied. "But I'd be happier if you'd let me stay and—"

His loving, open expression vanished. "No. And I don't want to argue about this again. I want you to go with Wroxton and *be* a duchess. If you can't bring yourself to do so, I'll leave and go—"

"No!" She squeezed his hands so hard he winced. "No, I'll do as you say, Papa. Just promise me—"

"Aye, I'll send word when it gets toward the end."

Josey winced. "*If*, not when, Papa."

He chuckled. "Aye, *if*. Now, yer duke is waitin' for ye and I'm tired."

"I'll come see you in—"

"I'll send word—don't come before, Josie; I forbid it." Jo hesitated, and he said, "Give me your word you'll obey yer old pa."

She ground her teeth and then gave a promise she wasn't sure she could keep. "Of course, Papa."

"Good girl. I want ye to remember you're as good as any of 'em, Josey—don't *ever* forget that. Yer Eddie Loman's daughter."

"I know, Papa."

"You've gotten used to bein' yer own mistress these past years and I'm at fault for allowing ye to help yer old pa instead of bein' a proper young lady with more Seasons, balls, parties—"

"But—"

"Hush and let me say my piece."

Jo bit her lower lip.

"Your new husband ain't a man to be bossed like yer old pa. His sort was bred to rule and he'll expect you to obey. Today you pledged before God and accepted him as yer lord and master." He paused, opened his mouth, closed it, and then opened it again with a slight grimace. "Rein in that temper o' yers, girlie. Be respectful, 'cause Wroxton won't appreciate you going at him hammer and tongs. I want yer promise you'll forget all the bad habits and words and things you picked up knockin' about in my shops— that ain't for a duchess."

Jo couldn't help smiling. "I know how to behave, Papa."

"I *know* you know—but I've *seen* how you get if you think you're bein' slighted."

Jo wanted to argue, but he was right. Hadn't she already needled the duke today—even *before* they were married?

"I'll behave like a duchess. I promise."

He gave her a weary smile. "That's good, love. Now give us a kiss."

Jo took care not to jostle him, inhaling the familiar scent of the person who loved her more than anyone else *ever* would. "I love you, Papa."

When she pulled away, her cheeks were again wet.

"Go dry your tears and put a smile on for your new 'usband. No man likes a Friday-face," he said in a gruff, thick voice.

Jo's lips trembled as she forced them to obey his command. "Yes, Papa."

"Off with ye." His lids drifted closed and his body seemed to sag into the bed.

Jo tiptoed toward the door and closed it without making a sound, slumping back against it. She wanted to run down the hall to her old room and crawl into her own bed. But this wasn't where she lived now. All her things were gone. Even her personal servants—her maid and footmen—were now at her new home.

Once again, Jo used her handkerchief to dry her tears. And then she straightened her shoulders and lifted her chin.

It was time to join the man her father had called her new lord and master.

CHAPTER 3

※━━◆━◆━◆━━※

It was dark by the time they departed the monstrous house on Russell Square. Although Beau had not wanted to, he'd insisted they stay and consume the gargantuan wedding feast Mr. Loman had arranged for them.

It was the most uncomfortable dinner in memory—celebrating an unwanted wedding while a man died an agonizing death above their heads.

Beau had been pathetically grateful for the presence of Lady Constance, whose incessant chatter had filled the gaudy, cavernous dining room. He and his new wife were both too consumed with their thoughts to make conversation.

Coward that he was, Beau had hoped the older woman would accompany them to Wroxton House and continue as a buffer in the coach. Hell, he'd consider bringing her to the nuptial bed itself if it would help settle his inexplicably hostile wife's feathers.

But he was not to be so fortunate.

When he lowered himself onto the worn bench in the

ancient Wroxton coach, it was only his duchess who sat opposite him.

Beau rapped on the roof with his cane and the battered old coach jolted forward.

With a little bit of luck they could ride the short distance home in silence and the pounding in his skull might ease. With a little bit of luck—

"I shan't be available for whatever you have planned tomorrow as I will be going over to my father's house in the morning. I will be spending the coming days there."

Beau sighed. *So much for luck.*

And then something occurred to him.

He squinted across the dimness of the carriage at her mulish face. "Am I mistaken, or do you *sound* different, *my dear*?"

She chewed her lower lip, her expression one of resentment and embarrassment.

Beau didn't wait for her answer—although he suspected it would be amusing.

Instead, he said, "I'm afraid that won't be possible. The house is rather at sixes and sevens, having been without a mistress for so long. I want it to be made ready for when we return in April," he lied. "I daresay you shall have your hands full with that." Beau bit back a groan; Lord, he sounded like a bloody idiot. He ignored her disbelieving expression and soldiered on. "We shall have an important dinner party toward the end of the week, so there really isn't going to be time for much else before we go."

"*Go?* I'm afraid I don't know what you mean. Go where?"

Beau briefly considered giving her the wretched letter that Loman had claimed would explain *everything*. But of course that was yet another promise the old bastard had extorted from him.

He took a deep breath and let it out slowly. "We will go to Wroxton Court—a sort of wedding holiday—where we can spend some time together and become acquainted." *And where you can begin a lifetime of hating me for taking you away from your dying father.*

"You want to leave London *now*?"

Beau winced. "I am right here. You needn't shriek like a costermonger."

"A costermonger." She repeated the words in a soft, almost dangerous, tone that made him suspect the word *costermonger* had not been the wisest choice.

She crossed her arms and glared holes through him, her mouth a supercilious twist. "I would like to know what you mean."

It had been a very, very long time since anyone had regarded him with such contempt. In fact, Beau wasn't certain that he'd *ever* been the recipient of such a look.

He discovered that he did not like it.

"I'm sorry, my dear. I thought my meaning was perfectly clear. But let me reiterate in simpler language: we are leaving for the country in less than a week."

She shook her head, not bothering to hide her—in Beau's opinion—justified confusion. "But isn't your family coming? Why invite all of them here if they are only going to have to turn around and leave?"

It was an excellent question and one Beau could not answer sensibly thanks to her stubborn ass of a father.

"That is not your concern," he said, quite truthfully, if not exactly tactfully. "I have decided there is no reason to stay in town."

"My *father* is reason enough to stay," she said between

clenched teeth, her eyes narrow and her lips tightly compressed.

Her father is dying, Beau reminded himself; the least he could do was show a little compassion.

"I am sorry," he said, meaning it and fiercely wishing Loman were here to bear the brunt of the idiotic promise he'd extorted. "I understand you wish to attend your father in his ill health. However, he has asked that I get you out of London as quickly as possible."

She gasped. "I don't believe you."

Beau's eyebrows descended. "I beg your pardon, Your Grace, but did you just accuse me of *lying*?"

His duchess opened her mouth—no doubt to say something scathing—but then closed it again. Her jaw worked from side to side a moment. "I'm sorry," she said, not sounding in the least apologetic. "I know you wouldn't lie because it would be against your *gentleman's* code."

Beau was still pondering what had obviously been a dig when she said, "Please forgive me." Her face was twisted in gut-churning agony.

"Of course," Beau said reflexively, his response a product of breeding.

"But you must see that I cannot do this."

"I'm afraid I don't see that at all," he lied, seething with fury—not at her, but at the architect of this asinine situation. But he had given his bloody word, hadn't he?

"Not only has your father requested it, but I am your husband and the man you just promised a few scant hours ago—before God and all of Christendom—to honor and obey. If *I* say we are going to the country, your only response is to ask me when we leave."

He could see by her rapidly rising and falling chest and

flaring nostrils that the methods he'd always employed to command his men might not be the wisest with his wife. She was skittish—like a high-strung filly—and justifiably so: her father was dying.

Compassion, Wroxton.

So he tried again. "I know this is—"

She jerked forward in her seat, the sudden action making him recoil. "You know what I think?" She obviously didn't care, because she didn't wait for an answer. "I think you can't *wait* to tuck me away in the country, can you? Bury me far from the judging eyes of your *friends*—your *mistresses*. I daresay you'll take me to your wretched pile of stone and *leave* me there while you come back here and immerse yourself in debauchery and pleasure." Her eyes flared with something resembling hatred. "And you'll do it all using *my* money. *That's* what I think."

Beau was stunned into speechlessness. What kind of female brought up the vulgar topic of money and then hurled it like a cannonball at her husband of barely a few hours? Was this a foreshadowing of what his life would be like? Engaging in shouting matches with this—this—ill-bred, ill-mannered, and ill-natured *shrew*? Was this what—

Compassion.

Beau gritted his teeth against the flood of anger trying to escape. "You are free to believe as you choose," he said acidly.

"Well, thank you for *that*," she sneered. "For a moment I thought—"

Beau jerked forward, his abrupt action mirroring hers. "You are free to believe as you choose," he repeated softly, "but that does not mean I wish to *hear* it. In fact, you may feel free to keep observations about my intentions—debauched, pleasurable, or otherwise—to yourself."

"You'd like that, wouldn't you?" she lashed back. "A sweet, obedient little wife who does your bidding without demur?" She laughed and the sound dripped bitterness. "If that's what you thought you were getting, you are *sorely* mistaken." Sparks flew from her eyes and Beau realized she looked almost attractive when her face was animated rather than grief stricken.

Anger, he knew from personal experience, was a far easier emotion to deal with than grief.

So, really, Beau thought as he eyed her thunderous expression, keeping her furious at him rather than grieving for her father would be doing her a favor.

In fact, it would be easier for both of them.

Beau gave her a smile he knew to be smug and infuriating. "How prescient you are, my dear. I *would* like a sweet, obedient, and *quiet* little wife. You would do well to keep in mind that I always get what I want." Beau was impressed he could utter such a ridiculous claim without laughing out loud. When was the last time he'd gotten *anything* he wanted?

He thrust the self-pitying thought aside and continued, "Right now what I'd like is for you to relinquish this distasteful subject and concentrate on behaving in a way that befits your station, as we are almost at Wroxton House."

Her eyes flashed. "Well, I'm *not* finished with this *distasteful subject*."

"Are you *quite* sure you wish to have this conversation right now, Your Grace?"

* * *

Jo understood the warning beneath his soft words and knew he was right: she would *not* present herself in a positive light in her current state and should wait until her temper cooled.

But then the words *befits your station* came back at her.

"I *would* like to have this conversation right now. May I remind you, *Your Grace*, that this *distasteful subject*, as you so charmingly put it, is the reason there are no longer dunning agents swarming your dilapidated pile of bricks."

The nostrils of his fine, aquiline nose flared and his pupils shrank to specks. He nodded. "Very well, let us put an end to this tiresome discussion once and for all."

Jo shivered at his silky tone.

"Yes, I married you for your money—did you only learn of that today? Is that why you're behaving with such hostility?"

Jo flinched at his cold loathing.

"If that is the case, I'm sorry you were misled. It is true, I married you for your great pots of money—money derived from trade and industry. Money—as you so *charmingly* pointed out—that has already settled a mountain of ancient bills and will soon be spent on *dilapidated* houses along with a hundred other things. Money your *father* labored and sweated for." His lips curled into a cruel, sensual smile and he leaned even closer and said, "Money *I* will be—" He stopped, extracted his watch from his pocket, and squinted at it before turning to her. "Money I will be laboring and *sweating* for myself in less than an hour."

Jo gasped and a wave of heat slammed into her. Had he really just said—

"Now." His face was so devoid of even a hint of sensuality that she must have misinterpreted his meaning. "Is that about it on the subject of *your* money? Or did I leave anything out?"

Jo opened her mouth, but his *sweating* comment had captured her vocal cords along with the rest of her body.

"I'm going to take your silence for assent and move along. So, while I traded my person for filthy lucre, *you* traded *your* person for my title and position—as well as a good-faith promise that my blood will one day *soon* mingle with yours in the veins of our children."

Jo's body clenched at the words *our* and *children*. She pressed her thighs together to suppress the distracting tingling, but the action was less than helpful.

"Would you agree with that assessment? Again, please correct me if I'm wrong."

Hysterical laughter rose up in her throat as Jo briefly— and insanely—wondered what he would say if she told him his status and title had *nothing* to do with the reason she'd married him.

Wroxton cut her a stern look that should *not* have amplified the distracting sensations coursing through her body but did. "When I ask you a question, I expect the courtesy of an answer."

"Yes, money for status, *Your Grace*," Jo retorted. "You are correct, just as I suspect you are *always* correct."

His lips curved into a cold smile. "Such spousal faith in my unerring judgment is commendable," he drawled. "You may consider the subject of money and status permanently closed."

"And what will you do if I have the audacity to reopen it?" Jo whipped back before she could stop herself—a not uncommon problem and one that often landed her in trouble.

He sighed, as if bored, but his penetrating blue gaze said otherwise. "I do not make threats, Your Grace."

Before Jo could form an answer—not that she had one—he turned from her, hardly waiting for the carriage to come to a full stop before flinging open the door, hopping out, kicking down the steps, and offering her his hand, along with a frigid smile.

"Welcome to Wroxton House, Your Grace."

Jo glared at her reflection in the mirror while Mimi tamed her hair into charming curls.

When Jo had told her not to bother, the older woman had looked so shocked you would have thought Jo had proposed going down to dinner naked.

"Don't you want to look lovely for your husband on your wedding night?" she had asked—a question that only a maid who'd once been one's nurse would be bold enough to ask her mistress.

"Wroxton doesn't even see me, Mimi. All he sees when he looks at me are pounds, shillings, and pence." *And an ill-tempered shrew.*

And whose fault is that?

"Oh, tush!" Mimi scolded. "You're his duchess." The older woman hesitated and then added, "I pray you won't let yourself be goaded into unbecoming behavior, Miss Josie. You know how you are."

Jo didn't bother confessing that Mimi's warning was too late.

She had no idea why she was so bitter and furious toward him. Wroxton had been correct in the carriage—

Jo had *known* he was marrying her for money. He'd never tried to pretend otherwise.

His behavior today hadn't been disparaging; he'd not singled her out for rude treatment. No, he treated her with the same high-handed arrogance he'd used on his friend, an *earl*, for pity's sake; the vicar, a man of God; Lady Constance, the impoverished niece of a duke; the servants; and anyone else he'd come into contact with. The man was simply autocratic to the bone—a duke, in other words.

And Jo had known all that before she married him.

Not only had she known about his commanding, dominating behavior—it was what *still* woke her in a sweat far too many nights.

Yes, Jo had gotten exactly what she wanted and now Wroxton was *her* commanding, dominating husband. So why was she chafing at his authority? What kind of woman schemed and dreamed to get something and then behaved as if she didn't want it?

An idiot, that's what kind.

Jo couldn't argue with that unkind assessment.

The unflattering truth was that Jo wanted him, desperately, and she hated herself for wanting him.

"Besides, Your Grace," Mimi said, breaking into Jo's irksome thoughts. "Just because His Grace doesn't love you *now* doesn't mean he won't come to love you. He can't fail to fall in love when he knows the real you. Take my word for it, Your Grace, these hoity-toity marriages usually work out for the best," she said, speaking from no experience whatsoever.

Jo snorted but didn't bother arguing; Mimi was one of only two people in the world who actually *did* love her.

Something in the older woman's words had caught at

her: Mimi said the duke would love the *real Jo* once he knew her. Was it possible Jo was behaving like an argumentative toad because it was safer to pretend to be somebody else rather than to risk his rejecting *the real her*? Was that what she was doing? Sabotaging her marriage before it had a chance to fail?

Jo chewed her lip as she ran through the day, her mind lingering on the way she'd accused Wroxton of lying and then continued to bicker even though she'd *known* the plan smacked of Edward Loman.

Good Lord, even a besotted fool like Jo knew the last thing Wroxton wanted was to spend two weeks cooped up in the country with *her*.

No, Papa had bullied—or likely guilted—the promise out of him and then Jo had treated him like a monster because of it. No wonder he'd been so furious.

Apologize.

Jo bit back a groan at the thought of apologizing to such a superior, haughty man.

You'll catch more flies with honey than with vinegar, girlie.

Jo smiled grudgingly at her father's voice, even though it was only in her head. She could still remember her response to his annoying proverb all these years later: *Now why would I want to catch flies, Papa?*

"There, that's better, Miss Josie," Mimi said, catching Jo's eyes in the mirror and forgetting to *Your Grace* her. "When you smile, you're as lovely as any of those snooty great ladies."

Jo didn't bother to correct her maid's gross inaccuracy; at least two people in the world believed her to be beautiful.

She studied her hazel-eyed, snub-nosed round face and

tried to see herself as the warrior-god in the adjacent room saw her.

Jo grimaced; she knew *exactly* how he saw her: *he didn't.*

Wroxton hadn't remembered her from five years ago in spite of the fact that they'd attended at least fifteen of the same balls and parties *and* spent a week in the same country house.

Lord. That time in the country.

The duke had no recollection of that week yet Jo still cherished—*gloated over* would be more accurate—the vivid memory of *him* in her mind's eye, as if she'd been burnt by the sun. No, it was more scorching than that; it was an all-too-brief image so sinful and erotic that Jo had never shared it with another living soul.

It was *hers*.

Unfortunately, it didn't really belong to her, because it wasn't Jo Wroxton he was writhing with in that haunting, arousing memory. Wroxton had had eyes for only one woman that summer, and it hadn't been Jo. No matter how diligently Jo had tried to excise Lady Victoria from her cherished recollection, she'd never been able to erase the other woman.

For all Jo knew, the duke might *still* only have eyes for Victoria, now his widowed sister-in-law.

Jo grimaced. *I suppose that makes dear Victoria my sister, too.* Once upon a time, claiming a connection with the most beautiful, vivacious, and sought-after woman in London would have made Jo proud and pleased. But that was back when she'd still been stupid enough to believe a woman with Victoria's background and breeding would ever befriend someone like her.

Jo chewed her lip. Did Wroxton still love Victoria? The

thought made her ill, but she could not ignore it. Would the duke have married Victoria if such a union wasn't forbidden by law?

"You're squirming," Mimi scolded. "I'm almost done."

"I'm sorry," Jo murmured.

Jo knew the dukedom had been teetering on the brink of financial collapse even before Jason Halliwell died in a hunting accident that everyone knew wasn't an accident.

So, no, even if the law didn't forbid it, the new duke would not have married Victoria. The family needed a great deal of money or they would lose everything, even their ancestral seat, a castle that had been theirs for seven centuries.

Jo was fortunate they needed so much money, because it was the only reason a man like Wroxton would ever condescend to marry somebody like her.

Beau handed his valet the razor and took the steaming cloth to wipe his face.

He scowled as he recalled his brief, heated exchange with his bride in the carriage earlier—the very same willful woman who awaited him on the other side of the connecting door.

Beau experienced a sudden urge to jump into his bed, yank the covers over his head, and hide the way he used to do when he was a boy and Jason had scared the hell out of them both with some ghostly bedtime story.

Jason. Beau shook his head at his foolish, tragic, dead brother—yet another subject he did not wish to think about tonight.

He blotted the unwanted thoughts from his brain the same way he blotted up the soap and water on his face.

Tonight was his wedding night, and, God willing, the only one he would ever have. In a few moments he would bed his new wife—a maiden—for the first time. Beau wasn't worried he couldn't bring her physical pleasure, but he *did* worry they would bring the animosity that flared so quickly and easily between them into their marriage bed.

Beau refused to have a marriage like that of his mother and father—or Jason and Victoria, for that matter. He simply *couldn't* live in such a union. He didn't just want a body to bear his children; he wanted sex, companionship, and yes—he even wanted affection. Not just wanted—he needed those things, and he refused to feel ashamed for his needs.

Even when he'd kept mistresses, he'd retained them for long periods of time. He disliked nameless engagements in brothels, although he'd certainly gone to such women to slake his urges when he'd had no other choice.

Beau pictured the woman who awaited him on the other side of the door.

Not only did his wife spring from a class of people he had no experience with, she was also far from his physical ideal. Beau was an inch over six feet, almost fourteen stone, and possessed a vigorous and demanding appetite in bed. His wife was small and slight and Beau would need to leash his passion and take care not to hurt her.

He sighed. Josephine Loman—*no,* Wroxton—was not the woman of his choice, but she *was* his wife and only a spoilt child yearned for things he couldn't have. He was married now and it was his duty to make the best of what he had.

He ran a brush through his close-cropped hair and grimaced at his reflection; he supposed he should grow it out now that he'd fully rejoined civilian life. But to tell the truth, living on a battlefield for almost a decade tended to alter a man's perspective. Beau simply did not *care* about which haircut—a Brutus or a Caesar—would suit him best. When it came to clothing and his person, he was neat and clean but not ostentatious. He would have horsewhipped any officer of his who'd gone through twenty cravats in search of a perfect knot.

"Your Grace." Dobson appeared behind him with the blue silk robe Beau's last lover—Celine, a French widow ten years his senior—had given him.

Celine had been a beautiful, proud woman from a family almost as ancient as his own. She'd also been a sensual woman who'd been uninhibited, demanding, and open-minded in the bedchamber, just the type of lover he enjoyed.

But she was part of another life and Beau had locked her away in a cupboard with all his other memories. The woman in the next room was his present and would, he hoped, become his future. The new Duchess of Wroxton was a proud, prickly woman who was quick to see slights where there were none meant. But she was also clever and lively and—if not beautiful, she possessed youthful vitality and might actually be quite pretty if she ever stopped scowling.

Beau could treat her with affection and respect and she might become his companion and lover. Or he could treat her as his father had treated his mother: as nothing more than a vessel for his children while he took his pleasure elsewhere, living apart once she'd given him the requisite heirs. Beau knew that, in large part, it was a man's choice what to make of his marriage.

Dobson hovered off to his side, drawing Beau from his morbid thoughts.

"That will be all, Dobson."

Beau picked up two glasses and the bottle he'd chosen from the cellar, took a deep breath and exhaled slowly, and then knocked on the connecting door and entered his duchess's bedchamber.

CHAPTER 4

—◆—

There was a light knock on the door that connected their rooms before it swung open and exposed her husband standing in the open doorway. Jo tried not to gawk at the dizzying sight of the Duke of Wroxton wearing only his dressing gown. In *her* bedchamber.

"Good evening." Her husband glanced from Jo to Mimi, his golden brows slightly raised.

"You may go, Mimi," Jo said hoarsely, unable to look away from her husband—as if he were a hallucination that might flicker and disappear.

He strode into the room, not exactly smiling, but no longer looking at her as though she were some kind of burr stuck to his stocking. Not that he was wearing stockings—or much of anything really.

"I'm sorry," Jo blurted.

His glorious blue eyes narrowed. "I beg your pardon?"

"About what happened in the carriage—I, er, well, I was distraught, but that's no excuse for blaming you. I—I know my father and I know he has ways of getting what he wants. I shouldn't have blamed you, Your Grace."

His lips curved into the slightest of smiles and Jo was horrified by her body's reaction to even such a miserly little thing as that. If she didn't take care, she would be a puddle at his feet.

"Why don't you write him a letter in the morning and put your case to him." His lips twitched. "After all, you are his daughter; I daresay you inherited some of his remarkable powers of persuasion."

Jo's face heated at what was surely the most tepid compliment a bridegroom had ever paid his bride on their wedding day.

His piercing gaze swept her body and heat crept up her chest and throat as he made a leisurely, and thorough, perusal of her person.

Jo's breathing quickened. What did he make of her? Did he think she was trying to turn a sow's ear into a silk purse by wearing such a beautiful nightgown? That was the notion that had flickered through Jo's mind when she'd seen her reflection in the glass.

The lace on the gown—the color of honey—cost more than a factory worker would make in a lifetime and it made even her scrawny figure appear shapely. The warm shade made her skin look creamy rather than pale and freckled.

And it was also remarkably revealing, so she was grateful she'd put the matching—and more concealing—dressing gown over it before he'd come to her.

By the time his eyes reached hers, Jo knew she was visibly shaking. His beautiful, stern face softened and he closed the distance between them, the blue silk of his exquisite robe whispering as he walked.

"You look beautiful." His warm voice and unexpected

words fed the fire that had smoldered in her belly ever since his wicked threat in the carriage.

Sweating . . .

Well, the fire burned lower than that, she acknowledged with yet another wave of heat that made her drop her gaze to her husband's bare—and yes, beautiful—feet.

"I know this marriage is not what either of us would have chosen," he said, blithely unaware that his words were like a bucket of freezing water over the fire inside her. "But we are man and wife now and I would rather we live in harmony."

Jo nodded dumbly, grateful he was at least oblivious to the explosion of pain his words had detonated inside her. What had she expected? A declaration of undying love?

"I would like to make a go of our marriage—Josephine. May I call you Josephine—when we are alone or among family, of course?"

Why bother telling him that nobody had ever called her Josephine? What was he supposed to call her? A pet name like Jo or Josie?

He paused, and Jo knew he was waiting for a response. It wasn't love he was offering, but at least it wasn't dislike. Wasn't that good? Why did his words twist like a knife?

"And of course you must call me Beaumont," he went on when she said nothing.

Beaumont. Not Beau, as his friends called him—as *Victoria* had called him—but Beaumont.

Jo squeezed her eyes shut; could she not keep that horrid woman out of her thoughts even on her wedding night?

"Don't be frightened, Josephine."

Her eyes snapped open. "I'm not frightened."

His mouth pulled up slightly at one corner. "Liar," he

said, with something that looked like desire flaring in his eyes.

That was impossible; she was imagining things. Jo turned back to his feet, which were far easier to read—at least correctly.

"Look at me, Josephine."

She tried to lift her head, but her neck wasn't obeying.

To her surprise, he chuckled and took her chin, gently but firmly tilting her face up, *making* her meet his knowing gaze. Her duke was a consummate aristocrat: a powerful, masculine man born to command and bred to expect obedience as his due. His faint, sensual smile told her more clearly than words that her puny efforts at resistance amused him. They both knew the truth: her body, like all her other possessions, belonged to him, to do with as he pleased. The knowledge terrified her, but it also—thrillingly—freed her. It freed her to stop struggling, stop fighting; there was no point in opposing him: she was his.

As suddenly as he'd taken her face in his hand, he released her, the absence of his touch leaving her breathless with relief and yearning.

"I will pour us some wine. It will help relax you."

Jo could have told him it would take more than wine to relax the coil of need, want, and fear that was knotted inside her.

But she didn't. Instead, she took her glass with a murmured, "Thank you."

"Come, let's sit in front of the fire." He took her hand and led her to a worn and faded settee, then sat down beside her.

Her father would never have possessed a piece of furniture so threadbare and battered in his house. But somehow this ragged old sofa looked more sophisticated than all the expensive, sparkling items with which he'd filled his brand-new mansion.

Poor Papa, he never could understand—

"You look so serious," the duke said. "What are you thinking?"

"Why? So you can tell me to think something else?" Jo squeezed her eyes shut and cursed her big, impulsive mouth.

"Look at me, Josephine."

Jo opened her eyes to find him regarding her with amusement rather than wrath.

"Can we call a cease-fire for tonight?"

"Yes, of course. I'm sorry. I'm just accustomed to—"

"Getting your own way?" he suggested gently.

A surprised laugh escaped her. "Yes," she agreed. "I blame it on my father, who indulges me terribly."

"Ah, but that is what daughters are for." He took a sip of wine, his eyes wandering over her, not with disgust or disappointment, but rather with . . . *interest*? "I have to confess I am accustomed to getting my own way, as well," he said.

"I hadn't noticed," she retorted before she could stop herself.

He threw back his head and gave a shout of rich, masculine laughter. It was so shocking—laughter from a man who never seemed even to remember how to smile—that Jo could only stare.

His eyes were still shining when he looked back down at her. "You aren't the only one to have noticed. My mother's last letter used the words *draconian* and *dictatorial*."

Jo couldn't help smiling. "I daresay you are accustomed to having hundreds of men obey your bidding."

"Yes, well, I suppose it might take me a little practice

to learn you are not like my soldiers. Are you willing to bear with me?" he asked with a teasing look that sucked the breath from her lungs.

"Perhaps," she said, hoping he didn't notice the feverish quaver in her voice.

He brushed her jaw with the backs of his fingers, the intimate gesture freezing the breath in her chest. "We will be together until one of us dies, Josephine. I do not want to look ahead and see years of strife." His fingers continued their intoxicating caressing. "I want you to be my companion and my lover."

Jo swallowed—or at least tried to—and made a sound somewhere between a choke and a gasp.

One corner of his ridiculously shapely mouth pulled up and his hand went to the base of her neck, his finger stroking lightly over her thudding pulse.

"It is natural to be nervous. I suppose you have been warned—probably by Lady Constance—that what happens tonight is something to be endured, a business that should be conducted swiftly and under cover of darkness."

Jo nodded. Yes, that was certainly what Lady Constance—the only woman ever to speak of such matters to her—had told her yesterday.

"That is not how it will be with us, Josephine," he murmured, his fingers continuing their distracting exploration of her jaw, throat, collarbone. "We can give each other a great deal of pleasure—if you are receptive."

Jo wondered what he would say if he knew he'd *already* shown her that—five years ago.

Fortunately, he didn't appear to need her to say anything. "I want our marriage bed to be used for loving—no arguments or disagreements should be allowed to creep in between us. We have plenty of other places to discuss such matters."

His words did something to her vision and the room shifted around her; he wanted to keep a place for loving— with *her*?

"You should see your expression."

"Why?" she blurted.

"You look stunned that I would suggest such things."

"I am. I mean, I agree," she amended hastily.

His lips curved into a full-blown smile that threatened to make her eyes cross: here was the Beaumont Halliwell of five years ago.

"So agreeable," he murmured. "What have you done with my feisty wife?" His big, warm hand cupped her jaw, the gesture making her feel cherished and precious.

He stood and extended his hand. "Come to bed," he said. "And *breathe*," he added with a glint of humor in his eyes. "I don't want an unconscious bride on my wedding night."

Jo followed him on numb, clumsy feet to her bed, a large four-poster with hangings as old and faded as everything else in the room. Everything except her husband. *Beau*, she mentally corrected. In her mind, at least, she would take the liberty of calling him Beau.

"I want this off," he said, his large fingers remarkably deft as he unfastened the row of tiny buttons and then slid his hand beneath the silk dressing gown and pushed it from her shoulders. A low hum emanated from his chest and his eyelids lowered as he took in her body. "You are small, but exquisite," he said, almost to himself.

He turned her around without any assistance from her, which was just as well, as her mind was still grappling with the word *exquisite*, when applied to her.

While his fingers worked, his mouth lowered to her neck and he trailed hot kisses from her nape down the nobs of her spine. "I want you to tell me if I frighten or hurt you, Josephine," he murmured, his breath hot on her ear. "There will be some pain for a moment—that can't be helped. But I want the rest to please you—make you forget yourself."

He sucked the lobe into his mouth and rolled and nibbled, tugging with his lips before releasing her and returning to her throat, which he proceeded to bite and suck and lick, sending hot sparks of pleasure up and down her body.

His hands slid beneath the lace and Jo trembled when he stroked her sides, from breasts to hips, back and forth, his touch firm but soft. He lowered his mouth to where her neck met her shoulder, taking a mouthful of skin between his lips and sucking.

Jo let her head tip back, her neck boneless. She didn't realize he'd pushed the gown from her body until she felt the silk and lace puddled around her feet.

"Turn around," he murmured against her throat. "I want to look at you."

"W-why?"

His lips curved against her skin. "Because you are mine." He trailed kisses up her neck. "And because I want you."

"Uh." That was all she had; the rest of her brain needed to move her feet.

His jaw flexed as his flame-blue eyes roamed over her naked body. "You're lovely," he said thickly, as if he was actually . . . aroused.

Jo's head became so light she worried she would faint if he kept looking at her that way, so she dropped her eyes to the sash of his robe and encountered visible proof of his desire.

Her head jerked up. He was smiling, one eyebrow cocked in challenge.

Well.

Never one to shy from a dare, Jo fixed her eyes at chest level and tugged on the silken sash, staring as the two sides fluttered open. Just as he'd done, she slid her shaking hands beneath the silk, her damp palms skimming one of his stiff nipples and making him hiss in a breath.

His skin was warm and infinitely softer than the silk of his robe, the light dusting of golden hair springy beneath her fingers. Her entire body was trembling as she pushed her hands over hot, sculpted muscle, her fingers discerning an imperfection that her lust-soaked mind took a moment to decipher: a battle scar.

Jo stood on her toes and shoved the robe off his shoulders, her eyes widening at the feast before her.

"A bit banged up, aren't I?" he murmured, his hand sliding around her jaw and pulling her forward. His mouth captured hers with a softness she'd not expected, his lips dropping light kisses, gently coaxing and stroking until she was open, his tongue seducing hers until she was inside him, exploring the silken heat.

Jo closed her lips around the tip of his tongue and sucked.

He groaned and slanted his mouth, plunging deeper, his free hand sliding up to cup her breast, palming the round curve while she threaded her fingers into his short, curly hair.

She shoved her body against his and shuddered when she felt the hot brand of his shaft against the softness of her belly.

"My God, you feel delicious," he whispered, his teeth

grazing her jaw while his thumb brushed her erect nipple, again and again and—

He made an impatient grunt and slid his arms beneath her shoulders and legs, lifting her onto the bed, which was when Jo saw the lower half of his body for the first time in five years—at least outside of her dreams.

He was larger than she remembered, thick and ruddy and extending an alarming distance from his lean, powerful hips.

As Jo stared, he grasped the shaft and Jo's head jerked up. His lids were heavy and his lips slightly parted, the powerful muscles of his biceps flexing and bulging as he gave himself several quick strokes and then paused.

"Yes, touch me, Josephine," he said, which was when Jo noticed her hand was halfway to his body.

He released himself and Jo replaced his hand with hers.

He hissed as if her touch burned, his hips thrusting toward her. He felt just the way he looked, silky hot skin sliding over a hard ridge that actually pulsed when she moved her hand.

The crown had a fascinating slit that was weeping, a drop of slippery liquid, sticky and—

"None of that," he murmured, taking her by the wrist and carefully removing himself from her grasp before grabbing her hips and tossing her farther up the bed.

Jo yelped at the sudden powerful gesture, aroused by how effortlessly he handled her body.

He climbed up onto the bed, towering above her on his knees, giving her a vista she would not be forgetting in her lifetime—acres of pale skin, stretched over corded, ridged, living steel.

"Clasp your hands behind your head," he ordered.

Jo hesitated.

"You will like it," he assured her.

Of course he was right. The action not only lifted her breasts high, their stiff peaks jutting, but also left her feeling wickedly exposed.

He lowered himself to his hands, his body caging hers.

Jo cried out when the wet heat of his mouth closed on an aching bud and he sucked and tongued her to hardness, alternating breasts until she was squirming with pleasure. He propped himself on one arm and his free hand reached between them to skim the sharp bones of her pelvis on the way to her belly, where he began to caress her. He swirled in ever-increasing circles, until the tips of his fingers brushed the tangle of brown curls, making her jump.

"Shhh," he whispered, his mouth fastening on to a nipple and sucking hard enough to draw a low moan out of her. All the while his wicked hand was moving until he settled over her mound and cupped her, his middle finger stroking up and down the seam of her lower lips, stroking and stroking and—

"Open for me," he whispered, his knee pressing at the juncture of her tightly clenched thighs.

His second knee joined the first and he nudged her legs wider and wider—

"Yes, just like that," he praised when she could spread no farther.

He sat back on his heels, his hands caressing the sensitive skin of her inner thighs from her knees to her sex, consuming her with his eyes. Never had she felt so exposed, so stripped bare, so *naked*, and she started to lower her hands.

"No, keep them there. I like the way you look," he said, moving from her thighs to her nipples, pulling and stretching the hard little buds until her entire body hummed, her back arching off the bed. "I wish you could see yourself, Josephine—you are so very desirable laid out before me."

His face was intense and stern, every bit of his attention focused on *her* as his eyes followed his hand's progress from her breast over her ribs and trembling stomach, across the thin skin of her pelvis toward—

Jo's entire body tightened as his finger slid between her swollen lips, brushing that part of her that sometimes woke her in the middle of the night.

"So wet," he said in a husky and reverent voice. His finger caressed from her core to her body's entrance, and when he breached her with the tip of his finger Jo jerked in surprise.

"Shhh, sweet," he murmured, "I'm going to relax you—prepare you to take my body." His strokes were rhythmic, each a little harder, probing her a little deeper with every pass, until his thick finger slid all the way inside, his hand beginning to pump in slow, deep thrusts. Jo's muscles eased around him and her body relaxed, her hips tentatively pulsing to meet each thrust.

"Yes, Josephine, take what you want—use me," he whispered as a second finger joined the first, the uncomfortable burn only momentary before the friction was pleasurable, the motion hypnotic.

Jo hadn't even noticed he'd lowered his body over hers until she felt the puff of hot air on her sex. Before she could move or close her legs or do anything, his tongue pushed between her folds and his lips closed around her throbbing peak. Jo sobbed as he sucked, his hand still moving in controlled thrusts, until her hips began to buck wildly.

He gave a breathless laugh and pulled away just as a

wave of pleasure slammed into her. And then again and again.

Beau loomed over her once more. "Take me in your hand, Josephine, and put me at your entrance."

He was harder and wetter now and his hips jerked when she dragged her hand up and down, her thumb discovering more slickness on the fat crown and swirling it around.

He made a sound that was half moan and half laugh. "I want to be inside you."

Jo stared up into pupils so huge there was barely a corona of blue. She lifted her hips and pressed him against her entrance.

And then he began to enter her, far larger than two fingers.

Jo squirmed and dug her fingers into his shoulders as he pushed deep inside. She bit her lip to keep back the whimpers at the burn and stretch, her hips bucking, this time to get away as he sank deep and then held her full.

"It will only hurt for a moment, sweet," he promised, lowering his mouth over hers, invading her with deep, languorous strokes of his tongue that mimicked what was to come.

Jo stopped squirming when she noticed she was no longer hurting—just full and . . . *his*.

Her body clenched at the thought and he jerked inside her.

"God, that feels good, Josephine."

Jo shuddered at the way her name sounded on his tongue; how was it possible? All this passion—for her?

"Am I hurting you?" he asked tightly, his voice tense.

"No," she whispered, only lying a little. The fullness in her pelvis was odd—even a bit uncomfortable—but it was also *so* delicious.

"You're small—so tight," he purred, his hips beginning to pulse, only lightly at first. "I want to fill every part of you," he hissed, his thrusts smooth and strong. "Tilt your hips, Josephine—take me deeper, as deep as you can."

Jo did as he bade and he groaned, his hips beginning to drum.

Jo clenched her teeth but reveled in the signs he was losing control—his movements less precise, his breath coming in harsh gasps, and the part of him that was inside her was so very hard. This was all *her* doing; *she* was the reason he looked less and less like a cool aristocrat and more like a feral, earthy, primitive savage. Jo was stripping this powerful, beautiful man of his rigid control and making him become something fierce and *hers*.

"Yes," he grunted, his muscles stiffening beneath her fingers as his movements turned brutal, the bed shaking alarmingly beneath them.

He gave a hoarse shout and buried himself to the hilt, holding her pinned while his body shook with the force of his climax.

Jo could feel him stiffen inside her each time he spent; each jerk was a little weaker than the last, until he was almost still.

"Yes," he whispered one last time, and then shuddered.

Yes, she echoed silently but fiercely. *Yes, you are finally mine.*

CHAPTER 5

———◆◆———

Beau woke with a start, instantly aware he was not in his camp bed. No, he was home now—in London.

He held a warm, small body in his arms, her back pressed against his chest, abdomen, and already-interested groin.

Indeed, it was his hard cock that must have woken him. It was snuggled between the firm globes of her ass and clearly had ideas of its own.

The candles were still burning, so he knew it couldn't be late. He turned just enough to see the clock; he'd only slept for an hour. Beau laid his head back on the pillow and listened to the sound of her breathing. His *wife's* breathing.

Her body had been a joy—and her sensual and curious nature promised a great deal of pleasure for both of them.

His cock throbbed, reminding him of the feeling of plunging deeply into her tight sheath; Beau wanted to take her again, but she would be sore. And she was too innocent and inexperienced to pleasure him in other ways—not yet, at least. His lips curled into a smile at the thought of the things he would teach her. Eventually.

She shifted in her sleep, rubbing against his sensitive shaft and causing him to suck in a breath.

He would never be able to sleep in this bed.

He carefully untangled their limbs, amazed when she continued to breathe deeply even as he climbed off the bed, his weight making the worn mattress shift and shudder badly.

As Beau bent to pick up his robe and slip it on, he decided a new mattress would be one of the first things he would buy with her money.

He snuffed the candles and made his way toward the sliver of light beneath their connecting door. Dobson had left two candles burning and Beau extinguished the one in the wall sconce.

He lowered himself onto his bed—this mattress no improvement over the other—and laced his hands behind his head, staring up at the cracked and peeling plaster ceiling.

Unless Josephine could convince her father to relent, they'd be heading to Yorkshire in a week. Beau had already sent a message to his mother to stay at the castle. The only reason he'd given in to his mother's request to travel to London at this time of year was because she'd made him feel like an ogre for denying his sisters the treat of coming to his wedding.

"Ha!" he snorted softly. Some treat today had been.

He shook his head as he thought back on the gruesome day. What a bloody gudgeon Loman was to conceive of such a stupid idea.

Beau was even angrier at himself that he'd let the old bastard bully him into agreeing to it.

Both father and daughter had the same broad streak of stubbornness running shoulder to shoulder, but the old man had decades more experience. If it came down to a struggle between father and daughter, Beau suspected he and Josephine would be heading north shortly.

He was looking forward to going home, as he'd not been to Wroxton Court in five years.

But thinking about home made him think about Victoria and the letter she'd sent—three entire sheets—alternately gushing about his return and scolding him for not coming directly to see her, as if they were long-lost lovers looking forward to a reunion.

Well, clearly she was.

"Bloody hell," he said, closing his eyes against the drama he was sure awaited him.

Other than this recent letter, he'd not spoken to Victoria in five years. Beau had no doubt that she was just the same, which was to say just as beautiful, seductive, selfish, manipulative, and devious as ever. Beau's mother shared the last three qualities on that list with Victoria. So, two demanding Duchesses of Wroxton awaited him.

And then there was the one he was bringing with him. Beau shook his head. *Good God. What man deserved to be stuck with three bloody duchesses?*

Although it was unfair to class Josephine with the other two. She was stubborn, yes, but she was not selfish. Indeed, the fierce devotion she showed her father was awe-inspiring. Neither of his parents had been cruel, but neither had they moved any of their children to such heights of affection or fidelity.

No, it was distinctly unjust to put Josephine and Victoria in the same category.

Escaping Victoria's trap had been the biggest piece of luck in his life. Even a cannonball to the skull was preferable to a life shackled to the woman who lurked behind Victoria's beautiful mask.

He'd felt guilty for years that poor Jason had ended up saddled with her, but his brother had steadfastly refused to learn from the mistakes of others.

Even after Beau told Jason that he'd been bedding Victoria the entire month of their betrothal—his besotted brother had still believed Victoria's declaration of love and had wanted to marry her.

Well, Beau hadn't been much wiser when it came to the siren. He should have known she was trouble when she turned up naked in his bed, only a week after he'd met her. She had been far from a maiden, but then Beau had never had an interest in virgins, and he'd enjoyed Victoria's lusty, adventurous, and somewhat deviant habits, which had nicely matched his own.

Victoria's marriage to Jason had been like pairing a cobra with a kitten.

Poor, sweet, weak Jason. If there was a man less suited for a dukedom than his brother, Beau didn't want to meet him.

Beau had known there were financial troubles years ago and his suspicions had been confirmed earlier this week when he'd skimmed the ledgers at his solicitor's office.

His brother couldn't be blamed for all of the debt, but Jason had barreled headlong into a financial disaster that might have been, with careful management, staved off for another generation.

Now those worries were all over.

An odd pang of foreboding stabbed at Beau as he

considered his current situation. He knew he'd been wallowing in self-pity since he'd inherited last August; he'd never wanted the title and had looked forward to a long and satisfying career in the army.

And yet as he looked around him now, he had to admit his blessings were many. He had his health—a bloody miracle after a decade on campaign—a vast fortune at his disposal, and a wife who showed a good deal of promise, at least in the bedchamber.

As for her argumentative nature, Beau felt confident he could bring her to heel along with the rest of his argumentative, fractious relations. Indeed, other than her lineage, Josephine would fit right in with his squabbling siblings.

All in all, Beau's situation was far better than he ever could have expected. That should have made him happy—and it did—but it also made him uneasy to be the beneficiary of such munificence.

Beau recalled a small war-torn village in Portugal, where he and his men had received the evil eye from the villagers. *That* was the level of superstition he was feeling at this moment—he was worried because he was actually quite happy.

Beau chuckled at the ridiculous thought and snuffed the candle: he was no peasant and he needed no talisman to protect him from evil.

CHAPTER 6

———✦———

Jo was eating alone in the breakfast room when she heard boots out in the hall. She wasn't surprised when Beau came into the room dressed in top boots, snug buckskins, and a black claw-hammer that lovingly sheathed his exquisitely formed torso.

"Ah, good morning," Beau said, his lids lowered as he looked down at her. Something about his expression sent vivid images from last night flickering through her mind.

"Good morning, Your Grace," she murmured, hot faced.

"Did you sleep well?" he asked, a subtle twist to his lips.

Jo glanced at the two footmen beside the door, but they might have been stone carvings for all the emotion showing on their impassive faces.

"I did, thank you," Jo said, proud of her cool tone. If everyone else could demonstrate such sangfroid, so could she.

"I hope you will forgive me for bringing the smell of horse and dirty boots into your breakfast room," he said, coming close enough that she could smell the salty, horsey, leathery scent of him, which hit her directly between the thighs.

"Er." Jo couldn't think of a single thing to say.

He smiled and then stunned her yet again by dropping a light, husbandly kiss on her cheek.

Jo stared at her mostly empty plate and concentrated on not making any mortifying noises.

"Coffee," he told one of the footmen before turning to the chafing dishes. "Do you ride?" he asked her.

"Er, yes," she admitted. "But not particularly well."

"You haven't spent much time in the country?"

"No." *None, really—except that week I spent with you five years ago. Do you remember that, Beau?* Jo swallowed a giddy laugh. What had come over her this morning?

Her husband: *that* was the *thing* that had come over her.

The *thing* turned, holding a full plate in his hands. He took the seat across from her—so there would be no escaping.

"I thought your father owned several houses around the country?" he asked, buttering a thick slice of bread.

"Yes, but they are all in cities. Bristol, Manchester—" She shrugged. "I'm afraid I really don't know where they all are."

His eyebrows rose as he chewed a mouthful of bread and then washed it down with coffee. "You never traveled with him?"

"Rarely." She hesitated and then said, "My father is not the sort of man who travels for pleasure. His trips are, *were*"—she grimaced—"mad rushes that revolved around business and meals with other men like him. I wasn't needed as a hostess on such journeys."

"But you did act as his hostess here in London?"

Jo raised her eyebrows. "Tell me, Your Grace, is this your way of asking if I know how to plan a dinner or seat a table?"

"So prickly," he said, a faint curve to his lips as he chewed.

Her mouth curved in an answering smile. "You are correct. *As always.*"

He chuckled but didn't comment.

Jo realized they were speaking like a real husband and wife.

And then the good humor drained from his face. "Did you receive any response to the message you sent last night?" he asked.

The question was like a stone crashing down on her head.

How could she be laughing and chatting while her father withered and died?

Jo cleared her throat. "No, nothing."

"I thought you hadn't," he said, taking a sip of black coffee before turning back to his plate. "He gave me a letter I was to give to you today and I also wrote to him myself this morning."

"Oh! Did you?" Jo asked, more surprised to hear that he'd made such an effort than she was to hear her father had sent one of his missives. Jo was accustomed to her father's brief correspondence; she knew whatever Beau had from him would likely not illuminate the current situation.

"If you come by my study after breakfast I shall give it to you," he said.

Jo nodded and then said, "Thank you for writing to him. That was very thoughtful of you," she added more quietly. "Perhaps you will make him listen to reason."

He gave a soft snort to show what he thought of that notion and raised a piece of ham to his mouth.

He was likely right, but Jo couldn't help feeling ridiculously pleased that he'd cared enough to write to her father.

Perhaps he's just doing all he can to avoid being closeted with you in the country for two weeks.

I refuse to believe that.

Oh, then it mustn't *be true.*

She would not let the evil little voice ruin her moment of happiness.

"Would you like to go to the theater this evening?" Beau asked. "I can't guarantee there is anything worth seeing, but—"

"I'd love to," she said, flushing at how eager she sounded.

But when Beau smiled at her, Jo was glad she'd let her enthusiasm show.

It was true her father was ill and being horrid to her, but at least some things in her life seemed to be going right. One *very important* thing—at least so far.

My husband likes me, she thought.

For once, the little voice had nothing to say to that.

Jo was busy working on an inventory for the house and making a list of things needed—a lot—when Wroxton entered her study.

"Ah, I was told I'd find you here." His rosy cheeks proclaimed that he must have just come in from the cold.

"Mmm," Jo said, finishing her train of thought before putting aside her quill and glancing at the clock. "Oh, dear! I had no idea it was so late." She put away the small book as he came over to her desk.

"I procured a box for a production of *The Tempest* that

begins two nights hence." He grimaced. "I'm afraid there simply isn't much else worth seeing."

"That's one of my favorites."

"Hmm, a tempest—why doesn't that surprise me?"

Jo still wasn't accustomed to this teasing version of her husband and had no witty response.

"In any event, don't have too high expectations, as this will be a production full of understudies rather than principals and a first night is never the best," he said, leaning against the wall beside her desk, the casual pose showing off his long, powerful body to mouthwatering advantage.

"What are you working on so diligently?" he asked.

"I'm making a list of things we'll need based on the inventory we started today."

"By your expression I'm guessing it is pretty grim?"

Jo reminded herself this was his family's home. "It's not so bad."

He smiled and pushed off the wall. "Liar."

The word reminded her of last night and she could see by the way his pupils flared that he was thinking the same thing.

He held out his hand. "Come here."

Jo lifted her chin, not because she didn't want to go to him—she wanted to *fling* herself at him—but because she wanted to go to him too badly.

"And why would I do that?" she asked coolly.

He slowly shook his head from side to side as he closed the distance between them, making her feel as if she were being stalked by a panther, until he was standing barely an inch in front of her.

Jo's eyes riveted on the place where his dark blue cutaway coat met his pantaloons: skintight buff pantaloons stretched over powerful hips and pelvis, which hid *nothing* of the magnificent body they covered.

Jo made a mortifying gulping noise and shut her eyes.

His voice floated down from above, darkly amused. "I *would* say that you should come to me when I bid you, *because I am your lord and master*. But I know that answer won't fadge with my willful wife. So I'll tell you the truth, Your Grace." He stooped, placed his hands around her waist, and lifted her from her chair in a smooth show of strength that was impressive and arousing.

Jo yelped and slid her arms around his neck as his mouth claimed hers. He moved one large hand from her waist to her bottom, his splayed fingers sinking into her flesh and pressing her tightly against his torso as he probed and stroked and kissed until she was breathless.

When he pulled away, his eyes were slitted and his smile was smug and sensual. "*That's* why you should come when your husband tells you to do so."

"Ah," Jo admitted hoarsely. "That's a *very* good reason."

Beau laughed, but his expression grew serious before he gently lowered her to the floor.

Jo's entire body stiffened, and not with passion this time. "What is it?"

"No, it is not that." He reached into his coat pocket and unfolded a letter. "Stowers gave this to me when I came in; he said it arrived two hours ago."

Jo stared down at the familiar handwriting:

Your Grace,

> *I sleep almost every minute of the day and those few minutes I'm awake I don't want to talk or cry or have gloomy, weeping mourners around my*

*deathbed. Tell my daughter that the father she
knows is gone—that this letter is causing me
physical pain to write and I just want my suffering
to end. Take my Josie out of town; you gave me the
word of a gentleman, Wroxton. See that you keep it.*

> *Yrs & etc.,*
> *Edward Loman*

The writing deteriorated alarmingly, barely a scrawl by the time it got to his name.

Jo looked up to find her husband regarding her with an unreadable expression. "Your father is a man of few words."

Jo gave an unladylike snort and refolded the letter before handing it back to him. "Yes, and those few words make his wishes patently clear. This letter is almost word for word the same as the one you gave me this morning."

"I am sorry, Josephine," he said, sounding it.

"As am I." More sorry than she could bear to think about; her father was forcing her to mourn him before he was even dead. *Stubborn, selfish, thoughtless man!*

Beau replaced the letter in his pocket and held out his arm. "Come, we must get ready for dinner."

Jo smiled to herself as Mimi took the last of the pearls from her hair. "Oh, Your Grace, I wish you had come up earlier. I need more time to—"

"You need more time to make me beautiful?" Jo teased. "I doubt there *is* enough time for that."

"Oh, hush, you shouldn't say such things about yourself," Mimi chided, her eyes flickering from her work to

Jo's reflection. "I was only going to say I would have liked to fix these curls again and—"

"My hair already looks grand, Mimi. I'm getting ready for bed—not a ball."

"Aye, well, bed is more important, Your Grace," she said with a look that made Jo's cheeks heat. Jo looked away, down at her lap and the turquoise silk of her evening gown. Beau had commented on it before dinner, his eyes glinting with approval as he'd taken her into the cavernous dining room.

"Perhaps I should find a nightgown in this shade, Mimi. Even I have to admit I look well in this color."

"Not *well*, Your Grace—you look just like an angel."

Jo laughed at the woman's ridiculous comment, but inside she was singing as she recalled Beau's expression from earlier. Of all the colors in the rainbow, this shade made her hair a more interesting red-chestnut and her eyes a mysterious green rather than their boring hazel. Tonight she had looked her best for him—far better than she had on their wedding day.

Your father is dying and you are thinking of gowns. What's wrong with you?

Heat rushed to her head, accompanied by a sharp ache in her chest.

Yes, he is dying! And he has made the worst experience in my life even more agonizing with his cruel, horrid behavior. I refuse to let this crush all the joy out of this evening.

The thoughts were so ringing and clear that Jo wondered for a moment if she hadn't spoken them aloud. But Mimi was smiling to herself and happily fussing.

It would be impossible to banish her worry and grief entirely, but Jo made a vow then and there to enjoy tonight and the time she and Beau spent in bed. As he had said last night, it was a place only meant for loving.

Jo smiled. Yes, she—

The sound of voices and several pairs of feet running interrupted her thoughts.

"What was that?" she asked, cocking her ear toward the hall door and then getting to her feet. "Hold a moment. I want to see what is amiss."

"Your Grace, your gown is undone in the back—"

"I just want to take a quick look. I won't go out in the hall." She opened the door in time to see one of the chambermaids scurrying down the hall toward the guest rooms.

"Wait—" Jo grimaced, struggling to put a name to a face, but she came up blank. Still, the young girl came to a screeching halt and spun around.

"Yes, Your Grace?"

"What is the matter?" Jo asked.

"A chaise and six have arrived, Your Grace," she said, her eyes glinting with excitement. "The Duchess of Wroxton has arrived."

"The duke's mother is here? Is she alone? Have His Grace's siblings come with her?"

"Not the dowager, ma'am, er . . ." She hesitated, her face a study of confusion. "Well . . ." She shook her head. "I dunno how she is called now—the *other* dowager duchess?"

Jo would have laughed if she hadn't felt on the verge of casting up her accounts.

"You may go," she said, as the girl was clearly anxious to be off to fulfill some order.

Jo shut her door softly and collapsed against it.

Victoria had arrived.

CHAPTER 7

———◆———

"I thought you'd be pleased to see me," Victoria said, her lovely face displaying pain, surprise, supplication, and a not-so-subtle suggestion of the erotic pleasures that awaited him.

She blinked her huge eyes up at him, her hands still resting on his shoulders after she'd rushed in and flung herself into his arms.

Thank *God*, she'd not done so out in the foyer with a half-dozen servants hovering.

When Beau took a step away, she followed, laying her cheek against his chest, her soft body melting against him. Whatever scent she wore—something floral and light and feminine—was the same as it had been five years ago and it invaded his senses, bringing a welter of memories in its wake.

Not all of those memories—or even most of them— were good.

Beau laid his hands on her shoulders and put her gently but firmly away from him.

There were tears on her cheeks.

Bloody hell! She'd not been playacting.

Beau pressed his handkerchief in her hand, as if that would somehow stem the flow. "Come now, none of that. Of course I am pleased to see you," he lied with all the conviction he could muster. "Why don't you have a seat," he said, eager to put his desk between them.

She arranged her voluptuous body on the chair closest to him, her sinuous feline movements causing the predictable stirring in his groin. It didn't seem to matter to his cock that Beau mistrusted and disliked the woman.

Victoria was a siren in the classic sense of the word, and her soft, alluring curves were more deadly than even the sharpest reef.

Beau had no intention of falling prey to her lures, but he knew that would require a tiresome vigilance—and it would also be wise never to be alone with her like this. Not that he didn't trust himself, but, really, why take any chances?

So he cut to the chase. "I don't understand the purpose of this expensive visit."

Her turquoise eyes opened wide. "Expensive?" she asked, but then laughed. "Oh, you mean the chaise." She shrugged, the provocative gesture rippling through her voluptuous body. "You can afford it now, can't you? Besides," she continued before he could answer, which was just as well, "how am I expected to travel—by mail coach? Are you going to stint me, Beau? Keep me on a small allowance? A short *leash*?"

Beau knew her provocative words and suggestive smile were meant to remind him of what had once been between them. He had to admit he experienced a slight flare of heat at the memory of their bedroom games, but the heat was quickly extinguished by all the other memories of their shared past—and the fact that he now had a wife.

"There was no reason to make this journey, but there are at least a dozen I can think of for you *not* to come to town at this time of year."

"Ah," she said, giving him a lingering scorching look. "I *see*."

Beau sighed. "What do you see, Victoria?"

"You wanted me to be waiting for you at Wroxton Court when you came home." Her eyes smoldered. "You wanted me to come to you, just as I used to do."

Beau felt an unpleasant tingling in his scalp at the thought of Josephine finding Victoria tied to a bed in his chamber—or in his chamber at *all*. They'd only been married a day, but he somehow suspected infidelity would not be something she'd tolerate without a fight. Especially not under her own roof.

"I wanted you to do as you were told, Victoria," Beau corrected. "Did you not get my response to your letter?"

"I *did* get your letter and it was *positively* draconian, darling!"

"And so you decided to disobey me." It was not a question.

She shifted and sat up higher, reminding Beau of a hen fluffing its feathers. "You're angry with me." Her plush lower lip quivered. "I think you'd like to *keep* me in mourning—keep me for yourself—sequestered in Yorkshire, panting for you. I suppose now that you're married, your *wife* will want to install me in the Dower House just to keep me away from you—and *you'll* allow it."

"Wroxton Court is your home and you never need to leave it—you know that. You are a Duchess of Wroxton." He caught her gaze and held it. "But you are not *my* duchess, Victoria, and I will not tolerate any disrespect toward Josephine."

Her chest rose and fell but it didn't draw his eyes from hers. As veiled as her gaze was, he could see the struggle—*feel* the tension—taking place inside her.

"Now, tell me why you have made such an arduous journey when you will only find yourself housebound?"

Although, now that Beau thought of it, leaving her in London might be best for everyone.

She flashed him an accusing pout. "I know you didn't want me here for your wedding—because of what we once were to each other. And perhaps still are." She paused to allow him to confirm her suspicion.

Beau did not.

Victoria tacked smoothly. "The truth is it has been a wretched winter, brutally cold and dreary. I knew your mother wouldn't allow me to come with *her* when they took the old coach down—you must know how unfairly she judges me. She has *always* hated me."

Beau wisely reserved comment.

Victoria shrugged, the action drawing his attention to her magnificent breasts, which threatened to leap from what had to be the most seductive mourning gown in Christendom.

"Besides," she said when he continued silent, "I have not seen Jo in forever. You know how close the two of us once were when we were in school together—*like sisters*."

"You were schoolmates?" Beau kept to himself the opinion that it strained credibility to believe two such different women were ever friends.

"Of course that is where we met, but we became so much more after leaving Bath. Not only did we go to all the same parties, routs, and balls, but even that rather wonderful week at Lady Edelson's country house." She paused significantly, as if Beau wouldn't recall the things they'd done at that party. "But I'm sure you recall darling Jo at that party as fondly as I do."

Beau wanted to curse and stomp. *Good God—a bloody* house *party?* He'd already surmised from Moreton's comment at the church that he must have met Josephine that summer. But a house party?

"Oh, no!"

His head jerked up and he saw her eyes widen at whatever she saw on Beau's face.

That was when Beau *knew* he would have made a dreadful diplomat.

Goddammit! How can I be such a bloody idiot?

With very little effort, it seemed.

A tiny triumphant smile flitted across Victoria's face before she raised an elegant beringed hand to her mouth, drawing attention to perfect bow-shaped lips that lovelorn, besotted fools—thankfully *not* Beau—had written odes about.

"Oh, Beau! Never tell me you did not remember she was at that party?"

His wretched face heated. But at least she thought his lousy memory was limited to the party and not his wife's very existence.

"Well, that's understandable, Beau. We *were* rather distracted back then." She gave a throaty chuckle. "That is something of an understatement, isn't it, darling?"

Beau ignored her question.

"Please tell me she does not *know* you don't recall her being at that party, Beau. How *crushing* that would be."

Yes. And how eager you look to crush *her with such information.* He sighed. So there was yet another uncomfortable piece of information he would have to disclose to his new wife before Victoria could wield it like a weapon.

"We were not speaking of my wife," Beau said, taking charge of the conversation before it careened any more out of control. "We were speaking of *you*, Victoria, and what I'm going to do with you."

"I've got several ideas as to—"

"Don't," he said softly but with enough menace that even she should know he was not jesting.

She cast her eyes modestly down as he studied her. Yes, it *was* better that she was here. After all, he hardly wanted her around when he took Josephine up to Wroxton Court for their wedding trip.

Josephine.

God help him. How was it possible he hadn't remembered her from five years ago? If what Victoria said was true—always debatable—that meant he'd seen Josephine more than once or twice.

Josephine would have realized he'd forgotten her when he failed to mention their prior acquaintance. Beau grimaced, mortified to think how much embarrassment, if not pain, his omission had likely caused her.

"I brought Sarah with me," Victoria said, her words jolting him from his orgy of self-flagellation.

"Good Lord, Victoria! What could you be thinking to drag a four-year-old on a cross-country journey at this time of year?"

Her beautiful face crumpled and she sprang to her feet, rushed around his desk, and dropped to her knees beside his chair.

"Oh, Beau—she is our *daughter*!" She grabbed one of his hands and brought it to her smooth cheek, nestling into his palm like a kitten. "Don't you want to see her? We made such a beautiful child together and—"

"Victoria." Beau tugged on his hand but she'd latched on to him like a bloody shore crab clinging to a rock. "*Victoria*," he repeated through clenched teeth.

She gazed up at him through eyes sheened with tears. "I can see you are still angry with me for what happened back then and you have every right to be. But I love you—it has always been you."

Beau stared in openmouthed wonder as a fat tear slid down one cheek and her lip trembled. The woman could cry on command—he was sure of it.

"Haven't you thought of me even a little? I've spent so many days—and nights—wishing things had been different. Wishing *I* had acted differently." She gave a violent shake of her head, the action sending her glossy black curls dancing. "You can't know how hard it was. Jason wouldn't leave me alone—even though he knew I was yours. He badgered me and—"

"Enough," Beau said, revolted that she would tell such lies about his dead brother—a man who'd wandered into her snare with all the awareness of an infant.

Her eyelashes fluttered, scattering tiny diamonds onto the sweet curve of her cheek. "I'm sorry; that was wrong of me." Her hands clutched him hard enough to grind his bones together. "But don't punish me for what I did. Haven't we both suffered enough? And now you've been forced into this dreadful marriage—"

"Victoria," he warned.

There was a soft knock on the door and Beau knew before it opened who was on the other side.

CHAPTER 8

———◆———

"Oh," was all Jo could think to say as she stared at the tableau: Victoria kneeling beside her husband's chair like a supplicant before her king.

Beau stood and helped Victoria to her feet before turning to Jo, his expression thunderous.

"Why, hello, Your Grace," Victoria said coyly. "You look just as lovely as ever."

Jo almost laughed at her masterful insult.

Beau, on the other hand, wasn't in the mood for banter. His face looked carved from stone. "What did you need, Josephine?"

Jo flinched under his ice-cold anger but held her ground. "I'm sorry to disturb you, Wroxton, but Her Grace's little girl—Sarah?" She cut Victoria a questioning look.

Victoria nodded, her full lips curled up at the corners, her expression that of a cat that had just licked up an entire bowl of cream. At Beau's feet.

"Yes, what about her?" Beau prodded.

"She is crying—very upset, in fact—and is asking for a turtle?" Jo raised her brows.

Victoria's expression snapped from lazily sensual to irritated and she huffed. "It's *Tuttle*, her old nurse." She cut a glance up at Beau, who was staring down at her, his face turned in such a way Jo could not see it. Victoria gave him a melting smile. "I told her that big girls didn't need their nurses."

"You left her nurse in Yorkshire?"

Victoria's brilliant smile dimmed at his obvious disbelief. "It's not as if I didn't bring a girl to look after her, Beau. But Tuttle is too old to travel. Besides, it's time Sarah started behaving like a little lady, not an infant."

"Good God, Victoria, she is not yet five years old—she *is* an infant."

"My, what a wonderful father you will make, Beau." Victoria's lips pulled up on one side into a sensual, wicked smile that made heat gather in Jo's belly; she could only imagine what such a come-hither look would do to a man.

"Go see to the girl, Victoria. I will arrange for the housekeeper to send a suitable servant to assist whomever you brought with you."

Beau turned away from her and strode toward the door, holding it open for her.

Victoria's smile faltered at his autocratic dismissal, her expression shifting to mute outrage as she flounced toward the door.

Jo bit her lip to keep from smiling. So, her duke was highhanded with everyone, even a woman whom he'd once loved and still might.

He closed the door and returned to his desk, his expression distracted. "Was there something else, Josephine?"

Jo blinked. "Um, I thought . . ."

"Yes?"

I thought you might want to tell me what you were doing with Victoria on her knees? Or even why she is here?

Jo stared up into his face. It was expressionless now, but he'd been far from impassive in bed last night, and even this morning when he'd kissed her at breakfast.

Perhaps Jo was making a mountain out of a molehill and he really did not care about Victoria as he used to.

But why had she been kneeling beside his chair?

"I want to have a word with Mrs. Stowers. Please send her to me when you leave," he said, impatient.

Jo gritted her teeth. "Of course, Your Grace." She spun on her heel, but his hand caught her upper arm.

"Come here." He slid his other arm around her body and pulled her to him, holding her trapped as he stared down at her, his gaze intense. "I apologize for being short with you."

He blinked after the words came out, as if he'd surprised even himself.

And then he lowered his head and captured her mouth, taking her with the sort of savage, wits-obliterating kiss at which he excelled. His eyes were dark when he released her.

"Go ready yourself for bed, Josephine. I will join you in three-quarters of an hour."

Beau's duchess was in bed when he entered her room. She was wearing a faded pink and white flannel nightgown buttoned up to her chin, and a scowl.

Beau paused for a moment to take her measure before

speaking. She no doubt believed such a garment would dull his ardor. But the truth was he preferred his women naked and he viewed any gown—ugly or otherwise—as an impediment to be immediately removed. Still, she was obviously trying to make some sort of point and it would be unwise of him to ignore it.

She watched him in silence as he came toward her bed.

He held out his hand. "Come sit with me."

Her jaw tightened for a long moment before she pushed back the covers and did as he bade.

Beau led her to the settee and sat beside her, as he'd done last night. Something about her expression made him feel it was best to keep her within arm's reach.

"You are angry with me," he said. "Tell me why."

"Why? So you can then tell me I am not *permitted* to be angry?"

Beau supposed he deserved that. "Last night we agreed we would not take strife to our marriage bed. I wish to make love to you tonight—do you not want me in your bed?"

Her eyes widened and her lips parted.

Beau did not rush her. It was important they begin as they meant to go on. And the beginning was now.

"I am angry," she admitted. And then she met his gaze and added in a quieter voice, "And I do want you."

The ferocious wave of arousal that swept his body stunned him as he looked into dark eyes that told him more plainly than words just how much she desired him.

But they must attend to business before pleasure.

He took her hand and kissed her palm before saying, "I collect it is Victoria?"

She nodded, her lips pressed together and her eyes—so

THE DUKE'S TREASURE   201

hot with desire only a moment before—clouded with deep unhappiness.

Beau found the prospect of discussing one woman with the other repellant and had hoped to avoid it. But he knew Victoria would take the first opportunity to tell his wife they'd once been lovers—if Josephine did not already know about that from long ago. Victoria was a woman who would delight in teasing and taunting Josephine in the years to come, and it was up to Beau to at least provide her with the truth before Victoria could spring it on her.

"You're angry that she has come without an invitation?"

Her eyes flew to his. "You didn't invite her?"

"No. In fact, I specifically ordered her *not* to come."

"Oh," Jo said, and then gave a halfhearted shrug, as if she wanted to say something but had decided against it.

"Josephine, you must tell me what is wrong. I'm not the sort of man to catch subtleties. Or even *un*subtleties."

She smiled faintly at that. "I was disconcerted, and yes, a little angry, when I came into your study and found her—"

"Kneeling so dramatically at my feet," he finished for her.

"Yes. And then you looked so angrily at me when I interrupted you that—"

Beau lifted a hand imperiously. "Wait—please. I want to be sure I understand. You thought I was angry at *you* for interrupting that annoying little drama?"

"Yes."

He gave a bark of unamused laughter. "I was *relieved* to see you, Josephine. I was furious with Victoria—for disobeying me and coming to London, for behaving like an actress in a pantomime and dropping to her knees, for any number of reasons. But I was not angry at you."

Her cheeks wore twin spots of red and she remained uncharacteristically quiet; Beau had no idea how to interpret her reaction, so he continued.

"When I came in here tonight, I didn't know you were upset about Victoria until I asked you about it. I wondered why you were looking so unhappy and angry in your bed but assumed you were stewing about your father's behavior and my unfortunate part in it."

"You *did*?"

"Yes, I did. Likely because, as my own mother put it, I am a dictatorial, draconian clod."

She choked on her laughter.

"So you see how easy it is to perpetuate misunderstandings if you do not talk?"

"Yes."

"Now, I want to speak of this irksome matter—Victoria—only this once and then I want to put it behind us."

Her lips twisted into a bitter smile.

"I know what you are thinking: dictatorial. But the truth is that talking about her or dwelling on her is not something that gives me pleasure. I would rather learn about *you* and talk about *us*. Do you understand?"

"Yes, Beaumont."

He frowned. "Nobody uses that except my mother—call me Beau."

"You told me to call you Beaumont."

Why was she looking at him with her mulish expression? "I did?"

"Yes, just last night."

"I have no recollection of that."

"Ah, so you are not infallible, after all," she quipped. "Or perhaps you are losing your mind?"

Beau laughed, genuinely amused by her spirit. "I fear it is the latter, as I have never been wrong before. But you will call me Beau from now on."

She rolled her eyes, flattened her hands palms down, and made small gestures of obeisance. "Yes, master."

"Actually, I prefer that to Beau."

"I'm sure you do."

Beau was enjoying himself, but they needed to finish with Victoria.

He gave Jo a stern look. "I do not love Victoria. I thought I did—long ago—and maybe I did." He shrugged. "But whatever I felt for her died almost as long ago."

He took Jo's hand again and raised it to his mouth, permitting himself a more lingering kiss, licking the soft, damp skin of her palm, her salty taste unexpectedly erotic.

Her pupils flared and her small, shapely mouth parted in a way that made him imagine putting something in it.

Beau set the entrancing image aside for later and turned back to the far less appealing matter at hand.

"I know, *now*, that you and I met several times when I was home on leave five years ago." He kissed each of her fingers. "I am sorry I do not remember you—not only because I suspect it causes you pain, but because I would *like* to remember you; I *wish* I remembered you. But those weeks were . . . well, suffice it to say I have forgotten more than I remember about that time. You are the only memory I regret losing, Josephine. I hope you believe that."

She gave a jerky nod.

"I know Victoria is . . ." He hesitated, choosing his words carefully. While he wanted to alleviate his wife's worry, he did not wish to insult his brother's widow or disparage her.

He felt a light pressure on his hand and looked up from his thoughts.

"I know how Victoria is. We were once friends—of a sort—or at least I thought we were." She shrugged. "I don't like her, but she is now my family and I know she might live with us for some time before she remarries, or the remainder of her life if she doesn't. You have my word that I shall always be civil to her."

Beau nodded and then braced himself to make a more uncomfortable, but necessary, confession.

"I suspect Victoria will take the earliest opportunity to tell you that Sarah is my daughter."

She appeared to have no words at the ready, and Beau could not fault her reaction.

"We were lovers that summer—after I asked her to marry me. I'd suspected my brother was infatuated with her, but I had no idea she was toying with both our affections until I caught them together."

"Oh." Her eyes were round.

"Yes, that was my response," he said wryly. "I'm ashamed to admit I had been so besotted that I hadn't known what she really wanted until that moment: to marry a duke, not his younger brother; she used me to get to Jason. I'm sure a more observant, less *draconian*, man"—he smiled slightly—"might have noticed signs, but I missed them all. Regardless of what happened between her and Jason, I stood ready to honor my offer of marriage. Jason would have none of it. He told me he loved her and she loved him. So—" Beau shrugged. "That was an end to it and I left for the Continent that very day—voluntarily shortening my leave by two weeks."

The tawdry tale seemed to hang in the air between them.

"I'm so sorry," she said. "That must have been awful."

"I'm not sure you understand, Josephine. I didn't flee the country because I was broken-hearted. I fled because I felt so guilty at my lucky escape—guilty that poor Jason was *not* so fortunate." Her eyes widened and he nodded. "Yes, the reason I didn't return for five years was not because I was so brokenhearted that I couldn't face the woman I'd lost; it was because my mother wrote regularly to regale—and blame—me with stories of their disastrous marriage. Tales of how Jason and Victoria were behaving with a recklessness that was endangering the future of the dukedom." He shook his head. "I can never know if Jason really did slip and shoot himself, or if he did it on purpose. I desperately hope he was not in such despair as to take his own life. But my brother was never strong. The enormity of his situation would have crushed him. My mother told me how Victoria flung the truth of Sarah's paternity at him at a family gathering. Now, as for whether the child really is mine? None of us could know that—you understand that Victoria was with both of us at the same time?"

"Yes," she said, not with revulsion but something else in her eyes. "I understand."

"I will have to live with the burden of what I've done for the rest of my life and—"

"What burden? You mean your brother's possible suicide?"

"Yes, of course."

"What did he do to jeopardize the security of your estates?"

He shrugged irritably. "Gambling, horses, the usual run of costly pursuits."

"Did you make him do those things?"

Beau frowned, and then realized where she was going. "No, you are correct, I did not."

"So claiming responsibility for his death is—Well, it's ridiculous."

Beau bristled at her tone.

"No, don't become angry or offended. I'm just reminding you that everyone is responsible for their own actions. How old was your brother when he married Victoria?"

"Thirty-five."

"So, old enough to make his own decisions." She dropped her chin and gave him a challenging stare. "It is arrogant for a person to believe they are responsible for other people's decisions."

Beau couldn't help laughing. "Ah, so I am arrogant, am I—along with draconian, dictatorial . . . what else?"

"Authoritarian," she supplied.

"Hush," he said, pulling her closer and then lifting her small, soft body onto his lap so that he was cradling her. "You are trying to assuage my guilt and that is very kind and commendable and wifely." He kissed the tip of her nose, amused when her skin once again turned fiery.

He held her at arm's length and pointedly looked from her body to her face. "Did you wear this hideous nightgown to express your displeasure?"

She gave an adorable gurgle of laughter. "Yes, is it terribly obvious? I just thought—"

"I want it off. Now," he said, standing and lifting her to

her feet along with him. "Do you want to dress in a way that pleases me, Josephine?" he murmured as his fingers made quick work of the few buttons.

"Yes, of course." Her voice was flatteringly breathy.

"Then you will wear this for me in the future." He lifted her gown over her head and flung it aside.

"I want you waiting for me in *nothing* from now on." He stared down at her naked perfection and tugged on his sash, shrugging his robe to the floor, his cock hard, thrusting, and eager to possess her.

"You are beautiful," he said, his eyes roaming her flushed skin. "I need to be inside your body. Now."

She glanced from Beau to the bed on the other side of the big room, taking a hesitant step toward it.

Beau caught her hand and pulled her back. "No. Here and now." He dropped into the chair behind him and held out his hands, amused by her shocked expression. "Straddle my thighs, Josephine. I'm going to teach you how to ride me."

There were pulse points in Jo's body that she'd never known existed. And every single one of them was thudding at his touch, his words, and—most of all—the sight of his long, thick arousal curved against the quilted musculature of his abdomen.

Beau took her hands and pulled her down ungently onto his lap, shifting and positioning her until Jo's bottom rested on the hard bones of his thighs, his hands sliding from her knees to her sex, pushing her legs wide, exposing her, his blue eyes blazing and hungry.

Jo stared every bit as hungrily at the masculine riches before her.

"Take my cock in your hand, Josephine."

Her head jerked up and her thighs instinctively tightened.

He eyed her from beneath heavy lids with a faint, challenging smile, as if he were curious to see her response to such a vulgar, inappropriate word.

A proper lady would be offended, Jo knew, but her body adored his crudity.

She slipped her fingers around his hot, silky shaft and gave him a tentative stroke.

"Harder," he demanded, flexing his hips and shoving himself into her tightened fist. "That feels so good," he said raggedly. Jo stroked her thumb over his tiny slit and he groaned and bucked, so she did it again, and again.

"Yes, Josephine, like that," he murmured, his hand moving from her thigh to the damp tangle of curls.

Jo grunted and inched closer when he stroked that *already* very stimulated part of her, his skilled fingers knowing exactly what to do to send her down the path to ecstasy.

She noticed her hand had stopped and resumed her measured stroking, her other hand tracing the distinct grooves on his abdomen, which flexed exquisitely with each pulse of his hips.

But then her body began to shake and her head tipped back, her fist slowing and slowing and—

Beau covered her limp hand and stayed her motions, his other hand driving her toward her climax.

"Come for me while I watch you, Josephine."

Her body exploded at his coarse command and for a brief eternity there was nothing in the world but bliss.

Jo was still floating when she felt something breach her entrance.

"Are you too sore for me here?" he whispered, stroking and probing with his middle finger.

"No." She shuddered as yet another wave of pleasure washed over her. "I want you . . . Beau."

"I like the sound of that," he growled, grasping her hips and lifting her. "Say it again."

"I want you, Beau." Jo grabbed on to his powerful shoulders, her fingers unable to penetrate the hard, tightly woven muscle.

"Watch me as I take you," he ordered her, his heavy-lidded eyes dropping to where he was pressed against her opening. And then he entered her in one smooth thrust.

Unable to look away from the place where they were joined, Jo cried out as her body struggled to accustom itself to his thick length.

"Beautiful, isn't it?" he gritted, holding her impaled for a long moment before pulsing his hips in sharp thrusts. "I've thought about being inside you all day long," he said while they stared at the mesmerizing sight of his slick shaft sliding in and out of her body. "Did you think of me today, Josephine? Did you want this?" He lifted her hips up until only his crown was inside and then brought her down hard.

"Yes," Jo gasped, shuddering at his powerful assault.

"More?" he hissed, his fingers digging painfully into her bottom as he lifted her again.

"Oh, yes, please, I—"

This time, when he brought her down, he met her with an upward thrust.

"Oh God," she moaned, vaguely shocked at her words.

Beau gave a wicked, breathless laugh and commenced to work her without mercy.

Jo clung to his shoulders, her body a willing and eager sacrifice to the ferocity of his lovemaking. This was not like the night before—this was a primal, thrilling claiming that would leave her bruised and sore, and Jo reveled and rejoiced in each savage thrust.

This was what she'd wanted; *this* was what her body and soul had craved for five long years. *This* was exactly as he'd been the night she'd spied on him.

Except tonight, he wasn't passionate and unrestrained with another woman, but with *her*.

At long, long last, he belonged to her.

CHAPTER 9

———◆———

Jo's first thought when she woke was that she'd once again slept through her husband's departure. Except this time she knew he couldn't have departed much more than a few hours ago. He'd been insatiable last night. But then so had she.

She was grinning like a fool when another, far less pleasant, thought hit her: Victoria was here.

"Ugh," she said aloud, dropping back onto her pillow.

Don't let her do this to you; don't let the manipulative witch add to all the other difficult, unpleasant matters you need to deal with. The voice, for once, was kind and soothing.

And it was giving her excellent advice.

There was no reason to fear Victoria. Beau's explanation last night had not only rung true; it had been heart wrenching. He did not love Victoria and he did not wish that the law allowed a man to marry his sister-in-law.

Jo would need to adjust to Victoria's presence as the

other duchess was likely to live with them at Wroxton Court.

Thinking about Beau's castle made Jo think about her father, and thinking about her father was like a punch to her midriff.

He really *was* going to die without ever letting her see him again. It was hard to comprehend. Each time the thought came to her, it was just as painful and shocking as the first time.

Yesterday she'd seriously contemplated taking a hackney to his house and pounding on the door. They'd have to let her in, wouldn't they? If only to stop the racket.

She groaned. But she'd promised her father. And while she wasn't a gentleman, her word still meant something to her. So here she was, getting closer to leaving him every minute.

Mimi had already started on Jo's packing and the trunks and boxes were a pointed reminder that the hours were ticking past, faster and faster.

Jo would leave and her father would die here alone.

Why was he *doing* this to her?

Because of her mother? Watching her mother wither away from consumption had been painful, but Jo had treasured those last weeks and months with her. Why did her father always believe he had to protect her from everything?

Jo contemplated pulling the covers over her head, but it was past nine already, time to get up. She shoved back the blankets and hopped out of bed just as the door to Beau's dressing room opened.

"Good morning." It was her husband, clad in yet another glorious robe, this one a dull gold and black. He was holding a tea tray in his hands. "I guessed you might be awake. I thought to surprise you."

Jo gaped. Yes, she was certainly surprised.

His lips curved into a wicked smile and his gaze dropped to her chest.

Jo yelped and dove headfirst into bed, yanking the bedding up around her.

His warm laughter came closer and she heard the rattle of crockery before he said, "Come out of there. I've got your robe at the ready and I've closed my eyes."

Jo's face heated; how could she possibly be shy after the things they'd done last night?

"What are you doing here?" she asked rudely.

But he only chuckled again. "I was trying to be husbandly rather than draconian. Now come out of there."

She emerged slowly to find him holding the robe, but his eyes were wide open.

"I thought you were going to close your eyes."

"I did close them. I didn't say I was going to *keep* them closed."

Jo snorted, trying to slide from the bed and into the robe without exposing her body in the process, and making an acceptable job of it.

She tied her sash and his hands landed on her shoulders and turned her around.

"There—better?" he murmured, swooping down to kiss her with a mouth that tasted fresh, not like a stale trunk as she suspected hers did.

"You've cleaned your teeth," she accused when he pulled back. "And your hair is damp."

"Yes, I am guilty of cleaning myself," he agreed. "Come," he said, taking her hand and leading her toward the seating area in front of the roaring fire. "I am not only trying to be husbandly. I also wanted to demonstrate I'm not just decorative, but also useful. So I nipped down to the kitchen and fixed this tea tray."

Jo gave a very unduchesslike snort. "You did no such thing."

"Well, all right—but I *did* ring for the tray, which is quite strenuous."

"Now *that* I believe."

"I don't know why you doubt my ability to do basic things like make tea," he said. "I've been a duke for less than a year—and a spare for thirty-four years before that." He stopped and cocked his head. "I just realized that I don't know your age."

"I will be twenty-four on my next birthday. I suppose most married couples—the ones who courted normally— know that kind of thing beforehand, don't they?"

"Perhaps," he drawled. "But I think we got to the more interesting parts of the marriage before most *normal* couples."

Jo gasped.

"You really are quite amusing to shock, you know."

"Well, I'm pleased that I *amuse* you."

His eyelids lowered in a way that made her feel as if she weren't wearing any clothing. "You do amuse me, Josephine. As well as intrigue, please, entertain, and arouse me."

Josephine opened the teapot for the ninth or tenth time, the lid rattling noisily in her shaking hands.

Thankfully, he didn't appear to notice.

"We were talking about something else when I became distracted. Ah, yes, my utility. I'll have you know that I made tea for myself while trudging across the Continent."

"What, twice?" she teased.

"At least three times."

Jo's face was not scalding, so she risked a peek at him. "You might have only been a duke since last August, but you have a very ducal air."

He squinted at her. "By *ducal* you mean, er, what was it? Draconian and—"

"Dictatorial," she finished for him. "How do you take your tea?" she asked.

"Light and sweet."

Something in his tone made her look up; he was wearing a lazy, suggestive smile, his eyes hooded.

Jo swallowed and dropped her eyes to the task at hand. "How interesting—since you take your coffee black."

When there was no answer, she looked up. His lazy smile was gone and his expression arrested.

"What is it?" Jo asked.

"You know how I take my coffee," he said quietly.

"Well, yes, I noticed at breakfast yesterday."

He nodded slowly but did not speak, so Jo resumed her work. "Did you ride again this morning?" she asked.

"No. Come look." He held out his hand and pulled Jo up, leading her to the window.

When he yanked open the drapes, they both waved their hands to displace the dust.

"Good God," he said, coughing. "That's dreadful. Look outside," he ordered.

At first she thought it was the thick cloud of dust motes. But then she realized it was snow—and a heavy snow, at that. The square below had already been cleaned at least once, but already more deep snow had accumulated: it was a snowstorm.

Jo looked up at her husband, who wore a slight, mysterious smile. "Do you think this will keep up?"

"The sky certainly has the look of it. If this continues we shall be snowed into the house."

Jo's face broke into a grin.

"I thought you might like that," he said.

All this snow meant no travel.

Of course it also meant that Jo was snowed in with Victoria, but at least she didn't have to leave London. Not that it mattered, since she couldn't actually *see* her father, thanks to his orders.

A warm hand took her chin and tilted her face up. "If you wish to send another letter to your father, I can deliver it when I go out after breakfast."

"Where are you going on a day like this?" Jo blurted before she could stop the nosy question.

But her husband did not look annoyed at her question. "I need to go to the Home Office to take care of a few details, and I also need to see my solicitor." He hesitated and then added, "I'm terribly sorry about Victoria being here just now, and I shan't make you manage her all day on your own. I'll come back as soon as I'm able." He hesitated and then added, "I know this is a rough time for you, Josephine."

"It is. But—Well, you are being very kind." Jo had wanted to say that being with him made things better, but she'd lost her courage at the last moment.

"And when I return, you might show me just how good you are at that—" He gestured to the heavy gilt and marble chess table her father had given her for her birthday last year. It was a gaudy thing that she'd only brought along because it reminded her of him.

"You play chess?" she asked.

"Yes, and charades and spillikens, as well. I assure you that I'm quite human when you get to know me."

Jo laughed at his mock affronted look. "I didn't mean to say it like that. I just wouldn't have thought you'd had much spare time, being on campaign for so long."

A shadow passed over his face. "Oh, there was always time. Too much, sometimes." He shook himself and gave her a dry look. "I must confess I'm not very good."

"Neither am I," Jo lied. Her father loved the game and they'd played every night since she was eight years old. She was going to enjoy besting her magnificent husband for a change.

Jo held out his tea and he leaned forward to take it. He took a sip and gave her a look of pleased surprise. "Perfect, thank you."

Jo felt far too happy for such mild praise.

"We shall have to eat dinner with Victoria, of course."

"Of course," she murmured, trying not to think about it.

"But I think we might be excused for retiring early. Right after dinner, in fact." He shot her a wicked look that sent sparks of excitement throughout her body. "After all, it is our wedding holiday, my dear."

CHAPTER 10

———❖———

"That was a lovely dinner, Jo."

Jo had just stepped foot on the stairs, pitifully eager to get up to her room. But she turned at the sound of Victoria's voice. Although Jo knew the truth about her husband's affections, she still could not bring herself to enjoy the other woman's company. She'd successfully spent the day avoiding her, but of course she'd had to suffer through dinner—a meal at which Victoria had monopolized the conversation, either not realizing or caring that she was the only one talking.

"Thank you."

Victoria laughed, the sound enticing and musical. "I do hope you will call me Vix—and I have always thought of you as Jo."

"Of course," Jo said, already knowing she'd never use the pet name. But there was no reason to be churlish.

Victoria laid a hand on Jo's arm, and it took all her willpower not to jerk away.

"I hope things will not be awkward between us because

of my relationship with Beau," Victoria said in a loud whisper.

Victoria really was a snake—beautiful, but a snake all the same. It made Jo weak with gratitude that Beau had pulled her fangs so quickly; otherwise comments like this would have her and her husband at loggerheads every single day.

"We are sisters, Jo—there should never be awkwardness between sisters."

Thanks to her husband, Jo was able to give Victoria a genuine smile of amusement. "I'm looking forward to it."

Victoria recoiled slightly, a puzzled notch between her spectacular eyes. But she recovered smoothly.

"I'm so pleased to hear it. I really was excited for you when I heard you were finally going to achieve your dream of marrying a Duke of Wroxton."

"I beg your pardon?"

Victoria's eyes grew big with obviously feigned surprise. "Oh, I just meant that I know things didn't work out for you with Jason." She chuckled. "That naughty boy."

"I'm sorry, but what are you talking about?" Jo demanded.

"Are you ready to go up, Josephine?"

Jo turned to see her husband standing just behind Victoria. When she didn't answer immediately, his eyes narrowed and he looked from Jo to Victoria to Jo.

Whatever he saw on Jo's face made his stern expression soften. "You go up, darling. I'll join you shortly."

The same caressing look and loving endearment that sent Jo's pulse racing caused Victoria's full mouth to tighten with displeasure.

Jo knew she was grinning but didn't care. "Good night,

Victoria." She didn't wait for a response before turning on
her heel and floating up the stairs.

Beau's head ached as he dried his wet face and then
slipped into the robe Dobson held out. He nodded his head
in dismissal at his valet, his mind on the woman he'd left
down at the bottom of the stairs—when it *should* be on the
woman he would be joining in only moments.

Damn Victoria! How dare she try to thrust her way
into Beau's more than satisfactory marriage bed? Oh, not
that he hadn't expected it. He'd meant what he'd said about
Victoria always being welcome in his homes, but that
didn't mean she would have free rein to torment his wife.

Beau had seen the disparaging looks she'd given
Josephine earlier, the way she'd monopolized the conversation, speaking of past events that only served to under-
line how close she and Beau had been that summer, and
how Josephine had not been part of it.

Making his marriage work with such a strong-willed
woman as his wife would be challenging in itself; the last
thing he needed was a meddling ex-lover.

Victoria was a bloody menace. The sooner her mourning was over and Beau could find her another husband, the
better.

He had no idea what she'd been saying to Josephine on
the stairs, but it would likely be another evening in which
he would need to put out a fire that Victoria had started.

"Dammit all to hell," he muttered as he strode toward
the connecting door, not knowing what he would find, but
girding himself to expect the worst.

He yanked open the door.

Josephine was curled up in a chair by the fire reading,

but she looked up and smiled when he entered. So, she was not armored in flannel. Instead, she was wearing a lovely confection that had obviously been purchased with him in mind.

Well.

"You look like a thundercloud," she said.

Beau snorted. "Do I? I'm beginning to realize I would have made a dreadful diplomat with such a face."

She grinned and put a placeholder in her book before setting it aside.

Beau lowered himself into the chair across from her, wanting to sort things out before getting to the real business of the evening: which was stripping that nightgown from her body and teaching her something new.

"I'm sorry, Josephine. I know this isn't much of a wedding holiday for you. Between your father and now—" Beau composed himself. "What did she say to upset you?" he asked.

"It doesn't matter."

"Josephine."

She sighed. "Fine, she said something about being glad I finally got what I wanted—a Duke of Wroxton." The look she gave him was more than a little hurt and slightly accusing. "I don't know what she meant, but I'm sure she shall enjoy sticking me with pins for her own twisted entertainment."

If Victoria had been in front of him at that moment, Beau would have throttled her.

Here was yet *another* vow the old man had extorted from him. But at this point, was he really breaking his word by explaining what their vicious sister-in-law meant? By speaking now he wasn't exposing the truth; he was only stopping a problem before it got worse.

"Please, tell me."

Perhaps he was becoming weakened by all this emotional turmoil, or perhaps he was just sick and tired of always finding himself on the wrong side of the argument with this woman. It really didn't matter. What mattered was that he needed to ameliorate at least a little of her unhappiness, even if it meant breaking his word. If he didn't tell her, Victoria would—as Josephine said—stick her with pins. He could not be a party to that.

So he took a deep breath, and prepared to tell her one more thing to hurt her.

Jo had never seen an expression like this on her husband's face: it was bone weary, and she dreaded learning whatever had made him that way. Perhaps it would be better if she told him she didn't want—

"Your father made a marriage contract with my brother—five years ago. Jason broke their agreement. It wasn't a legally binding agreement, of course—not without your signature or knowledge—but Jason couldn't have known that when he married Victoria, thus breaking his word."

Jo didn't know what she'd been expecting Beau would say, but this certainly hadn't been it. She'd started shaking her head before he'd even finished. "Even my father could not be so arrogant."

Beau said nothing.

"I cannot believe this! Just when was he going to tell me? When he dropped me off at the altar?"

"If it is any consolation to you, he deeply regrets his actions."

"Oddly, that is no consolation at all," she said, her voice shaking with anger.

"I can't blame you for being angry."

A horrid, nasty, slimy thought shoved its way into Jo's frazzled brain and her head whipped up. "Is that why you married me? Did he pressure you to save your family's tarnished honor?"

He sighed. "It's long over with, Josephine. What matters is that we are married now, and it seems quite happily—at least for the past forty-eight hours, or so."

"I guess that is my answer," she said, ignoring the thrill she felt at his "quite happily" comment and keeping to the subject at hand.

"Fine, here is your answer. It *was* part of my reason for marrying you. First off, your father approached not long after I learned of the horrible financial disaster Jason left. Not only did his offer seem like a godsend, but then he told me about what Jason had done. If your father hadn't known my brother, I suppose he never would have approached me. And we never would have married. Would you have preferred that?"

Jo looked into his handsome face and knew he was right: they *were* getting along and their marriage showed signs of only getting better, but—*blast it!* Just who did her father think he was?

Edward James Loman, that's who, he would have said.

Jo took a deep breath and flung herself off into the void. "I am glad that I married you."

The corner of his mouth pulled up into an almost boyish smile. "Thank you," he said softly. "As am I. So does how we got here really matter?"

"I don't know," she said. "I just—" She flung up her hands. "No, you are right. Once again I'm acting angry at the wrong person. It is my father, and not you, who is responsible for this."

Beau held out his hand. "Come here. I don't want to sit across from you—I want to be in bed with you. Inside you."

His words tore the air from her lungs, and her legs were wobbly when she rose from her chair.

Beau sucked in his breath when she stood. "Good God."

Jo looked down; she'd forgotten she was wearing this particular nightgown, a pale blue and very sensual creation with sheer panels in strategic places.

"Do you like it?" she asked, recalling with a shiver what he'd said the night before—that he wanted her naked.

He stared as if enraptured. "I might have to revise my opinion about fancy, lacy nightgowns. There is something about this one—it covers you, but with a suggestion of nudity that almost makes you look *more* naked."

Jo didn't think her head could become any hotter.

"Turn around," he said.

She put her hands on her hips. "Has anyone ever told you that you are very bossy?"

"No. But I have been called draconian and dictatorial. Does that count?"

She laughed and then twirled in a circle for him.

He made a growling noise and took a step toward her, dropping his mouth to suck on her hard nipple through the lace panel.

Jo swooned. He was so . . . so—Oh, she didn't know what the word was. And she didn't care right now.

"It's very becoming," he said when he stood up, his robe sliding to the floor and exposing his arousal. His eyes were riveted to her body. "Now take it off."

Her hands were shaking badly, so it was fortunate the gown had only three ties to loosen before she could pull it over her head. Once freed, she flung it aside and moved toward the bed.

But he caught her hand and tugged her back. "No," he said, capturing her mouth in a kiss that was more of an assault. Jo met him stroke for stroke, their teeth clashing in their urgency to get deeper inside each other.

Beau wrenched himself away and then pulled her toward the sofa.

"Kneel and put your hands on the back of the settee," he ordered.

She blinked, dazed.

"Do it, Josephine," he said when she gaped up at him.

Her limbs were jerky, but she took the position.

He made a noise of approval. "This is a breathtaking view of your body." His hand slid from her hip over her flank and then paused to cup her breast, thumbing her aching nipple while his other hand slid between her thighs.

"You are so wet for me," he murmured into her neck, biting and kissing and licking while he pulled her tightly against his chest and drove her ruthlessly toward her climax.

When she began to shake and cry out he kneed her thighs apart and entered her with a punishing thrust, riding her hard while teasing another orgasm from her just before burying himself to the hilt and emptying deep inside her.

They were lying side by side, faceup on her bed, the cool air beginning to chill their sweaty bodies.

"I am not usually so impatient, my dear. Thank you for indulging me."

"I daresay you can find a way to make it up to me," Jo said lightly.

He turned toward her. "Look who's cheeky."

Jo grinned and turned on her side to face him, propping her head in her hand.

He tucked a lock of hair behind her ear.

"My father sent nothing again today."

"I'm sorry."

"Oh, he's so *stubborn*."

Beau's lips pulled up on one side. "I wonder if it runs in the family?"

Jo smiled, pleased by his gentle teasing. She loved lying in bed and talking with him almost as much as she loved his body and what it could do to her.

"Tell me about yourself when we first met—did you only have the one Season?" he asked.

"Yes—and that one was *more* than enough. My father hounded me mercilessly the next year, but I stood firm."

"So, stubborn in other words?" His blue eyes crinkled at the outside edges.

"You used to smile like this a lot back then," she said.

"Hmm, did I? Well, I suppose I was younger then."

His face had subtly tightened and Jo knew he was probably thinking about the things that had stopped his smiles. Like the jagged pink scar on the right side of his chest.

She reached out and touched him lightly. "What happened here— Er, that is, if you don't mind talking about it. I don't mean to pry," she added when he fixed her with the impassive look she'd decided she didn't like very much because it was a mask, a defense.

"It is from a bayonet, not deep or life threatening. Tell me, why just the one Season? What did you plan for your life before your father sought me out? Or was I only the latest offering in a long line? Did he bring suitors and leave them at your door, like a cat leaving a mouse?"

They both laughed at that image.

"I had three other offers that Season," she confessed, "and a few others over the years. But you were the only one he brought to me—Well, who knows? Maybe there were a dozen others and they all begged off at the last moment."

"Shhh," Beau murmured, kissing her deeply and thoroughly, until when he finally pulled away she couldn't recall what they'd been discussing.

"What happened that Season to make you hate society so much?" he asked.

She shrugged. "I don't particularly care about such things—parties, balls, society functions, moving from London to Brighton to the country and then doing it all over again, but my father became obsessed with the aristocratic set. Oh, *he* didn't want to join them, not that they'd ever accept him even though he buys and sells peers the way he does ships and—" Jo stopped when she realized what she'd just said. "I'm sorry. I didn't mean—"

"Shh," he said. "You don't need to apologize for the truth." He cocked his head at her, absently stroking her side with his hand, making Jo want to purr. "You keep saying *them*. You do realize you are now *them*."

"Not really. I'll never be *of* your class—you know that. And I'll never be of my father's class. I'm neither fish nor fowl. I am destined to spend my life on the fringes—any entrée I have is thanks to you."

His gaze became uncomfortably acute. "I don't understand why you agreed to this marriage. You never really cared about becoming a duchess, did you?" Jo swallowed and his eyes narrowed, making him look like a predator who'd just caught scent of his prey.

God. How had this conversation started?

"You said something earlier—that I used to smile more. How did you know that? I suppose we must have seen each other often—in particular at a house party." He grimaced. "It infuriates me that I don't remember any of our interactions. I know I was distracted, but I don't understand how I didn't see you, but you saw me."

Jo felt her deceitful face heating.

His eyebrows shot up. "Why are you turning such a charming shade of pink?"

Jo raised her palms to her flaming face.

"Josephine?" he asked in a voice that warned he would have it out of her. "What is it?"

Why not tell him? Hasn't he already confessed enough of his own embarrassing secrets?

She dropped her hands. "I was never outgoing—I rarely spoke unless somebody dragged me into a discussion. It was just too mortifying to know that men only spoke to me because of my money." She shrugged. "You never saw me because I never once spoke to you. In fact, I usually hid when you were around."

"But why?"

She snorted. "Ask Victoria."

His eyes narrowed.

She swallowed several times. "I didn't mix with your set, Beau—not normally. The only reason I was invited to that party—my only house party—was because Lady Edelson had a son she wanted to marry off."

His brow creased and then he snorted. "Not Bertie? God. Tell me she didn't want you to marry—"

"Yes," she ground out between her teeth. "She thought I'd be perfect for her dipsomaniac half-wit son, Bertie."

"Ah."

Jo couldn't stand the pity on his face. "I didn't know

anyone there except Victoria." She snorted. "I say *know*. That's not really accurate. She only paid me any mind when I could be a foil for her beauty—as if she needed one." She cut him a glance from beneath her lashes; he looked pensive. Whatever memories talking about that party stirred up, they weren't entirely happy ones. Jo wanted to ask him how *he* liked having to relive the past but then recalled that what she was about to tell him was entirely her fault, not his.

Jo rolled onto her back and stared at the canopy, unable to look at him while relating this embarrassing tale. "It was a dreadfully tedious party for me and the last of its kind I would ever attend. The group, you probably don't recall, broke into eight couples whenever the opportunity presented itself. Bertie and I were to be the ninth couple, but he wasn't exactly challenging to dodge. Anyhow, a person could hardly walk a step without encountering— well, you know."

She risked turning to him.

"You must know that women were—still *are*, I'm sure—mad for you. It's rather nauseating, really."

He actually blushed. "Er—"

"I wasn't the only one who enjoyed looking at you— we all did. But, for some reason, Victoria thought it was the most amusing thing she'd ever seen—a little merchant scrub like me admiring you from afar."

He looked dazed.

"Victoria talked about you—told tales of what you two did." Jo's breathing was rough. "She dropped several hints—I know she wanted me to see it."

"It?" He frowned. "What?" And then. "No. Please tell me you didn't—"

"Yes," she hissed, releasing the pent-up frustration,

anger, and jealousy of five years into one word. "Yes, you and Victoria."

His lips were parted and he was shaking his head. "Er, I thought we were in the—"

"Carriage house," she finished for him.

"She *told* you we went up there?" he asked with no little disbelief.

"Yes."

"Good God. Were there more of you watching?"

Jo could not believe his question. "I. Don't. Know."

He recoiled slightly at her angry tone. "And where did you hide?" His expression said he really didn't want her answer.

"In the wardrobe. Across from the bed."

"Ah." He nodded, his lips tightly pursed. And then he dropped his arm over his face, his nose in the crook of his elbow, his bulging biceps hiding everything except his chin, and his body shook.

"Beau?" she said, turning onto her side and laying a hand on his arm. "Are you all right?"

He shook his head, choking.

He was crying?

And then she heard a snort and recoiled from him as if he'd spat fire at her. "You're *laughing*?"

He dropped his arm and gave up trying to hold back, laughing until there were tears in his eyes.

Jo crossed her arms over her chest, which reminded her she was nude, so she sat up and pushed herself toward the edge of the bed. "I'm so pleased to amuse you."

"I'm sorry," he said in between gasps of laughter, his hand catching her upper arm and holding her like an iron shackle. "I daresay you were dreadfully shocked— perhaps frightened even. But, darling"—Jo shivered at that naturally given endearment—"you were the one who *went* there. Did you know what we would be doing?"

"Well . . . *yes*, I suppose so," she ground out, even her ears burning now.

"So then whose fault was *that*?"

Jo seethed. "Let go of me."

"I can't," he said, shaking his head, his expression regretful. Jo squirmed, but her attempts didn't even budge him.

"Where are you going, Josephine?"

"Nowhere, it seems."

He pushed out his lower lip, tilted his head, and gave her a rueful smile. He looked so adorable Jo wanted to hit him.

"Is it dreadful of me to laugh?"

"Why would you think that?" she retorted sarcastically, struggling mightily to maintain her glare.

His lips curled up at the corners in a satisfied smirk and he flexed his arm, the action pulling her slowly but inexorably toward him.

"What are you doing?" she asked in a voice that was far from commanding.

His nostrils flared. "Did you like what you saw, Josephine?"

She gasped, her face blazing. "Of course not."

"We really must cure you of this disturbing propensity to lie," he said, his eyes narrowed as he easily pulled her onto his hard, hot body. "I'm going to check and see if you really are as repulsed as you say." His free hand slid between her thighs as if it had every right to be there, as if her body belonged to him.

He thrust a finger into her slick passage and groaned, the sound rumbling deep in his chest. "Wet and hot."

Yes, Jo thought as her mouth whimpered and her body

arched against his, her hips wantonly begging for more. There was no point fighting it: he could do or say whatever he wanted to her and her traitorous body loved it.

"My Josephine," he murmured, kissing her neck while his powerful hips pulsed suggestively beneath her. "You're on fire for me and your cunt—"

Her body stiffened and a scandalized shriek burst from her at the coarse word.

Beau just chuckled. "Oh, Josephine—you *act* shocked, but your *cunt* is telling me something completely different. You're wet and swollen and clenching just *thinking* about the things I did all those years ago." He lowered his mouth over her neck and bit her, hard. "Just how will your body respond when I do those things to *you?*"

Jo made a mindless gasp and he began to move in measured, deep thrusts.

"Have you pictured yourself spread out on a bed like that ever since, Josephine? Naked, exposed . . . vulnerable," he whispered, his hand never stopping. "Am I the man in your fantasy? I hope so. Am I cruel? Wicked? Relentless?"

Jo bit her lip hard enough to taste metal. She would not—she would not—

"I would tie your wrists . . . restrain your ankles . . ." he murmured, his voice hypnotic, his breath coming in rapid, heated puffs on her throat. "If I had you bound that way . . . what do you think I would do . . . Josephine? Do you think I'd make you . . . come?"

"I don't—I, no, I—" Her voice was ragged, barely a whisper.

"No?" His hand paused. "Do you want me to stop?" he asked in the same mild tone he might use asking if she cared for another lump of sugar in her tea.

"Please." She shamelessly ground her sex against his motionless hand.

Again that wicked chuckle as he resumed his exquisite torture.

His other hand was no longer restraining her—she noticed belatedly—and it slid between their bodies and found her hot, pulsing core as surely as an arrow found its target.

Jo couldn't catch the sob that broke out of her as he effortlessly pushed her toward her crisis and she shuddered and shook until she lay like a limp rag on his chest.

"I think that is what you want, isn't it? To come when I will it . . . your every pleasure mine to command."

His finger slipped from her sheath.

"No, don't go," she begged. "Please—"

"Shhhh, I'm not going anywhere, my lovely, needy darling," he whispered, positioning something bigger and hotter against her entrance. "This is what you want," he told her.

"Yes."

"Yes," he agreed, "and I'm going to give it to you. Hard."

He took her with agonizing slowness, making her feel each and every inch, his body sinuous and undulating, his thrusting slow, lazy, deep.

"Tell me the way you want it," he said, his voice strained, his body slick with the effort of resisting his own need, but his motions smooth, thorough, controlled.

"Please," she whispered.

"Tell me," he ordered through gritted teeth.

"I want you . . . *hard*, Beau."

He flipped her onto her back before she'd even stopped speaking, their faces a bare inch from each other.

"*Josephine*," he whispered, his lips curving into a smile. "You want it hard, my wicked, wanton, wonderful wife?"

Jo tilted her hips and wrapped her legs around his body. "Hard," she whispered.

And that's exactly what he gave her.

CHAPTER 11

———❖———

Jo woke up with a smile, her body so twisted and tangled in the bedding that she didn't bother trying to get free but luxuriated as last night came back to her, piece by exquisite piece.

Ah. Last night.

He'd taken her one last time, slow and languorous. And then he'd whispered something about a park, a pond, and skating, before slipping away into the gray light of dawn.

Jo hugged herself. He knew—he knew everything about her, no more secrets, nothing to hide, just . . . her and Beau.

She lazed and stared up at a threadbare canopy that had somehow become precious to her over the course of the last three days. Even the memory of Victoria's unwanted presence could not dim her happiness.

But the door to Jo's constant worry about her father and her burning need to see him was never quite closed.

She would go today—even if they didn't speak—just to *sit* with him. She groaned at the well-trammeled path of thoughts that appeared before her, and turned onto her side.

But she couldn't avoid it, no matter which way she turned or what she did.

Jo would be enjoying herself—either during her delicious evenings with Beau or even while going through cupboards full of worn linens with Mrs. Stowers—when all of a sudden it would hit her like a brick to the head: Her father was dying. Alone.

Jo managed to subsume most of her guilt beneath anger—after all, it wasn't her fault he'd locked her out of his life—but sometimes a wave of despair would wash over her and she would begin to flounder, to drown.

She slowly untangled herself from the bed linens, debating whether to have breakfast in her room. But no, stewing alone was ill-advised. Jo scowled. Of course stewing with Victoria would hardly be better.

But she couldn't allow the other woman to make her a prisoner in her own house so she heaved herself out of bed, rang for Mimi, and dressed.

Nobody except Stowers was in the breakfast room when she arrived.

"His Grace went out but said he would be back well before noon," he reported. "And Her Grace is breakfasting in her chambers."

Well, thank heaven for small favors.

"I'll have some coffee, Stowers," Jo said, taking a plate and perusing the selection of food in the chafing dishes.

Jo's face heated at the memory of the prior evening, and she found herself grinning like a fool as she nibbled a slice of toast. While her husband's autocratic ways would likely annoy her on occasion, she couldn't help enjoying his commanding ways in the bedchamber.

He was certainly dictatorial, but it was always for their mutual pleasure, never selfish. And it was—

The door to the breakfast room creaked slowly open and then stopped.

Jo and the footman—Michael, one of the servants she'd brought with her—gave each other curious looks.

He'd taken a few steps toward the door when it creaked open a little more. It was Victoria's little girl, Sarah.

"Well, hello again," Jo said, smiling at the little girl—who was crying and appeared to have been doing so for some time. "Are you looking for your mama?" she asked when the child simply stood planted, her lips turned down, her little hands clutching a doll of some sort.

Sarah shook her head. "Turtle."

"Ah." Jo pushed back her chair and went to the child, dropping to her haunches and bringing herself to eye level. Whoever Sarah's father was, the little girl was the very image of her beautiful mother. Her enormous blue eyes leaked tears, her thick black lashes heavy with drops of water, like branches after a heavy rain.

"Do you want to sit with me? Perhaps have a little breakfast?"

Sarah hesitated, her brow furrowed deeply.

"Your dolly looks hungry," Jo said. "What is her name?"

Sarah looked down at her hand, as if only then remembering what she held. "Her name ith Thally," she finally said.

Jo bit her lip and looked up at Michael, who was grinning.

"Has Sally had her breakfast?"

Sarah shook her head.

Jo stood and held out her hand and the little girl took it as trustingly as—well, as a child.

* * *

A short time later, after Michael fetched two cushions from a nearby room for Sarah's chair, the little girl was seated beside Jo, chattering away, her hands and face smeared with strawberry jam.

"Won't you have a bit of egg to go with your, er, jam?" Jo asked, lifting a forkful and moving it back and forth, the way Mimi had done to entice her to eat when she was little.

The door flew open, banging against the wall and making both Jo and Sarah jolt in their chairs.

Victoria stood in the doorway, looking magnificent in a dressing gown of shocking scarlet silk, her unbound hair flowing to her waist, her blue eyes flashing as they took in Jo and her daughter.

"Mama, look!" Sarah held up her doll, whose face was also jam stained. "Auntie Jo gave Thally an' me jam."

A young maid, who'd been hidden behind Victoria, sidled around her. "Come with me, Lady Sarah; you've got a breakfast waiting upstairs."

Sarah's face became instantly mulish. "No."

"Sarah!" her mother ordered, making Sarah, Jo, Michael, and the young maid all start. "Go with Lucy. Now."

Sarah slid from the chair, sullenness in every line of her body and every movement. She stopped halfway between the breakfast table and the anxiously waiting maid and turned back to Jo.

"Thank you for breakfast," she said with the dignity of a duchess, and then took the maid's hand and disappeared into the corridor.

"You—" Victoria pointed at Michael. "Out."

He glanced at Jo before moving even a muscle, and she gave him a reassuring smile and nodded.

The door hadn't even closed behind him before Victoria began. "If you think you can poison my daughter against me—as you've done with Beau—you'll find you are sorely mistaken. And, as for Beau and what we share with each other—" Her eyes narrowed to slits. "If you believe it is over, that he has shifted his affection, his *desire*, from me to you—" She gave a snort that would have done a racehorse proud. "Well, then you are more naïve and foolish than I thought you five years ago. And if—"

For the next three minutes and forty-five seconds—Jo knew that because she watched the large clock behind Victoria's shoulder—her sister-in-law vented her not inconsiderable fury.

Jo could see she was winding down—her breathing slowing and her magnificent bosom no longer heaving—when Victoria demanded, "Have you nothing to say for yourself? Or will you just sit there like a bump on a log?"

"First, I wasn't trying to *steal* your daughter's affections," Jo said coolly, having to look up several inches to meet the statuesque woman's furious gaze. "I'm not sure it is even *possible* to steal a child's love for a parent. What did you want me to do when she wandered into the room, crying? Toss her into the street? Sarah was scared and lost and looking for her nurse. Again."

Victoria's mouth tightened into a pucker at the not-so-subtle reminder, the action causing her to bear more than a passing resemblance to the back end of a pug.

"And as for the rest of your . . . *tirade*, I will only say this. We are not dogs and Beau is not a pork chop."

Victoria's mouth opened.

"I refuse to tussle over him as if he is an inanimate object with no will of his own. He chose to marry me and he is my *husband*. If you are angry about that, you will have to manage your anger in some other fashion than ranting at me like a fishwife in my own house. Let me remind you, Victoria, that you once had his affections and threw them away. You are a very lovely woman—quite the loveliest I've ever seen, as a matter of fact. You would be even more attractive if you did not use your beauty like a club and bludgeon everyone with it to get whatever you want."

"You mean the way you've always wielded your money?" Victoria demanded, her smile triumphant at delivering such a solid hit. "Do you think a man like Beau would have married a woman like *you* if she weren't wealthy?"

"No," Jo said, almost laughing at Victoria's stunned expression at her honest—and disarming—admission. "But that is neither here nor there, now, is it?" she asked gently, actually feeling sympathy for this unhappy woman, who'd certainly let the best man she would ever encounter slip through her fingers. "He is my husband, Victoria. And you cannot change that with this sort of behavior. You only end up shaming yourself with your dog-in-the-manger ways—"

"I will *not* be insulted by such as *you*!" Victoria's face was an unattractive brick red, and her chin was wobbling in a way that threatened, for once, the arrival of genuine tears. She pivoted on her heel and stormed from the room, leaving the door swinging open in her wake.

Good Lord! Jo dropped into her chair, her heart pounding as if she'd been running. But then she noticed that the tight feeling she had in her chest whenever she saw the other woman—or, indeed, even thought about her—had eased considerably.

She stared sightlessly at her half-eaten plate of food, trembling in the aftermath of such an outpouring of emotion. She had, at long last, stood up to Victoria. And it had not been as terrifying as she'd always feared.

No doubt it was her marriage to Beau that was responsible for emboldening her—or at least partially. But Jo wanted to think it was also that she was five years older and wiser and could see what was truly important in life.

Victoria had been right about one thing—Jo had not only used her money as a shield to hide behind but also blamed many of her problems on it that Season. Any man who'd shown any interest in her—and there had been several—she'd despised as a soulless fortune hunter.

Didn't Victoria have to contend with something similar? Did she always wonder if it was only her beautiful face and body a man wanted, rather than the person inside it?

Jo wasn't foolish enough to think this was the last time she'd have such an encounter with the tempestuous woman. But at least she no longer felt like an insignificant, ugly, powerless insect, as she had five years ago.

Stowers appeared in the doorway and hovered, the majestic butler's posture uncharacteristically hesitant.

"Please, come in." Jo smiled. "Ah, my coffee."

When he set the steaming pot on the table, Jo saw there was a letter on the tray.

Her chest tightened before she even saw the direction on it.

"This just came for you, Your Grace."

It was her father's butler's handwriting and she snatched it from the footman's hands.

"Thank you, Stowers," she murmured. In her haste, she

tore the letter in half as she opened it, and had to hold a piece in each hand to read it.

Your Grace,

Mr. Loman spent an extremely difficult evening and it was questionable whether he would live to see this morning.

Jo gasped and surged to her feet. "Oh, Father!"

"Your Grace?" Stowers's voice came from far away.

The doctor was with him throughout the night and I feel morally bound to tell you that he cannot live out the day. If you wish to see him, you must come now.

> *Respectfully,*
> *Fanning*

Jo ran from the room, colliding with a footman carrying a bowl of apples.

She didn't stop but darted up the stairs toward her bedchamber.

"Josephine?"

It was Beau, and his voice was coming from the foyer.

She hesitated a second but then charged ahead, even faster. If he knew what message she had, he'd keep her from leaving. He'd given his word as a gentleman.

Jo sped past a startled maid and yanked open her door.

Mimi, who was sitting by the fire mending, let out a surprised squeak.

"He's dying, Mimi. I'm going to see him and nobody

can stop me." She grabbed the first cloak her hand landed on, a black velvet opera cape.

"Oh, Miss Jo, not that. It's freezing out there and you'll catch your death," Mimi said, flying past her to grab a wool, fur-lined cape, which she tossed to Jo. "Don't you go anywhere, Miss Jo! I'm fetching your hat and gloves," she yelled from inside the dressing room.

Jo hooked the clasp shut just as her door opened.

Beau paused in the doorway, his brow creased with concern. "What is going on, Josephine? Why didn't you answer me?"

She turned away and he strode toward her, lifting her chin. "Is this about your father?"

She jerked her chin out of his hand. "You can't stop me. I will fight you; I will bite and claw and kick and—"

"Miss *Josephine*!" Mimi was standing stunned with the fur hat and gloves in her hands. "That is not the—"

"I will take you," Beau said. "Come along."

Jo stared up at him. "Is this some sort of trap?"

Mimi squeaked at her rude question.

But Beau was calm and quiet. "No, Josephine, it is not. Are you coming? Because the carriage has just gone back to the mews and we might be in time to catch it before the grooms unharness."

He held out his hand and Jo gave him a tremulous smile and put her hand in his.

CHAPTER 12

———✦———

Beau stared at his wife, who looked ready to come apart at the seams.

For the first time in his life he was breaking his word. But he was doing it for *her*. He simply could not bear to watch her suffering, and for such a pointless, foolish reason.

He saw that she was shivering. "Make room," he said, shifting across to sit down beside her. She gave him a glassy-eyed glance as he slipped an arm around her. "The sun is out and you are in furs, but it is chilly. Let me warm you."

She hesitated only a moment before all the stiffness went out of her body and she melted against him. Beau closed his eyes as he pulled her closer, her small body and the unidentifiable sweet and spicy aroma that seemed to hover around her already familiar to him. And, yes, already quite precious.

Less than a week ago Beau would have scoffed if anyone had told him that not only would he come to *like* such an awkward little person—with whom he'd bickered from the start and had nothing in common—but also that she would actually begin to worm her way into his heart.

Was this the beginning of friendship? Affection? Love? He didn't know, nor did he need to have a name for it. All that mattered was that she was his wife and had become important to him—important enough to go back on a matter of honor. Because dishonor was more palatable to him than her pain.

Beau had known her so short a time, but already he saw her differently than he had only a few days earlier. Yes, she was small and delicate, but she was also fierce and passionate and strong. And there was something about her keen intelligence that transformed her rather average appearance into that of a woman who was compelling and beautiful in her intensity.

Yes, whatever man was lucky enough to earn her love, he would have it for a lifetime.

She murmured something against the heavy wool of his greatcoat.

"What was that, my dear? I couldn't hear you."

"Thank you," she said in a voice husky with anguish.

He squeezed her tightly to him, ashamed he'd held on to his foolish pride so long. God save him if Loman was gone before they got there.

"Papa?"

Jo sank to her knees beside the bed, her heart threatening to explode in her chest. She looked up at Doctor Philpot, who hovered near the end of the bed. "Is he—"

"He is alive, Miss, er, Your Grace. But he has rarely

been conscious these past three days. He is in a great deal of pain so I have given him all the relief I have to offer."

Jo knew what he meant; she could smell the sickly sweet odor of the poppy.

"Can he hear me?" she asked, unable to take her eyes from her father's skin, which was like gray tissue paper, his chest moving so little she had to squint to detect any breathing.

"I don't know, Your Grace," the doctor admitted.

Jo took her father's hand, which was as fragile and light as a dried-up leaf. "Papa," she whispered. "Can you hear me?" A hot tear slid down her cheek, followed by another and another.

Beau's warm, strong hand landed on her shoulder and gave her a gentle squeeze. "Leave us, Doctor. We will summon you if you are needed."

Poor old Doctor Philpot's eyes widened, whether at Beau's arrogant command or simply being addressed by a duke Jo couldn't have said.

"Yes—yes, of course, Your Grace."

The door shut behind him and Beau said, "Here, Josephine."

She stood to find he'd pushed the chair right up to the bed.

"Thank you," she said, not having to release her father's hand to sit.

He soundlessly brought a second chair and set it beside hers, and then he took her free hand and held it with both of his. He did not speak, but his very presence—like a fierce guard dog—gave her comfort.

"Papa," she whispered without much hope. "Can you

hear me?" She choked on a sob and Beau raised her hand to his lips.

"Do you think he can hear me, Beau?" she asked without turning.

"Yes."

Jo turned at his simple, certain answer. "You do?"

"Yes, I do. I think he is deriving comfort from you right now. I think he feels you holding his hand. I think he is glad we disobeyed his wishes and you are with him. But I think he is tired, Josephine. Too tired and too weary to express the depth of his love for you. Talk to him. Just because he doesn't answer, it doesn't mean he is not listening."

Jo turned back to her father's shell of a body and stared at his wasted face.

"You made me *so* angry keeping me away, Papa, but I know why you did it—because you love me." Her vision wavered and she couldn't blink away the tears—they were coming too fast and there were too many.

"You loved me more than anyone will ever love me, Papa," she said, her words garbled and broken. "And I will miss you so much. So much. So—"

Jo dropped her forehead to their joined hands and sobbed as if her heart was breaking. Because it was.

EPILOGUE

Yorkshire, Five Months Later

"Help! Beau—I need help!" Josephine shrieked in between peals of laughter as the three mastiff pups Beau had given her for her birthday chewed on her bare toes.

"Coming, Your Grace," Beau called out, carefully reeling in his line.

Once he was finished, he balanced the rod between two highup branches in a nearby tree—a place where it wouldn't attract teething puppies and meet the same fate as his last fishing rod.

Beau approached the blanket where his lounging wife lay and the puppies scattered and then regrouped to attack his boots.

He gestured to his formerly glossy boots and cut her a martyred look. "You see what I suffer for your sake?"

She chuckled and Beau reached up and took his crop from the branch where he'd hung it—his *third* crop before he'd learned his lesson. He looked sternly at the three hounds and pointed to a spot *not* on the blanket and then tapped the leather upper of his boot with the crop, *thwap thwap thwap*.

They were young, but they were clever enough and eager to please and they all three sat, their tails wagging their bottoms, their tongues lolling.

"Good boys," he praised, and then snapped his fingers and all three dogs curled into furry brown balls, sighed and squirmed, and then dropped into sleep like the infants they were. Beau cut his wife a smug smile and raised his eyebrows in a *did you see that?* gesture.

"Good *boy*," Josephine said, her lips curved into a wicked smile. She patted the blanket beside her. "Now sit."

Beau smirked and then flopped down beside her. "Do I get a treat?"

She snorted. "I hope this is not how you plan to train our children—with a crop and snapping fingers."

"Why not?" he murmured, tapping her hip with the whip he still held. "It worked training you."

She gasped. "You beast!"

Beau gave her a hard kiss, inhaling her intoxicating scent. "You smell so good I could eat you," he said, licking her throat and then nipping her earlobe. "I think I will."

She yelped and gave a breathy laugh as he continued to lave and nibble.

"*Bad* boy, no chewing."

Beau growled against her damp skin and then tossed aside the crop, slipped his arm around her swelling middle, and carefully lifted her so that she was straddling him as he rolled onto his back.

"Mmm." She shifted and wiggled, rubbing a most interesting part of her body on a very *interested* part of his.

"Wicked, teasing strumpet," he muttered, pulsing his hips hard enough that he lifted her gently up and down, grinding his stiffening ridge against her soft heat. She heaved a contented sigh and then closed her eyes, a dreamy, sensual smile on her face.

Beau laid his hands on her small, rounded stomach, which he could not seem to stop touching, and she purred while he stroked her body instantly pliant.

At four months' pregnant she was as eager for him in the bedroom as he was for her. Of course he exercised more care with her now—ignoring her objections that she was not fragile—and he was teaching her there were other, less strenuous but equally rewarding, ways to pleasure each other.

"I suppose this is yet another day that I won't get the fish dinner you promised," she groused, her eyes sensual slits as she smiled down at him. "Sometimes I wonder if you actually come here to fish at all."

Beau ignored her accusation, his attention shifting from her belly to the hem of her skirt, which he began lifting.

"Oh," she said, her eyes opening wider. "Did I tell you Rexford is going to order the plow that one of Papa's manufactories makes?"

Beau smiled. Rexford—his steward—and Josephine got on like a house on fire. "No, is he? I wondered what you two were doing together out in the corn shed so often."

"*Tsk*, you shouldn't mock," she chided. "You'll see—I shall increase our yield threefold."

"Mmm-hmm." He slid his hands over her ankles and calves, grunting when he encountered the soft, warm skin of her thighs.

"Do you know what a mangel-wurzel is?" she asked, shuddering slightly as his thumbs brushed the sensitive crease that bordered her damp bush.

"Small, furry rodent—sharp teeth?" he guessed, smiling when she laughed.

"No, it's some plant he asked about."

Beau was actually thrilled by her interest in the property as well as the castle. His Josephine would never be a grand, regal duchess like his mother, or an untouchable siren like Victoria, but she cared about the people on the estate with an interest that was personal, and they adored her for it. So did Beau.

In the months since they'd left London—not long after Edward Loman's funeral—they had settled into a comfortable, active existence. No moss would be allowed to grow with Josephine. Of course they bickered. Often. But he'd worked on his habit of issuing orders like a colonel and she'd learned to be far less prickly.

"Did you read that letter I received from your mother, Beau?"

"Yes," he lied. It turned out that Josephine was something the Americans called a wrangler, but instead of livestock, his wife wrangled duchesses. It was one duty Beau had been eager to pass along—corresponding with his mother—and he avoided reading her bitter tirades, which were usually about Victoria, who was sharing the house in London with her.

It all worked out rather nicely, in Beau's opinion.

"She wants to take Nora and Evie to Brighton," she said. "I will miss them, of course, but it seems as if they should go, don't you think?"

"Yes," he said, this time in earnest. As much as he loved his little sisters, they were twin forces of nature and would have a better time in Brighton. Besides, Josephine would have entered her confinement by then and would need a little peace.

Beau and Sarah would be plenty of company for her.

While Victoria had stayed in the London house, Beau and Josephine had taken Sarah back with them. Victoria had been relieved to let her go, and Beau surmised neither of her parents had ever paid Sarah any mind. The little girl was starved for attention.

Beau didn't care whose daughter she was—he would try to ensure she didn't grow to adulthood as he and Jason had done, in a household where the parents were more interested in hurting each other than loving their children.

Love, Beau realized the night Edward Loman died, was as critical to life as food and water.

Although Josephine's father never regained consciousness, Beau would forever be grateful that he'd brought his wife to see the stubborn old man before the end. It had taught him there were, sometimes, things more important than a man's word of honor.

"Are you hungry, Beau?"

He opened his eyes and stilled his erotic stroking, already guessing his cock would stay hard for a little while longer. "Not for food," he admitted.

"I'm *starving*," his wife said, either missing or ignoring his rather blatant hint.

"Of course you are. It's been what? Two whole hours since luncheon?"

She swatted his shoulder. "Don't be beastly. I'm hungry all the time. I shall be twenty stone before this is over."

"A husband's duty is never done." Beau grunted and rolled her onto her back, giving her a kiss before getting to his feet. "Stay," he ordered—just because he enjoyed giving her orders, not because he actually believed she had any intention of stirring from her comfortable position.

"I shall fetch the basket. Try not to eat the blanket before I return."

"Ha!" She picked up her floppy straw hat and laid it over her face.

Josephine was right about one thing: Beau didn't come out here to this lovely secluded spot to fish. His real hobby was debauching his wife in broad daylight.

But today he had something else planned in addition to making her sob his name in ecstasy.

Beau unfastened the heavy basket and set the food out on a small blanket he spread close to where they were lying. Of course he had to pause a few times to deliver stern looks and finger snaps to the interested puppies.

Once everything was arranged to his liking, he took the last item out of the basket—a small velvet box.

Beau flipped open the lid and looked at the contents, even though he'd had the ring for two months now. It was a beautiful square-cut emerald that reminded him of the green lights in his lover's eyes.

He'd made a special trip into Leeds to purchase it the day after he'd first told Josephine that he loved her. The same day that she'd shocked him speechless with her own confession—that not only had she spied on his amorous adventures five years ago, but she'd begun developing a fancy for him back then, as well.

"Five years?" he'd said.

"Will you quit *saying* it that way?" she'd begged, her cheeks fiery. "You make me sound like some deranged person."

"Well, you are, darling. But still—*five* years?"

Beau had teased her, but the truth was that her love for her father—so enduring—had humbled him. And he was *not* a humble man. It had made him delirious with joy to have earned her love.

They'd both been wild and passionate that night, their physical pleasure heightened by their declarations. Beau wasn't sure why he'd not given the ring to her yet, but the time hadn't seemed right, somehow.

But it felt right, today.

He settled on the blanket beside her and she pushed back her hat and squinted up at him.

"I think I fell asleep," she mumbled.

"Well, you weren't eating, so you *must* have been sleeping—since that seems to be all you do these days."

Her hand slid up his buckskins and she stroked and squeezed, bringing him back to arousal with embarrassing ease.

Beau hissed with pleasure. "All right, all right. Perhaps that is not *all* you like to do," he admitted. He took her wrist and turned her hand palm up, placing the small box in the center.

"What's this?" she asked, and then quickly said, "If you say 'a box,' I'll hit you."

Beau shifted his aching prick. "Go on—open it."

"Yes, Your Grace." Her gaze stayed locked with his while her hands opened the box.

Beau rolled his eyes. "*Look* at it," he commanded when she continued to stare at him.

She smirked. "Oh, sorry, I was just waiting for your order—" Her eyes dropped to the ring and she gasped. "Beau! It's lovely." But then her brow furrowed and she looked up. "But why?"

"Does a man need a reason to buy the love of his life a ring?"

Her eyes turned liquid at his words.

"Besides, I never gave you a wedding ring."

"Yes, you did." She held up the plain gold ring he'd found in the family vault and had resized for her.

"That was temporary, until I could find something that suited you." He didn't tell her the real reason he'd waited— until he'd received the money from selling out his commission and could afford to buy her something with his own money. He knew it was a ridiculous fiction, as everything belonged to him under the law, but it had seemed important to him—at least at the time—not to buy his wife a ring with her own money.

She slipped it on and raised her glowing eyes. "It fits perfectly," she said, her lower lip quivering.

"If you weep I'm taking it back," he threatened.

A tear slid down her cheek and she flung herself into his arms and squeezed him hard enough to crack a rib.

"I love you, Josephine," he whispered fiercely. "I love you with all my heart."

"I love you, Beau. And I will treasure this ring forever."

Her words reminded Beau of those her father had said to him that day—the day of their wedding: *I have vaults full of money and mansions stuffed with costly frippery, but my daughter is my priceless treasure, Wroxton. And now she is yours to cherish.*

How right he'd been. Josephine was Beau's treasure now, and he would cherish her forever.

Please read on for a preview of

OUTRAGEOUS,

the next novel in Minerva Spencer's
Rebels of the *Ton*.

CHAPTER 1

———≈•≈———

London
1816

Godric Fleming, Earl Visel, vowed to kill his cousin Rowland when he got his hands on him.

He strode down the alley, feeling like a fool as his ridiculous cape billowed out behind him as if he were some Barbary corsair. Which was, of course, exactly how he was dressed—or at least the English public's perception of a corsair.

When he reached the alley entrance he gaped. "Good God."

The street in front of the Duke of Richland's house was crammed with dozens, maybe even hundreds, of carriages. No wonder Rowland hadn't been waiting for Godric near the duke's garden gate as they'd planned. Godric considered the mob of unmoving carriages, his mind as chaotic as the scene before him. Perhaps this mess was a sign he should call off his asinine plan? Perhaps there was still time to—

"Lord Visel?"

Godric spun around to find a huge boy dressed like a stable lad.

"Who the devil are you?"

"Mr. Rowland sent me to tell you the carriage is waitin' at the back entrance, my lord." The young giant hesitated. "Mr. Rowland said he needed to talk to you before taking the woman."

Godric clenched his jaws so tightly his head throbbed. It was a struggle to contain his fury; trust that idiot Rowland to bring in even *more* conspirators. It was bad enough the two of them were planning to kidnap the woman—now this *boy* was part of the plan? Who else had the fool told? The bloody *Times*?

"No." He shook his head. No, he would not do it. He *could* not do it.

"My lord?" the boy asked, his expression one of nervous confusion.

"Come along," Godric said, ignoring his question and marching toward the other end of the alley.

The oddest sensation filled him as he walked: as if he were emerging from a dense fog, his head clearing with each step and his vision shifting slowly into focus. His gait stuttered and the air whooshed out of his lungs as the enormity of what he'd been about to do hit him.

Good God! What the devil have I been thinking?

Why the *hell* had it taken him so long to realize he was behaving like a bloody lunatic? And why had he only come to his senses *now*—after scheming and planning and preparing for weeks?

Perhaps speaking to his prospective kidnap victim—Drusilla Marlington—earlier in the evening had begun to clear the madness from his mind? The young woman had

done nothing to him—they hardly even knew each other—
and yet he'd humiliated her and forced her into a marriage
with a man who'd been courting another woman.

And when her unwanted marriage had—against all
odds—showed signs of becoming a love match? Well, then
Godric had decided to use her *again* to get to the man she'd
married: Gabriel Marlington.

To be perfectly honest, her husband had done nothing
to him, either. Yet all Godric had done since returning
home to Britain was harass the man.

I've been telling you this for months, the dry voice in
his head observed.

"Blast and damn," he cursed under his breath. Sod it all
to hell; this was bloody lunacy. He would get in the carriage, go home, and try to forget these past few months of
insanity.

He would have a devil of a time with his cousin Rowland—a man so desperate for funds he'd ransom his own
grandmother—but Godric did not doubt he could handle
the little worm.

The hired carriage waited at the end of the alley, the interior darker than the night. Godric yanked open the door.

"We're going," he said to the figure sitting on the back-
facing bench. "I won't—"

Something hard slammed into the back of his head. His
vision exploded with red-hot pain and he staggered forward. "Wha—"

"Push him in, James!"

Big hands grabbed his shoulders and shoved. Godric
went headfirst into the carriage, turning his head just in
time to avoid landing on his face and breaking his nose.
Even so, the pain from the impact was so intense it was
nauseating and his stomach cramped, preparing to void

itself. He gritted his teeth to keep back the flood of bile while huge hands grasped his ankles and folded his legs up against his chest.

A face lowered over Godric's: huge blue-violet eyes creased in a frown, red lips, parted, a lock of silky black hair . . .

He blinked, "Y-you—"

"Hallo, Lord Visel."

Whoever was holding his ankles gave him a shove and his head struck the opposite door. The last thing he heard was, "He's out cold, James, but you'd best tie his hands."

And don't miss

NOTORIOUS,

the newest novel in the Outcasts series,
available now!

The cure for a willful wife . . .

Drusilla Clare is full of opinions about why a woman
shouldn't marry. But that doesn't stop the rush of desire
she feels each time her best friend's stepbrother, notorious
rake Gabriel Marlington, crosses her path. So imagine her
dismay when she finds herself at the hands of a scoundrel,
only to be rescued by Gabriel himself. And when Gabriel's
heartless—and heart-pounding—proposal comes, it's
enough to make Dru's formidable resolve crumble. . . .

. . . is a smitten husband.

She's sharp-tongued, exasperating, and—due to one
careless moment—about to become his wife. Still, something about Drusilla has Gabriel intrigued. First there's the
delicious flush of her skin every time she delivers a barb—
and then the surprisingly sensual feel of her in his arms.
Gabriel even finds himself challenged by her unusual
philosophies. And when he discovers a clandestine rival
for Dru's affection, his temperature flares even hotter. But
Gabriel has an even deeper secret of his own, and once
all is disclosed between the newlyweds, they will either
grow closer, be thrown into danger—or both. . . .

CHAPTER 1

———⊱◈⊰———

London, 1817

Drusilla Clare plied her fan, using it for its intended purpose—cooling—rather than its expected purpose—flirting. After all, who would flirt with her?

"Dru, you're doing it again."

At the sound of her name, she looked at her companion. Lady Eva de Courtney should not, by all rights, have been sitting beside Drusilla in the wallflower section of the Duchess of Montfort's ballroom. Eva was not only the most beautiful debutante in London this Season; she was also one of the most exquisite women Drusilla had ever seen.

But she was also proof that a hefty dowry and a gorgeous person were not, alas, enough to overcome a fractious personality or notorious heritage. Or at least her mother's notorious heritage. Because it was a well-known fact that the Marquess of Exley's first wife and Eva's mother—Lady Veronica Exley—had not only been a ravishing, mesmerizing beauty who'd driven men of all ages insane with desire and yearning; she had also been barking mad.

Eva, reputed to be every bit as lovely as her dead mother, had neither the desire, nor the charisma, to drive anyone mad. Except perhaps her stern, perfectionist father.

"What, exactly, am I doing?" Drusilla asked Eva, who had pulled a lock of glossy dark hair from her once-perfect coiffure and was twisting it into a frazzled mess.

"You're frowning and getting that look." Eva thrust out her lower jaw, flattened her lips, and glared through squinty eyes.

Drusilla laughed at her friend's impersonation.

Eva's expression shifted back to its natural, perfect state. "There, that is much better. You are very pretty when you laugh or smile."

Drusilla rolled her eyes.

"And even when you roll your eyes." Eva's smile turned into a grin. "Come, tell me what you were thinking when you were looking so thunderous."

Drusilla could hardly tell her friend she'd been wondering when Eva's gorgeous but irritating stepbrother—Gabriel Marlington—would make an appearance, so she lied. "I was wondering if Lady Sissingdon was going to fall out of her dress."

They both turned to stare at the well-endowed widow in question.

Eva snorted and then covered her mouth with her hand. Drusilla couldn't help noticing her friend's previously white kid glove now had something that looked like cucumber soup—one of the dishes at dinner—on her knuckle and a stain that must be red wine on her index finger. Drusilla could not imagine how Eva had managed the stains, as she had not been wearing her gloves to eat.

Eva's violet-blue eyes flickered from Lady Sissingdon's scandalous bodice back to Drusilla and she opened her mouth to speak but then saw something over Drusilla's shoulder.

"Gabe!" She shot to her feet and waved her arm in broad, unladylike motions.

Drusilla slowly swiveled in her chair while Eva attracted the attention of not only her stepbrother but everyone in their half of the ballroom. She knew she should remind her friend to employ a little decorum—it seemed to be her duty in life to keep Eva out of scrapes—but her heart was pounding, her palms damp, and her stomach was doing that odd, quivery thing it seemed destined to do whenever Gabriel Marlington entered her orbit. Something he'd been doing on an almost daily basis since the beginning of the Season when he'd begun escorting his sister— and, by extension, Drusilla—to every function under the sun.

He stood near the entrance to the ballroom as the majordomo announced him. His name—as always—sent a frisson of excitement through the crowd. The women in the room—young, old, married, widowed, or single— raised their fans or quizzing glasses, the better to watch him.

The men, also, took notice of his arrival. Especially the clutch of men who slouched near the entrance—as if they were undecided about whether they should remain at the ball or leave to engage in some vile masculine pursuit. The men closed ranks as Gabriel walked past them, like a pack of wild dogs scenting a larger, more dangerous, predator.

One of the group, Earl Visel, a man with perhaps the worst reputation in London—if not all of England—said something to Gabriel that made him stop.

The two men faced each other, Visel's cronies hanging back as their leader stepped closer to Gabriel. They were, Drusilla realized, both tall, broad-shouldered, narrow-hipped men, although Visel was pale, blue-eyed, and blond while Gabriel was golden, heavy lidded, and flame haired.

Whatever Gabriel said to Visel put the men behind the earl into a flutter, their gabble of voices audible even over the noise of the ballroom. Visel was the only one who seemed unconcerned. In fact, he threw back his head and laughed.

Gabriel appeared not to notice the reaction his response created among the ball denizens and scanned the crowd just like the Barbary falcon he resembled, his full lips curving into an easy smile when his eyes landed on his sister. His gaze kept moving and Drusilla couldn't help noticing how his expression turned to one of mocking amusement when he saw her. She told herself his reaction was entirely natural, especially since she had done everything in her power to provoke and annoy him for the last five years.

She also told herself that she disliked him because he was everything she despised in the masculine species: arrogant, too attractive for either his own or anyone else's good, assured of his superiority, and so accustomed to female adulation he would never even have noticed Drusilla's existence if she hadn't forced him to.

But she knew she was just lying to herself.

AN INCONVENIENT COUNTESS

———◆———

KRISTIN VAYDEN

For Rachel. Because you always remind me that I *can*, when I sometimes think I can't. You're the best sister ever, and I love you. Also for Grandma Hart, I miss you. Every stitch of bravery I have I learned from you.

CHAPTER 1

———◆———

Charles Brook, Earl of Barrington, lacked only one thing. Well, perhaps lacked more than one thing, but most of those could be acquired by his fists or by his bank account. However, his money couldn't buy the one thing he particularly needed at the moment.

Respectability.

He'd destroyed his, and had a jolly time doing it. In fact, he'd do it all over again if given the chance. However, it was rather bloody inconvenient to not have it, especially when the business partnership he'd been working toward depended on him acquiring said respectability.

And it had to be authentic, not the kind where he could purchase a courtesan's time, buy her new clothes, and fake a titled name. No. He'd tried that already.

Which, in the end, only chipped at his respectability even more. He needed a wife, and not just any wife, but the kind who made an English businessman think of sheep, and muslin, and all other English things. One who was virginal, pure, and . . . utterly dull. The problem was that he didn't know many of those types, avoided them like the plague actually. And time wasn't on his side either—another bloody thing money couldn't buy.

As he saw it, he had only one option: leave London and hope his reputation didn't precede him. Surely there was some remote village that had respectable daughters of gentlemen who didn't use his name as a curse word. His reputation hadn't stretched that far, had it?

Hope was a heartless bitch, and soon his plan changed from anonymity to finding someone just desperate enough to deal with the devil.

That he found readily enough, and in his own backyard—quite literally. It was after he had taken respite on his country estate in Sussex that he had picked up on an interesting article of news.

The small, rather shabby estate bordering his own was rumored to be for sale. It was rather odd, since he distinctly remembered the gentleman who owned it because the man had turned down his earlier offers of purchase years before. Then the gentleman had sworn to keep it in the family, which had struck Brook as peculiar. After all, the gentleman had only five daughters, no sons to inherit. Assuming the man meant a son-in-law, Brook had disregarded his words and moved along.

Could this mean that the son-in-law didn't want the estate? Brook made the decision to inquire further in the morning. After breaking his fast the next day, he donned his riding coat, and had his gelding readied from the stables. The black horse pawed the damp earth with impatience, mirroring his master's mood. The leather squeaked as Brook swung up onto the saddle, his horse sidestepping slightly. Soon Brook was at a gentle canter toward the edge of his property, riding along the narrow path that bordered the two estates.

It was a welcome distraction, to do something that was unrelated to his quest to find a respectable woman. Damn, if he weren't so invested in the venture already, he'd forget the whole business partnership deal and go about his life. But to do such would set him back financially, and he'd worked too hard to give up now. Besides, he had to marry at some point, and the ladies—if one could call them that—he'd spent his time with weren't the kind a gentleman married. And he was a gentleman, after all, if only in title.

A soft rain created humidity in the air that was far fresher than the air of London, and he slowed his horse to better enjoy the ride. The clouds scattered across the grey sky, allowing a slight blue to peek through. Perhaps the day would take a good turn; one could always hope.

As he approached the manor house, he noted the disrepair of the gate. Frowning, he passed by the useless thing, the gravel crunching under his horse's hooves as Brook paused just before the door. Swinging off the saddle, he then loosely tied the reins to a nearby post. The manor was clearly lacking some maintenance, which of course mentally required him to adjust the price he was willing to pay. He gave a solid knock on the door, and stepped back.

The door swung open and a maid gave a quick curtsey. "Good morning, sir."

Brook studied the young woman, noting the unruly curls that defied their pins, and her face flushed as if she'd been rushing to the door.

Or making love.

He gave his head a quick shake and focused on the issue

at hand. "Is the lord of the manor receiving callers?" he asked in his most polite voice.

The maid frowned, then glanced away. After a breath she met his gaze directly. "I'm afraid not, sir. He passed around three years ago."

Brook chastised himself for not inquiring further before showing up on their doorstep. However, as he considered it, this turn of events clearly made sense and made his options toward purchasing the estate even more promising. "My condolences to the family."

"Thank you."

"Would the lady of the house be available?" he inquired.

The maid twisted her lips. "She is indisposed at the moment, but you may relay any message you wish to give her to me."

Brook noted the directness of the maid, wondering if she was as impetuous to all the callers. She didn't have an air about her of servanthood; rather, she seemed to fight for dominance in the conversation, however quietly. He could sense the authority in her words. *Odd, that.*

"It's rather irregular to discuss this topic on the doorstep, but if you insist." He glanced up, then back to the girl. "I'd heard the estate is for sale, and I wish to discuss the prospect of purchasing it."

The color drained from the maid's complexion. "You've heard correctly."

He waited for her to continue.

She arched a brow as if daring him to question her further.

It was a strange impasse.

"If you wouldn't mind leaving my card for your mistress, so she may contact me if she is interested?" he said finally.

"Perhaps." She accepted the card, reading the name. "I remember you. Did you try to purchase the property a while ago?"

Brook nodded, curious how a maid was privy to such information.

"We aren't interested in your offer." The maid handed back his card, stepping back to close the door.

"Pardon." He put his foot in the way, keeping the door open. "I don't believe it's your place to say such a thing."

Fire danced in her green eyes. "Is that so?"

"Maids don't often make such decisions, and I'm quite certain if I notified your mistress—"

"I am the mistress, the acting mistress, thank you kindly," she bit off hotly. "And I'm quite certain I have all the authority needed to turn down your offer, sir. Now, please leave."

"You? You can't be more than fifteen." He spoke without thinking.

"I'm more than eighteen, sir, and more than willing to notify the magistrate if you don't *leave, now*." She growled the last words.

Brook stepped back, gave one final calculating gaze, then turned toward his horse. The door all but slammed shut as he mounted his gelding. As he left the courtyard, he glanced to the shabby gate and pulled up the reins on his horse.

All the pieces fell together, and with almost lightning speed he saw the full picture of opportunity.

Five daughters, a deceased father, a manor in disrepair— it was bloody perfect.

He turned back his horse to the front of the house, preparing his words carefully. He'd have one shot.

It had to be a good one.

Because time was ticking away, and this was as promising a situation as he was going to find on this short of notice, he could not delay. He knocked on the door, then took a step back.

"Yes?" The woman answered the door once more, her dark brows arching high over her eyes a moment before her gaze narrowed, and she started to shut the door.

"No, wait. I have a . . . proposition—"

"I don't wish to hear any of your—"

"I think you'll be interested in this one. May I come in," and for good measure he added, "please?"

The woman hesitated, just enough to let him know he'd won. At least this round.

As she opened the door, he took a step inside and met the gaze of a small girl, no older than eight. She hid behind another sister, somewhat older. As he was shown to the study just beyond the foyer, he took in the details that helped him formulate his plan.

The largest weakness he could exploit would be the care of the other sisters . . . he pushed away a slight twinge of his long lost conscience, and took a seat when offered. She kept the door open, like a proper miss. As she sat down, she folded her hands and eyed him shrewdly.

So perhaps this wasn't going to be as easy as he anticipated.

But he found the challenge exhilarating—the promise of a chase and reward.

It was rather enticing.

Motivating.

And if it worked, this arrangement would be exactly

what he needed. And, he told himself, it might be what they needed, too.

For a price.

Always a price.

Perhaps money *could* buy respectability; maybe money could buy everything after all. . . .

CHAPTER 2

———◆———

Miss Diana Lambson squinted at the ledgers before her. Perhaps if she stared hard enough, everything would make sense. Rather, that was the problem. It did make sense, and she was desperately trying to figure out a way to make it *not* make sense. For there to be some mistake, some hidden money in some account . . . to give herself, and her family, some semblance of hope.

But as she relaxed her gaze, the truth of it settled over her. The numbers didn't lie, and she was an excellent accountant. Ever since she took over the management of their accounts at the untimely death of her father three years ago, she'd been warning her mother about this possibility. There simply wasn't enough money, and there was too many of them.

Five sisters, one mother, and a dying estate. It wasn't much, but as Diana looked around her late father's study, it was dear, it was home. A home that would be lost to them if she didn't find some sort of relief for their immediate financial needs.

A knock sounded at the door. Diana quickly closed the

ledgers—it was no use for one of her sisters to worry even more than they already were—and bid the person enter.

"Is it bad?"

So much for closing the ledgers. Diana twisted her lips, trying to find a silver lining for her dear sister. "There's always hope."

"So, no." Emily bit her lower lip and padded into the room softly. Diana noted the newly mended tear at the sleeve of Emily's day dress. How long had it been since they'd had new clothes? It was a boon that she and Emily were finished growing, with all their former dresses handed down to younger sisters. "What are our options?"

"Don't you think we should discuss this with Mother?" Diana remarked, then held back a laugh at Emily's incredulous look. It was an accurate expression. Ever since the death of their father, their mother hadn't been able to work through even simple problems, let alone the management of their home. "Very well, our options are few. We could sell the estate—"

"If someone were to want it," Emily replied. "There's not much land. And it's not a complete solution. It would only take care of us for a little while."

"Or . . ." Diana gave her sister an impatient glare, even though she knew very well a person who wished to purchase it. But it wasn't a viable option. If they sold the estate, where would they go? "We could find work. I could employ myself as a governess, or—"

"A governess salary will only be enough for you, not an entire family, Diana. Even if you, I, and Sarah all found employment, we couldn't keep up financially."

Diana met her sister's gaze with a frank one of her own. "There's one other option."

"I refuse to call *that* an option. That's more of a jail sentence."

Diana agreed with her sister's sentiment, and felt a pinch of regret for even telling her, but Emily was her closest friend and she had to confide in someone. It was more of a sentence, but the payoff made the idea far more tempting than it should. She'd heard about Lord Barrington's reputation; her father had warned them all about him for years, going as far as to forbid them from riding on land that bordered his estate. It was much more than a reputation as a rake; he was known to be heartless in business, emotionless in pursuit of what he wanted. A cold shiver trailed down her back at the thought. Would she be just another acquisition? And why her? Was London so repelled by him that no desperate mama wanted him for a son-in-law? It was possible, but there had to be more. She'd have to find out.

"You can't be considering it, not truly." Emily walked around the desk and placed a light hand on Diana's shoulder. "Your spirit would break. We'd lose you, in more ways than one."

Diana shifted her shoulder so that Emily's hand slid off. "It would provide a solution."

"You're far more than a 'solution,'" Emily replied with an edge of fear.

The sound of footsteps made Diana push back the hopelessness of her thoughts. "Di?" Eva's voice was sleepy. "Why are you all awake? Is there something going on? Where's Tully?" Eva rubbed her eyes with the palm of her hand and stifled a yawn.

"Tully's in bed, like you should be." Diana stood and walked over to her second-youngest sister, enveloping her in a hug. Her curly brown hair tickled Diana's nose as she kissed the top of Eva's head. "Go to sleep, love. All's well."

"Are you sure? . . . Mama was crying earlier. She didn't know I saw her I didn't want to ask. She cries so much since Father died." Eva's arms stretched around Diana, and she glanced up with her chocolate brown eyes.

"I know, sweetheart. And Mama is just sad; we all miss Father."

"Are we going to move?"

Diana froze and then smoothed Eva's hair once more. "Where did you hear that?"

"Mama was putting some of the books into a crate." Eva spoke with the innocence and directness of a child.

"You have nothing to worry about. We're not going anywhere right now. Well, you are." Diana poked her little sister's side, causing her to jump and giggle. "You're going to bed."

"But I'm not that tired—" Her words were cut off with a yawn as she sheepishly smiled at her sister.

"I'll take you back to bed." Emily reached out and grasped her sister's hand. "We'll read a bit, and the next thing you know it will be morning."

Eva left with Emily, Diana watching their retreat with a fondness and protective instinct that outweighed every other obstacle. With a decisive nod, she returned to her desk and pulled out a fresh sheet of parchment and sealed her future. Buying her sisters' freedom at the price of her own.

CHAPTER 3

—◆—

Brook studied the flourishes of the pen on paper, a smile teasing his lips at the exhilarating feeling of conquest. He set the parchment down, and quickly dispatched a missive to his solicitor in London. Now came the details, which had to be perfect. They would be married in the country, so there would be no scandal as he brought her, unaccompanied, to London. For all his scandalous ways, he knew how to be proper when he wanted to be, when it suited his purpose.

He'd need a license as well. It would be rather time consuming to apply for one at Doctors' Commons. He'd apply for an ordinary license, providing the woman—Diana—was a member of the local parish. That would take care of that detail.

And finally, and most important, he dispatched a missive by express to Lord Walker, to notify him of his impending marriage. As he finished the missive, he signed with a near-violent flourish. Let the deal be done then; the acquiring of the entirety of Walker's estate in the Caribbean would then be his, and his alone.

Finally.

It was nearly five years he'd been working toward this goal, with the possibility of it so near, yet so far away. Each time the old man would hint at it, he'd change his mind. However, with the death of his son there was no one to inherit the business estate—and Brook had made an offer that was very difficult to refuse.

Yet Walker did. Foolish old man, sentimental to a fault, he had insisted the estate belong to a family.

Not a bachelor who would surely squander it.

As if Brook had squandered his fortune; no, he'd doubled it, tripled it even. But the old man wouldn't be moved.

And with every week that passed, Lord Walker's health declined.

Time was of the essence, and with Brook soon to be acquiring a wife, he would fulfill the stipulations put forth by Lord Walker.

The documents were already drafted by Brook's solicitor, and Walker had given his word to sign if the requirements were met. So close, Brook was so very close.

And yet so far away, in Sussex.

He dispatched all the missives, and steepled his fingers, holding them to his lips as he considered his next move.

Withdrawing another piece of parchment, he wrote a message to Miss Diana Lambson, soon to be Countess Barrington. He paused. It had a nice sound to it; he could get used to the concept, provided she understood that this was going to be a contract more than a marriage. Which was the reason for the missive. He toyed with the idea of telling her the details in person but rather wished to keep everything as concise and impersonal as possible, no attachments.

So he began:

Miss Diana Lambson,

I'm pleased you agreed to accept my offer of marriage. In the honor of being truthful, I wish to outline several expectations I have in such a contract as marriage. I assume you'll be amenable to them, since you certainly are not attached to me in any way.

First, this is a marriage of convenience. I do not wish for your attachment, nor do I expect it. However, I do require your respect and you to fulfill your wifely obligations and the obligations that come with the title of Countess of Barrington.

Second, I will require an heir, but after said heir is born, you are free to seek your pleasure however you wish. Which leads to my third requirement, that you will be aware that I will do the same.

In return, all debts of your family will be paid in full, with a small dowry designated to each of your sisters. Your mother will also be provided for; with your estate fully repaired, its reestablishment as a sheep farm will create an income for the estate's maintenance.

I trust you'll approve of the terms I've outlined. I plan to visit the local vicar to procure a common license, so that we may be married this weekend.

> *Yours—CB, Earl of Barrington*

Brook studied the letter, then dispatched it via messenger to the estate. It was half past ten, and he was quite certain he'd done more than a day's work in less than a few hours. It was a delightful feeling. If he were in London, he'd reward himself by visiting Celine in her cozy town house, taking the rest of the day slow and deliciously in her ample company. But he wasn't in London. He was in bloody Sussex. With a low curse, he noted the stack of estate business that needed his attention. Though reluctant, Brook prided himself on his attention to business, even the mundane type. Now, if he could only view this impending marriage as business, he might actually be good at it.

Pity he was pretty certain that this was one business venture he'd not find immediate success at. But as long as everything followed the outline in the letter, it couldn't fail too badly. Expectations were important, and as long as Miss Lambson's kept to the rational, he had nothing to fear.

He hoped.

After all, the worst that could happen would be that she'd fall in love with him.

Which was laughable. And he wouldn't even consider the idea of falling in love with her. After all, who in all of England fell in love with his wife? A courtesan maybe, a mistress, possibly. But to fall for one's own wife . . . impossible.

Wasn't it?

CHAPTER 4

———◆———

Diana knocked on her mother's dressing room door, clutching her fists afterward, reviewing her words carefully in her mind.

"Come in."

Diana exhaled, then opened the door. Her mother was still in bed, her frame small and fragile. "Good afternoon, Mama." Diana tenderly sat on her mother's bed and smoothed her hair from her mobcap. "Are you feeling better?"

Her mother had been up late. Having overheard some of the conversation between Diana and the Earl of Barrington, she had assumed they were selling the estate and had begun packing. Why, Diana wasn't sure. However, the exertion had taxed her already fragile mother and she hadn't risen from bed this morning.

"I'm a little better. Tell me, are we getting a good price for the estate?" Diana's mother asked, tears pooling in her eyes.

"No," Diana replied, then forced a smile. "It's actually

better than that." Patting her mother's hand, she continued. "I'm to marry the Earl of Barrington and he will, in turn, provide for our entire family. Our estate is safe, your daughters will have dowries, and you can stay here, in your home, Mama." Diana's lips stretched into a real smile, happy in the knowledge that her family would be safe, provided for, and in their beloved home. It was worth it.

It had to be.

"The Earl of Barrington?" her mother repeated, her expression confused.

"Yes."

"Do, that is, are we acquainted with him?"

"Slightly, enough that he wished to marry me."

"The name sounds so familiar. Does he own the estate that borders ours?"

Diana knew her mother was connecting the information in her mind, and before she could disapprove Diana changed the subject, hoping her mother's fatigue would win over her awareness. "How about some tea? Do you wish for some breakfast? I know we have some biscuits as well."

"Oh, tea would be lovely. Thank you. I'm so tired, I think I'll just rest a while longer."

"I'll have the tea sent up." Diana rose slowly from the bed, careful to not disturb her mother.

"Are you happy?" her mother asked, eyes closed.

A tear slid down Diana's face. "Yes."

And she was.

Because she would be giving her family exactly what they needed. And maybe it wouldn't be as bad as she feared: freedom was exactly what the Earl of Barrington was offering her, and that was an enticing compromise. He wasn't expecting her love, and she wasn't willing to give it.

A marriage of convenience. It was a fair bargain. At least, fair enough. As she closed the door to her mother's room, she sent her sister Tully to bring their mother tea.

She thought back to his earlier letter, and decided it was only proper to return the gesture. He'd written of his expectations, and it was only fair she outline her own. From the beginning, he needed to understand he wasn't marrying an English Wallflower; no, she was made of far sturdier stuff, and wasn't about to back down. She had expectations of her own. So it was with a bit of a saucy grin, and more than a little cheek, that she started her own letter. Let him know now just whom he was dealing with.

Lord Barrington,

Thank you for your letter. It was very clear, concise, and outlined the needed particulars. And, in following your fashion, I felt it was necessary I return the sentiment and give my own specifications.

First, I wish for all the particulars to be in writing, from a solicitor, delivered to my estate the week after we are married.

Second, I request immediate relief for my family's current needs, and I would kindly ask for you to assist them.

Third, in reference to your more private requirements, I agree.

My local vicar should be able to assist you with the common license, and you can expect that this

*weekend will be a good date for the marriage to
take place. I hope these particulars will suffice.*

Sincerely,
Miss Lambson

A sense of power filled her spirit at being able to dictate
her own needs in the situation. Maybe it wasn't as hopeless
as she thought. To have control of one's destiny was an
important aspect of life, and she cherished the sensation.
As she sent off the missive, she felt lighter, as if an entire
weight—in truth, the weight of the entire estate—was
lifted from her shoulders. Her family was safe, cared for,
and she'd have the power to assist wherever necessary.

It was the right decision.

She was giving up the option of ever falling in love, but
such was the cost for freedom. For certainly, if she were
in love, freedom would be compromised, and in this situation it was the smallest threat.

It was a lovely thing to have traded large, looming
threats for small ones.

Because it was truly impossible to think of falling in
love with the Earl of Barrington. She would be content to
find a way to simply like the man. Certainly that wasn't
asking too much?

CHAPTER 5

———◆———

As the valet made the final adjustments to Brook's wedding attire, the earl allowed his mind to review the past few days. It had been quite the full schedule, but everything had gone according to plan. The local vicar was quite accommodating to providing a common license, and agreed to a Saturday morning wedding. Of course, the several pounds in excess of his usual fee assisted with his cooperation. Everyone had their price.

In response to Miss Lambson's letter, Brook had offered some financial relief to her family. He had to admit that the letter had taken him by surprise. He wasn't one to underestimate someone, but he most certainly had Miss Lambson. She was daring, and knew what she wanted. It was an admirable quality, and he begrudgingly was impressed with her pluck. He only hoped it wasn't often aimed at him.

Though he wasn't too hopeful on that front. However, he expected their interactions to be of a minimal variety, even more so once an heir had been given. Though he was reminded that such things take time.

"All finished, my lord." His valet stepped back. Brook tugged on his waistcoat sleeve, then adjusted a few minor details and gave a curt nod to his valet.

As Brook took leave of his rooms and made his way to the waiting carriage, he noted that he was no longer to be the Devil's Bachelor. It was quite an end to an era, if he said so himself. But all good things had to come to an end, and at three and thirty it was more than time for him to settle down.

Not that he had any expectations of settling down; rather, he just wished for the appearance of such. It was a convenient thing to have appearances so deceiving.

The carriage pulled from his estate and took the main road to the local church. It wasn't a long trip, one he didn't require a carriage for, but after the ceremony it would be more convenient for the two of them to take the carriage back to his estate for the wedding breakfast. Cook had been planning in a fury for the past few days. After the breakfast, they would spend one more night at his estate, then travel to London, where all the necessary papers could be signed so that, finally, he would have Lord Walker's estate.

He could almost taste the money he would make from the venture, if tasting money were possible.

Miss Lambson was already present, as whispered to him by the vicar once Brook arrived at the church. The pews were sparsely filled, and he noted a rather fragile-looking woman surrounded by miniature versions of herself. Deducing the woman was his soon-to-be mother-in-law, he gave a curt nod of respect in her direction.

She returned the gesture, but the ladies beside her offered no such graciousness. Rather, he felt the animosity as if it were heat waves. Straightening his spine, he turned toward the back of the church as he took his place at the front.

In a few moments, the back of the church opened, allowing sunlight to spill in. A young woman approached, dressed in a faded light blue frock. As he turned his attention to the next in line, he saw the unmistakably frank gaze of his soon-to-be wife, Miss Lambson. Her eyes were calm, but her back was held in a rigid posture, betraying her emotions. He studied her, watching her approach with a grace that pleased him. In fact, he found that she pleased him in every way. Her dress gave advantage to her lovely feminine form and her hair was curled in such a fashion to draw the eye to her delicate features and rosebud mouth. If she smiled, she would surely be transformed from merely pleasing to beautiful, but he was not expecting such a boon as a smile.

No.

And he didn't wish for it either. It would merely complicate matters, and he had enough complications in other matters, no need for more.

She paused before the vicar, and met Brook's gaze. The strength and resolve in her regard were impressive, and as he took her hands when the vicar started he noted that there was no tremble.

Good. The last thing he needed was a hysterical, emotional female.

They repeated the required phrases, they prayed the required prayers, and sooner than he could have hoped, they were man and wife.

"You may kiss your bride," the vicar announced.

Brook watched as his new bride swallowed, then lifted her chin just slightly. The devilish part of him wanted to test her strength, her resolve, and take more than was proper, to really kiss her to simply see her reaction. And as per his usual, he followed temptation's whisper and bit back a grin as he leaned forward to seal their marriage.

He paused just before her lips, rubbing his nose carefully against hers. If he'd learned anything about women, it's that they love the small little bits of foreplay—a touch, a whisper, a stroke, a lie: it was all part of the game. She was expecting a quick kiss; let her learn now that he would do nothing quickly but would take his pleasure as long as he liked, even when just experiencing a kiss.

A sharp intake of her breath caused his smile to widen as he ran his nose down her cheek and then paused with his lips just at the corner of her mouth. Darting his tongue out just slightly, only enough for her to feel, no one to see, he tasted the corner of her lips, felt the softness as she parted them. He kissed her then, slowly, prolonging every moment, stretching time itself as he caressed her lower lip with a flick of his tongue, learning her flavor. He deepened the kiss, gauging her reaction, gratified when she didn't shy away but leaned in ever so faintly. Releasing her hands, he trailed his hands up her arms, teasing the exposed flesh between her gloves and where her cap sleeves covered her shoulders. Gooseflesh erupted along her skin, and he slowed his movements, trying to provoke more of a reaction.

A throat cleared.

The vicar shut his Bible with more force than necessary.

Brook wasn't amused but leisurely took his time and broke the kiss.

Her eyes were smoky with desire, her lips swollen and bee stung, her face flushed with pleasure, and in a moment of unguarded mental clarity he questioned if he'd ever seen someone quite so beautiful.

Pushing the thought out of his mind, he released his hold on her shoulders and re-grasped her hands.

"May I present Lord and Lady Barrington," the vicar announced; the lack of applause was a loud silence. Thankfully someone took pity on them and started to clap, leading the rest of the guests into the customary action.

Brook led his new wife out the door, to their awaiting carriage, and helped her alight, noticing that she'd been quite silent.

As he took his own seat in the carriage, he turned to her, expecting . . . something.

"Well, that was interesting," she commented, smoothing her skirt ever so properly.

"Pardon?" he asked, expecting a remark about his consummating kiss.

"I don't think I've ever seen Vicar Peters quite so flustered." She held a gloved hand to her mouth, and her body started to shake. Her hand moved to her eyes, as if trying to hold back tears.

Dear God.

No. No crying.

Of all the reactions, he wasn't expecting tears. Perhaps a good scolding, or a cold shoulder. He'd dealt with plenty of those in the past. However, to think that his kiss had actually caused her to cry, it was rather emasculating actually.

Then he heard a small snort.

Freezing, he was waiting to figure out just what the bloody hell was going on, and heard the most curious noise.

A laugh.

And not the simpering laugh of a debutante, no. A belly

laugh, one that was rollicking and full of life and joy and hilarity—he couldn't remember when he'd seen someone quite so overcome with laughter. Her face transformed into a wide grin, she covered her face, then removed her hand and reached over, smacking his knee playfully. "That was my favorite part. I'd kiss you all over again just to see his face. He's such a straight-laced pain in the . . ." She paused. "You can figure it out, I'm sure. But, dear Lord, it was glorious. Thank you." She sighed, recovering from her mirth.

And he stared at her, like a bloody idiot.

She was . . . happy? Not hysterical, not frantic, not emotionless, but . . . finding humor in something as mundane as irritating a local vicar. It was oddly endearing, disarming actually. He wasn't quite sure what to do with it . . . with her. He was used to calculating things—numbers, people, business transactions, and mistresses. Everyone had a price; everyone had a gamble they were willing to make; everyone had something that jaded them.

Except her, apparently.

And as they made the short journey to his estate, he realized a sobering truth.

He was in danger.

Danger of actually liking his wife.

CHAPTER 6

———◆———

She wasn't quite sure what was more entertaining: the look on Vicar Peters's face after that quite impressive kiss, or the look on her husband's when she started to laugh.

To say that Lord Barrington was surprised was an understatement. Once she had garnered some control over her mirth, she'd cast a glance in his direction only to find a slightly fading expression of panic that melted into a more relaxed grin. He must think her daft. Oh well, it was probably true, after all. Here she was, marrying someone she barely knew—for money. It was as simple as that. She and her sisters had often scorned the marriages of the London Ton as mercenary, and here she was doing the very same thing. It was sobering and humbling, but it was too late now. She might as well make the best of it.

"I have plans to leave for London in the morning," her new husband mentioned as they made their way to his estate.

"Am I to come with you?" she asked, not assuming anything.

His gaze, which had been fixed on the window, shot

to her with a piercing clarity. "Of course. You will be quite occupied once we get to London as well. We are to have a party to present you within a week, so please quickly acquaint yourself with Mrs. Highbury; she is the most sought-after modiste in London. I sent word to her as soon as your agreement was given to the marriage. She is expecting you, and will have several gowns you'll need fitted quickly. As the Countess of Barrington, I assume you understand the need for appearances."

Diana nodded politely, wondering if the man ever actually sat still. Already she had made several deductions about her new husband. It was clear that he was always thinking ahead, planning, making assertions and, she assumed, contingency plans if those original plans didn't work out as expected.

"I suppose the next logical question is: What do you want me to represent as your wife?"

His earlier words made her wonder just what part she was to play. A slight panic had tickled her fingers, causing them to go slightly numb as she considered that he might want her to be a fixture in society functions that would demand her conversation and intrigue skills to be much sharper than they were at present.

"I expect you to be at the pertinent social functions, and to meet the peers who will approve of my settling down. Nothing too trying, I'm sure."

"If it's so simple, why such articulate planning?" she asked, suspicious.

He tipped his head as if trying to comprehend such an odd question. "Planning makes all things go smoother. It's so much better when you know what to expect."

"I see." And she did. It fit perfectly into the picture she

was creating in her mind of how her husband worked. It also gave her the strongest impulse to rearrange his careful plans just to see his reaction. It was a childish notion, but it was a real one, nonetheless. She had expected him to be a devil-may-care type of person. Even the kind that tossed caution to the wind, and by sheer dumb luck fall into fortune. But that clearly wasn't the case, and it was oddly comforting as much as it was tempting to disrupt.

"As a general rule, I do not ask women what they are thinking. I've learned the foolishness of such an action, but since we are to be in close proximity for the foreseeable future, it would be helpful for me to learn the way your mind works." He gave his head a slight shake. "And honestly, your expression is quite unreadable and I find that frustrating."

"So . . . all that to say . . ." she encouraged, teasing, drawing him out.

"You're taking all this better than I thought. So I'm curious to see if you're actually as calm as you appear or if I shoul—"

"Wait for the daft part of me to surface?"

"I was going to say it in a more gentlemanly way."

"No need. Quite honestly, since we are, indeed, being honest, your reputation precedes you, and 'gentlemanly' is not quite one of the adjectives I've heard used to describe your person. However, you may rest assured that I'm an irritatingly calm person, my lord. Feel free to ask any of my sisters. I'm utterly rational at most times . . . *most times*." She arched a brow to punctuate her words.

"I see." He rubbed his chin. "I'd appreciate it if you wouldn't repeat the . . . adjectives . . . you've heard about me."

"I find it hard to believe that you're sensitive about a reputation that it seems you've worked quite hard to create."

"I'm not ashamed as much as I'm trying to . . . rectify it."

"Turning over a new leaf?" Diana asked, honestly curious as to why he would make such a drastic change.

"Something like that," he murmured as the carriage stopped just before his estate. In short work, they were entering the house and ushered to the dining hall where their wedding breakfast awaited. Her family would arrive soon, which would be a comforting balm. She wasn't overly nervous, oddly enough, but it was a welcome distraction. The carriage ride had illuminated much. Astonished, she found her new husband to be quite interesting, and even easy to talk with. Of course, it could be said that it was no shock he could talk with women easily, since he'd spoken with so many. However, it allayed some of her trepidation. If they could have a rational conversation, that was a good omen for their non-conventional marriage. And for him to be so detailed, it was interesting; truly all of him was interesting. At least he wasn't dull.

As he offered her the seat beside him at the head of the table, she sat carefully and waited till he was seated as well, then offered a smile.

He quickly returned it, then reached over and patted her hand.

As the other guests started to file in, Diana was thankful to realize that while she wouldn't ever love her husband, at least she might end up finding him a friend.

It was more than she had expected.

And she wouldn't ask for more.

CHAPTER 7

———◆———

The wedding breakfast had gone well, and he was sure the news was spread far and wide. It would only serve his purpose to have his marriage a well-known occurrence.

As he signed off one last missive, he bit back a grin. Some poor bloke at White's was probably losing a fortune right now. The peers of the realm often took bets on events and happenings. Surely someone had bet another that the Devil's Bachelor would remain unmarried forever. Gambling was a heartless mistress, and thus Brook had avoided it like the plague. Rather, he'd go watch, find entertainment and some willing courtesan, and discover delight in another way. There were much better uses for money.

No need to gamble it away.

He wrapped up his business in his study and paused at the bottom of the stairs. His wife was upstairs, waiting for him. It was both disconcerting and erotic, both sensations vying for dominance in his mind. She'd be easy to bed, no trial there. She was beautiful, with a sharp mind and wit. He'd gotten lucky, that was for certain. But he also was quite certain she was a virgin, which meant that, as a gentleman, he should go slow and make it a pleasurable experience for her. He knew that wasn't too difficult of a requirement, but the fact that he was . . . right . . . was somewhat flummoxing. It wasn't a debauched evening of illicit sex; it wasn't a courtesan, or a mistress trained in the art of seduction: it was his lawful wife. To take her virginity would be the right thing to do, holy and all, which was so very strange compared to how he'd lived his life. As he started up the stairs, he pushed the rather revelatory thoughts to the back of his mind.

Pleasure.

He would focus on the best part of it, and in that he'd help her find her own pleasure as well. As natural as breathing.

Yet he found his heart pounded a little harder than usual.

Knocking on his door, he waited for her to bid him enter.

At her request, he opened the door, and paused, taking in the scene before him.

She was sitting by the fire, her hair a dark cascade down her back and over her night rail, making a sharp contrast between the white of the cloth and the dark luster of her hair. She slowly set a book down on the table, then stood. "I wasn't sure when . . . you'd be here, so I borrowed your book. Don't worry; I saved your page." She pointed to the table and the book upon it. "It's quite a fantastic story."

He nodded, then tugged at his cravat. Never before had he interrupted a woman from reading, which only made him consider the caliber of women he'd been entertaining. "It's one of my favorites."

"Do you read many books? Fictional, that is," she asked.

"Yes, I confess to reading quite often; it's very . . .

relaxing . . . Diana." He whispered her name, watching as her eyes widened, then she nodded once, glancing back to the book.

She fit her name, he decided. Diana. She hadn't given him leave to call her by her Christian name yet, but as he was now her husband how could she fault him for such an innocent liberty? Diana. Goddess of fertility—he smiled at the appropriateness of the deity.

"That reminds me, what do you wish me to call you?" she asked, turning her gaze back to him.

He untucked his shirt, the feeling of freedom relaxing. Feeling more in his element, he shrugged. "My friends call me Brook, but you can call me by my Christian name as well, Charles."

She tipped her head slightly, studying him. "Charles." She spoke as if testing the word on her lips.

Hearing the sound of his Christian name on her lips was an interesting feeling. It was the name his mistress in London always used, and it didn't quite fit the moment.

"No." She twisted her lips. "Brook." Then she nodded. "Yes, I do believe I'll call you Brook, if you are comfortable with it."

It was a better fit, and he nodded his agreement. "Brook it is."

"After all, I do believe that with time, we might actually become friends. Forgive me for being overly optimistic." She gave a cheeky grin.

"Ah, the optimism is indeed overflowing. To be friends with one's husband . . . that is dangerous waters."

"Isn't it? I will have to watch myself," Diana teased, smiling.

"It would be wise," he added soberly, enjoying the light-hearted teasing. It was unexpected, but that was a common thread with her; "unexpected," "surprising," those were the adjectives he'd use to describe her if given the chance.

"I'm sure you're more than aware, but because I'm a painfully frank person, I'm going to remind you that this is . . . not something I've done before, so . . ." She blushed crimson, then glanced away.

Brook watched with rapture as she fumbled with the tie of her night rail. He couldn't remember the last time he saw a woman blush. It was enticing in a way he'd never imagined. A predatory smile threatened to break through, but he bit it back. "You have nothing to fear."

"I didn't say I was afraid," she replied quickly, her eyes darting up. "I'm not fearful of you."

He nodded, taking a step toward her. "My apologies. You're . . ." He made a hand-sweeping motion for her to fill in the blank.

"A virgin," she answered, then gave him a curious expression as if it were a rather insipid question.

"No. What I was trying to do was encourage you to elaborate; clearly you have something on your mind." He closed the distance between them. Reaching out, he pulled her hand away from the tie of her night rail and laced it through his.

"I'm quite sure I know the mechanics, but . . . I'm encouraging you to keep your expectations realistic. Let's just say that while your reputation precedes you, mine does not, and it would probably be a good idea for you to remember that."

He bit back a grin at her rather inarticulate way of describing her inexperience. "You are exactly what you should be, and will be exactly what you should be. Don't worry about . . . that." He made a concentrated effort to be kind; he could see her vulnerable expression and didn't wish to wound her. It wouldn't be in either of their best interests.

"Thank you," she murmured, tightening her grasp on his hand, then rose up on her tiptoes, kissing him before he had a chance to realize her intention. She mimicked the earlier kiss, and he would have bet his first pound that this was only her second kiss. But she was clearly a quick learner as he tutored her mouth with his. Her one hand tightened on his while her other started to trail up his arm to his neck, her hands threading through his hair.

It was a delightful discovery to find that his wife wasn't just accepting his attentions, but initiating them.

She leaned into the kiss, and he sensed a slight tremble to her fingers. Which only said that she was thinking too much, overthinking really. Which was utterly unnecessary. Sex was natural, it was instinctive, and soon she would realize it was as easy as breathing . . . when he was leading.

He would take it slow, but not too slow. The whole idea was to stop the thought process in every way, to just feel.

So with a smile that broke the seal of the kiss, Brook decided that the only gentlemanly thing to do was seduce his wife.

CHAPTER 8

———◆———

Diana's mind was spinning as she tried to think of how to kiss, how to hold his hand, how to move her hand up his arm without trembling, without seeming afraid.

If her stupid thoughts would just stop moving so quickly through her mind, she might actually enjoy some aspect of it! Yet as soon as she had the last thought, it was like something shifted in the air. The rather gentlemanly man she was kissing had released her hand and stepped back and was watching her with an expression that could only be explained by a sensation: burning.

And in an instant, her thoughts froze, her body started to hum, and she forgot how to breathe. Brook—it fit him—gave a devastatingly handsome grin, one that made her realize how so many women had fallen prey to his charms, and quickly swept her into his arms, his lips seeking the side of her neck, nibbling, breathing, tickling her sensitive flesh with his wicked tongue. Before she could properly appreciate the sensations coursing through her, he set her on his bed and quickly covered her body with his, clothing and all.

The pressure of him over her was heady. He sought her mouth with an intensity that was both delicate and consuming; it was a kiss that demanded surrender, and she was more than happy to wave the white flag. Her senses reeled, and her mind, once so overly analytical, could hardly keep up with all the movements of his fingers, his tongue, his hands, and before she could realize what his intentions were his hand had trailed up from her knee to her thighs, teasing the flesh that no one, save herself, had ever touched.

Good Lord, she thought, feeling wicked for wanting more, for not shying away when he touched her most intimate areas, when he teased her from within. Her hips rocked; she wanted, needed something . . . needed him. She kissed him with the fervor he demanded, gasped when his hand left her leg and reached up to cup her breast. Every touch set her aflame in a new way, and somewhere in the back of her mind she thought of how this experience was far better than she had anticipated.

Thank God.

He kissed her deeply, searchingly, then rose from the bed, quickly disrobing entirely, all while keeping her gaze, daring her to scan his glorious body.

When she didn't break eye contact, he used his hands to trail down his chest, causing her gaze to dart to the motion. Smooth skin, hardened planes, and masculinity that made her body tighten further filled her gaze, and she swallowed, a bit of her reservations falling upon her at the sight of his most intimate areas.

"Stop," he whispered, coming back to the bed and kneeling over her.

"Stop what?" she whispered. Dear Lord, was that her voice? That squeak?

"Worrying. All the pieces fit, Diana," he said against her neck as he shimmied her night rail up over her hips, then higher. He gave her one lingering kiss on her neck and commanded her to sit up. She leaned forward and watched as the discarded clothing fell to the floor. A shiver started at her toes, but it was short lived as every inch of her body was covered with his. He threaded his hands through hers, leaning down to tickle her breast with his tongue. Fire and need sliced through her like a blade, and belatedly she realized that he'd entered her, filling her entirely. The pain was gone as soon as it appeared, and all that was left was pleasure.

Dear Lord, the pleasure was exquisite.

The movements he began only escalated the indulgence of the moment, calling her higher, demanding something from her body she was all too willing to give. She arched against him, needing more, reaching for something she couldn't name as she tightened around him without knowing how, and lost her breath at the same time. His movements intensified, and a moment later he gasped against her, the ridged and sculpted planes of his back seized, and his breath came in short gasps as she finally came down from her own release.

He hovered over her, breathing against her neck, kissing her gently by turns.

All she could think was color.

All she could do was breathe.

And in that moment, Diana realized the truth that had ruined many a woman.

Sex didn't require love.

It didn't even require like.

But she was indeed afraid for the first time since they started their lovemaking.

Because while sex didn't require those things . . . she had the sinking sensation that it led to them.

And falling for her husband was out of the question.

Wasn't it?

CHAPTER 9

———◆———

The next morning, Brook watched Diana with an intrigued eye. The trip to London would take most of the day, arriving just before dinner at his London home, which afforded him much time to observe the creature that was his wife.

She had been a goddess in bed, reacting to every touch and sensation like she was meant for seduction. He'd nearly lost his control a few seconds before she finally found her release. It had been ages since he'd lost his own self-composure during sex, yet she bled it from him, demanded it, and he was powerless to silence her siren call. Part of him wondered if she was already carrying his heir; the other part hoped she wasn't. He was in danger of hoping for a long time of practice to procure said heir, which could lead to entanglement . . . for her.

Women had a hard time separating sex from love.

Hell, men did, too. But not him.

It was a means to an end.

And a delightful, pleasurable end . . . but an end nonetheless.

"Have you ever been to London?" he asked as the carriage swayed.

Diana glanced over to him from the scene the window afforded. "No. I have not. But I've heard much. How would you describe it?"

Brook blew out a breath, thinking. London often defied explanation or definition. But that was truer about London Society rather than London the city. "The city is rather looming and not as regal as we English would like to think of it. It's rather sooty, and, as in most other areas of England, it rains often."

"You'd think that would clear away some of the soot," Diana deducted.

"One would think. It's a kaleidoscope of culture, however. Plenty of opportunity to meet new people from different regions of the world. In that capacity, it will not disappoint."

"And what of the social strata?" Diana asked, her green eyes direct in their frank gaze. He knew what she was asking; it was what everyone who hadn't been raised in London would be expecting.

"You mean, is it as mercenary as often described?"

She raised a shoulder, pretending indifference, but her eyes spoke of a sharp interest. "More or less."

"Yes. Probably worse than what you've heard."

He watched as her eyes widened ever so slightly before she composed her reaction. "I see."

"Yes, but you do have one advantage."

"Oh? And what is that?" Her dark eyebrows furrowed slightly.

"Me."

"You?" She frowned; then understanding dawned on her features. "Because I'm married."

"Yes, but not simply that." He nodded. "You see, you're not just married, but married to me. You're not a threat to the other ladies vying for husbands, so you aren't competition. But you will draw the fascination of many—"

"Because?" she asked. Her controlled manners made him suspect she had her own assumptions on that quarter.

"I'm not exactly marriage material."

"I see."

A bit of an awkward silence stretched, and Brook had the distinct urge to tug on his cravat.

"Is that a label you've given yourself, or taken on because of others?" Diana asked with an interested tone, as if she was honestly curious.

About him.

It was satisfying. She had nothing to gain. She was married to him, and he'd already pledged his assistance to her family provided she fulfilled her duty. She didn't need to invest in him, yet she was, even if it was just simply asking a question no one else had thought to ask.

"That's an interesting question."

A laugh escaped her lips, drawing his attention to them. "And your saying that leads me to believe it has an interesting answer."

He tore his attention away from her lips, thinking about his answer. "Neither, actually."

"Ah, I do believe you have a story to tell."

"Are you sure you wish to hear it? It might not have a happy ending."

Diana glanced around the carriage. "We have nothing but time, my lord. I'm your captive audience, quite literally."

"Ah, but 'captive' implies I stole you away. You're here quite voluntarily."

"More or less," she added, but with a teasing manner that made her otherwise heavy connotation considerably lighter.

She adjusted her posture, and waved her gloved hand for him to begin.

Only Brook wasn't quite certain where to begin. Few knew the story; fewer even cared. But if anyone deserved, rather, was owed the truth, it would be his wife, so it was with a slight trepidation he started at the beginning.

"It was my destiny," he said succinctly. When he met her gaze, he paused for her to reply, but she didn't open her mouth, just waited. He continued. "It turns out my mother was quite . . . liberal with her attentions to suitors. It's well known amongst the ton, her exploits." He took a breath. It was an old story, but it was still concerning something he cared about, even if Diana never fully learned to care for him herself.

"When it was apparent that she wasn't just sharing my father's bed, it created the problem of speculation on my biological father. My father never quite accepted me as his blood heir, but without any other option and as to admit anything less would be quite humiliating—more so than a wife who couldn't keep track of her own partners—he opted to claim me as his own." Brook still remembered when his father sat him down and explained the whole sordid tale.

Brook had come home on holiday from Eton, a black-and-blue eye creating quite the stir. An altercation that ended in fisticuffs had given him a shiner, but the boy who called Brook's mother a whore was missing his front tooth.

It was then that Brook's father had told him that it was the truth. From that moment, his world shifted. As an adult, he could look back and see the lack of insight on his own part, but he'd made a subconscious decision. If given the choice between being the type of person his mother was or his father was, he'd always choose to be like his mother. She was infinitely kinder, laughed often, and was everything that was charming and lovely.

He shared the story with Diana, then paused, watching her reaction.

"What was your father like?" she asked, her expression almost unreadable.

"Calculating, cool, very good at business."

"So you clearly inherited his business sense."

Brook laughed without mirth. "That's exactly what he said." He paused, then repeated the words his father had spoken over his future: "'You'll have my sense; that much is clear. But I'm afraid you'll be just as much of a whore as your mother, and for that I pray you never marry and break someone's heart.'" Brook watched Diana's eyes widen, expecting for her to retract her earlier friendliness. It was better this way, he told himself. It was better for her to keep her expectations low, to know that he was incapable of giving anything more.

"Your father was heartbroken, wasn't he?" Diana's voice pierced through his musings.

"What?" He thought over her question. "He never seemed as such. Angry, yes. Heartbroken, no."

"Many times anger is what brokenness bleeds," she whispered.

"Pardon?" He'd never thought of it like that.

"When people are hurt, it often comes out as anger, not sadness. The blood of brokenness is anger," she answered. "It's something my grandmother would say when someone would be particularly nasty to her or someone she loved."

"Your grandmother was a gracious person."

"And your father was not," she answered. "So you took on those words, didn't you?"

"It was only natural. I was always ever more like my mother than father, if, indeed, he was my father. But I rather fancy that he was; we look an awful bit alike."

"So that is how you came up with the name the Devil's Bachelor?" she asked, her lips tipping into a smile.

His own lips betrayed a grin; it felt foreign but welcome. "And what is so amusing about that name? It's rather famous, I'll have you know."

"Clearly, since even I am aware of it!" she teased.

"Ah, yes, even the far reaches of Sussex have heard of my legendary name."

"We are far more knowledgeable in Sussex than rumored." She winked. "So did you give yourself the name? Or was it given?"

"A friend gave it to me our last year at Eton. It stuck, needless to say."

"And I'm sure you did nothing to deserve such a name," she replied archly.

To this he felt equal; his charm rose to the occasion and he was on level footing. He could banter; he could flirt; oh, how he could flirt. "Well, you can easily speak for yourself on such a thing."

Her skin flushed vermillion. "I suppose, but I'd rather not."

He chuckled. "So my reputation is deserved?" he couldn't resist asking.

"Yes." She met his gaze brazenly. "Which is a welcome truth."

He paused, not entirely sure how to interpret her last phrase, but chose to accept it as a compliment. "I thank you."

She gave a token eye roll, and it suited her. It wasn't exactly ladylike, but it fit the rather unladylike conversation.

Then, on impulse, he reached over and grasped her gloved hand, kissing her wrist tenderly. "Thank you," he whispered.

"For what?" she asked with a confused frown.

"For asking."

She slowly withdrew her hand as he released it. "I'd be a terrible friend if I didn't ask, my lord. And the fact that you even said 'thank you' tells me one thing in particular."

He tipped his chin. "And what is that?"

She tilted her head, regarding him softly. "That you need better friends. And lucky for you, I happen to know how to be a great one."

It was strange how he had been searching for a wife, never once expecting to find something vastly more important.

A friend.

CHAPTER 10

—◆—

Diana reflected on the trip to London as she gazed about her sumptuous suite of rooms in Brook's London home. It had been a curious ride to Town, but it was pleasant, far more so than she would have expected. They conversed, sat in comfortable silence by turns, and then they had arrived. Brook had taken care to introduce her to the staff, who had all worked hard to shutter their curious and surprised reactions. More than once Diana had to bite her lip to keep from releasing a smile of entertainment. But the staff had been more than gracious, and she was thrilled to have a few moments to herself in her rooms.

The past few days had flown by; with so many changes taking place, she desperately needed some time to just think, to be, to absorb it all. Exhaling a deep breath, she walked over to the large window. Drawing back the sheer curtain, she noted that her room faced the front of the house, affording her a view of the beautifully tree-lined Mayfair district. Glancing down the road, she could catch a slight glimpse of Hyde Park, or so Brook had said.

The glass was cool on her fingertips as she touched it,

mentally comparing the view to that from her window at home. How was her family? How were Tully, and Eva, all her sisters? Had her mother recovered from her earlier sickness?

Determined, Diana strode over to the oak writing desk and searched the drawers. Thankful that the desk was well stocked with parchment and ink, she wrote a quick letter to her sisters, asking for the particulars of their situation, and giving only the barest details of her own. She wasn't quite sure how to categorize it herself, so it was useless trying to tell someone else. She would feel so much better if she knew her family was well.

She had no reason to believe otherwise . . .

But it would be reassuring to know for certain.

She rung the bell for a maid, and after dispatching her with the letter, she was once again alone in her rooms.

Drat, it was so silent.

How was it that the silence was loud?

She supposed that she was far more accustomed to the constant chatter of her sisters, and it was painfully absent. Would Brook allow her to bring her sisters to Town? Perhaps even give them a Season? Yet as she thought it, she remembered the main temptation of her agreement with her husband: freedom. She would have the means and the freedom to beckon her sisters to London, and much more. It was liberating, yet at the same time, it was an insecure feeling.

Drat, everything had some sort of emotion attached to it. With a resigned sigh, she decided she needed an escape before the upcoming appointment with the modiste.

The staff was more than helpful to point her in the right direction to the library, and as she perused the shelves she realized what she was looking for: the book she had started on a nervous impulse in Brook's rooms as she waited for him on their wedding night.

It hadn't been a lie—the book was very diverting—and she wished there were another copy in the library, but all searching proved fruitless.

After exiting the library, she halted a parlor maid and asked if she was aware of her husband's whereabouts. The maid dipped a polite curtsey and pointed toward a large wooden door that presumably led to his study.

It was the first time Diana had sought him out, and she wondered how such a move would be received. Knocking, she waited.

"Enter," Brook called from inside, his voice muffled by the door. The brass handle was cool on her gloved hand as she twisted it and opened the door.

An older gentleman was sitting across from her husband; a wide, highly polished desk separated them.

"Diana." Brook spoke her name with surprise but not displeasure as he waved her inside and stood.

"My lord." Diana gave a proper curtsey.

"Allow me to introduce you to Lord Walker." He gestured to the older man, who rose slowly, his age evident in his stiff movements. His expression was kind, yet he studied her with a scrutiny that wasn't expected.

Diana gave another curtsey to the older man. "A pleasure to meet you."

"I hear congratulations are in order," Lord Walker started, shifting his gaze to Brook.

"Thank you, my lord," Diana replied, as Brook nodded in agreement.

"Tell me, Lady Barrington, how did you meet your husband?" Lord Walker asked, with more than a token amount of curiosity.

"Well, it's not a long story, my lord, but our lands border one another in Sussex. My family has known Lord Barrington's for decades." It was the truth, and she waited to see if he'd inquire further.

"I see." He nodded. "So your family is still in Sussex?"

"Yes, my lord. I have four younger sisters and my mother at home."

"Interesting."

"Perhaps, I rather find my story quite uninteresting, but it is dear to me because it's my own," Diana replied, offering a smile to the older man.

"Diana, did you need something?" Brook asked, pulling her attention away from the gentleman.

"Ah, yes. It's not important, though. I see you're quite busy. I'll ask later."

"Are you certain?" Brook asked.

She hesitated. "Actually, I was just wondering if I could borrow your book?"

Brook's brow furrowed; then understanding dawned. A secretive smile teased his lips and he glanced down. "It's on my nightstand. You're of course welcome to take it."

"Thank you." She blushed, her thoughts immediately going back to the events of the evening after her reading of the book. Turning her attention back to Lord Walker, she gave her excuses, then added, "It was a pleasure to meet you, my lord."

"It was a pleasure to meet you as well, Lady Barrington." He gave a meaningful glance to Brook, then sat back down.

Brook gave her a quick smile before sitting back down as well, and as she quit the room she heard the men's voices just before she closed the door.

"I had my doubts."

"And now?" Brook asked.

"Now I actually believe you." Then, so quietly she almost didn't hear it over the click of the door, "No courtesan you hired would dare dress in such a dress as that."

Diana paused just as the door closed.

Courtesan?

And what was wrong with her dress anyway?

She glanced down and studied her day dress, the one that wasn't patched here and there, and for the first time realized the faded nature of the fabric and the simple cut of the cloth. A maid walked by then, and Diana couldn't help but compare her dress with the maid's uniform.

And the maid's dress was honestly finer than her own.

It was then that she made two choices:

First, that she would inquire about the comment regarding the courtesan, though she was quite certain she wouldn't like the answer.

And second, that modiste appointment couldn't happen fast enough.

In fact, she was so preoccupied with the last statements of Lord Walker that she almost forgot about the book.

Almost.

As she retrieved the book from Brook's rooms, she laughed at the irony of her predicament. She had sought out Brook's book to distract herself, only finding that she needed distraction more than ever after finding him. And now, she feared, the book wouldn't provide enough escape for her mind.

Things were simpler in Sussex.

And she had the feeling it was only going to get worse.

CHAPTER 11

———◆———

Several days later, Brook still couldn't wipe the grin from his face whenever he thought of Walker's expression after meeting Diana. To be sure, the old man had suspected him, with good reason, of trying to trick him into believing the authenticity of their marriage. But after meeting Diana, the man was finally convinced, and what had done it wasn't her appearance, wasn't her ladylike manner; it was the fact that the blasted modiste hadn't come yet and Diana was still wearing her rather worn and faded day dress. And he would have bet several thousand pounds that the poor dress was her best one as well. Lord Walker accepted the authenticity of the marriage based on Diana's story and appearance, leaving the signed documents on Brook's desk before he left.

The sale had to be recorded, which would take place the day after the party Brook was planning to present his wife to the London Ton. It was amazing how long he had awaited this moment, and for so much to happen in such a short amount of time was overwhelming, in the best way.

Diana had continued to impress him, and each time he

thought of her coming into his study in search of that book, it made him smile.

In fact, he couldn't remember the last time he'd smiled so much. He wasn't sure if he liked or felt trepidation about such an emotion. The more pessimistic side of him was waiting for something to happen and steal all the joy away.

A knock sounded on his study door. "Enter." He glanced up from his musings and smiled a welcome to Diana.

"Good evening." He stood. "Is it time for dinner, then?"

"Almost." She gave a smile in return. Her day gown fit beautifully, tucking in and accenting all the right curves of her body, reminding him that the festivities of the night were only a few hours away. It was not hardship, bedding Diana. She had only become more engaging with each passing night, an equal partner who threatened to tempt him into caring more than just for the procreation of an heir.

He tempered his thoughts. "How was your afternoon?"

"Pleasant. I finished the book. Do you know if there's any more in the series?"

"Yes. And I shall get the entire set for you tomorrow." He left his desk and walked over to her, offering his arm.

"Thank you. And how was your afternoon?"

"Busy. But at least I wasn't planning the menu for the party tomorrow night."

"Ah, yes. That was my delegation." She sighed. "Thankfully your cook is far more knowledgeable than I, and made the whole project easy. I simply nodded," she replied with a laugh.

"Ah, you nod very well."

"Thank you. I'm quite proud of my skills. I've learned how to seem very obedient when I'm really not," she teased. "Ask my mother."

"I'll take your word for it." He started to lead them to the hall.

"Actually, I do have one question." Diana's voice stopped him short. She was tentative in her tone, very unlike what he'd come to know of her.

"Yes?" He turned to her.

"Lord Walker . . . as I was leaving he said something. . . ."

Immediately Brook knew what she meant. "Yes?"

"And I was wondering why he thought I would possibly be a courtesan, and if, perhaps, others would assume the same upon meeting me?"

It wasn't quite the question he was expecting. He had anticipated anger, frustration that there had been a courtesan—hell, many—before her. And probably would be more after they satisfied their contract. He was careful to formulate his reply. "Well, it turns out that Lord Walker has a piece of property I want very much, but he wished to keep it in a family. Meaning, he wasn't willing to sell it to me if I remained a bachelor with no heir to inherit."

"I see. So you . . ." She paused, then squinted with amusement. "Hired a wife?"

"In a way."

"And he found out."

"I hired a friend—"

"A courtesan friend," Diana replied archly.

"Yes."

"And he didn't approve? Shocking," she teased.

"He did not approve, or believe me."

She nodded. "Which leads to me."

"Which leads to you." Brook nodded. "And I must say, I did pretty well for myself." He hitched a shoulder. It was the truth, no need to steal her due credit.

Diana frowned. "Thank you."

He touched her forehead. "You don't look appreciative."

She shook her head. "I just didn't expect your thanks."

"Then apparently I've been very poor at giving it. Turns out we both gained something from the marriage. I was able to purchase the property, and your family was able to keep theirs." It was quite ironic actually, and thinking of it in such a way made it somewhat poetic as well.

"How very astute . . ." Then she grinned. "Even if you did try to hire a wife. Honestly, did you think that would be so easily pretended? How long would you have had her live with you?"

"I don't often have Lord Walker at my house, so it seemed like an easy farce."

"You're quite impressive at business, but in this, I must say you didn't do your intelligence justice."

"I do believe I'm insulted," he replied, arching a brow playfully.

"Friends are honest. And that is the truth, my lord. If a friend can't be honest with you, who can? Then you're simply surrounded by people using you, lying to you, et cetera. Honesty isn't a bad thing."

"When you put it that way." He grinned. "Then thank you for your honesty."

"You're welcome. I'm sure you'll return the favor someday, but I must say I wish you would have said something sooner. . . ."

"About?" He followed her as she started toward the hall.

"My dress. I think the maids are wearing finer clothing than I."

He gave a laugh. "I'm sorry; I didn't wish to offend."

"Instead you let me look like a poor cousin."

"A cousin you are *not*," he accented. "However, I do

believe the modiste has rectified the problem. Are you happy with your clothes?"

"Yes, and the dress for tomorrow is lovely, though I think people will expect that perhaps I *am* a courtesan. It's quite scandalous, but I admit that I do love it."

"I'm sure you'll do it more than justice, and no one will think of you as a courtesan. *The Times* and *The Courier* have run articles announcing the marriage and an abundance of invites have poured in. People know, Diana, and are all dying with curiosity to meet the woman who has ended my reign as bachelor."

"It wasn't hard," she said. "You had to convince me more than I you."

"They will never believe you," he joked, tapping her nose with his finger.

"That's because they don't know you. But don't worry; your secret is safe with me."

"Because we're friends?" Brook asked, watching her green eyes flicker to his.

"Yes. And friends keep secrets."

"Well then, I think it's only fair that I have a secret to keep about you," he traded.

They had made their way to the table, and he pulled out the chair for her, seating her beside him.

The footman poured a light white wine and served the first course of consommé broth. As he departed, Brook turned to her.

"So, a secret."

Diana narrowed her eyes as if studying his worthiness for such a precious gift. "I suppose the question is, which one."

"So you have many secrets."

"A great many, but most won't matter to you." She took a sip of her soup.

"Well, I think it's only fair if you share a secret that does matter to me."

"Why?" she asked, setting the spoon down.

This pulled him up short, and he glanced up, thinking. "Because it will prove I'm worthy of your friendship."

"And I can't just offer the friendship; you must prove yourself?"

Again, he paused, not quite certain how to proceed. "Yes?"

"Wrong. Try again." She picked up her spoon and dipped it in the soup.

Brook watched her, curious if she knew how unconventional of a conversation they were having. Never, in all his experience with women, had he ever had a conversation such as this. Such as were most of the conversations he'd had with Diana—and they hadn't been married a week yet!

"Is the question that difficult for you?" she asked, blinking at him.

He shook his head. "You should share a secret that matters to me, because I . . ." He paused. "You know what, I have no idea."

"When you can tell me, I'll tell you. It's only fair."

And as Brook watched his wife smile a grin of victory, he decided that sometimes losing wasn't as terrible as he originally thought.

But something tickled his mind, hinting that this wasn't the first time he'd lose in a battle of wits against Diana.

But that it was only the first of many.

Which should have scared the hell out of him.

Yet it didn't.

For the first time, the future looked better than he'd ever expected to see it.

All because of her.

Who'd have thought a wife could change so much?

And not just a wife: her.

CHAPTER 12

———❖———

The evening of the party arrived, and Diana struggled to keep her nerves in check. It would be the first ball she'd ever attended, if one didn't count the few country-dances to which she'd been invited. All day the servants had prepared the rooms, the food, the ambiance, to a fever pitch of perfection. The heady scent of roses and English lavender floated up the stairs and penetrated her rooms with its intoxicating scent. She winced as her maid tugged a few strands of hair particularly tight, and she inhaled a deep, calming breath.

I can do this.

It helped to know that her marriage to Lord Barrington had been announced in the proper way. At least she didn't have to wonder if people were looking at her askance, curious if she were another hired wife. No, she was a wife in truth, and in deed. She had no reason to do anything but hold her head high, but the trepidation of her introduction to the London Ton was daunting. She wasn't expecting acceptance, but it would be nice not to be ostracized. However, she didn't keep high hopes for anything; it was better to expect nothing and have something pleasantly surprise her.

Like her marriage to Brook. Her expectations were very small, if any. And he'd surpassed each one, beyond what she dared hope. He was kind, attentive, but she didn't read into his care to believe him sincerely attached to her. She did indeed hope that he viewed her as a friend, as an ally at least. She had offered her friendship, without expecting anything in return. She only wondered if he knew how to accept such a gift without strings attached. It was a pity.

"All set, my lady," the maid whispered reverently, and Diana hesitated to glance into the mirror. She'd been watching the progress of her hair but had been lost in her thoughts and missed the final touches.

A smile teased her lips, and she took in all the details of her appearance. Her chestnut brown hair was twisted, curled, and woven with small pearl strands, the contrast between light and dark stunning. Her green eyes were accented by the smallest hint of a blush in her cheeks, and the gown.

Good Lord.

She'd been speaking the truth to Brook when she'd said it made her feel like a courtesan. The shoulders were barely covered by the smallest whisper of emerald fabric, and the décolleté dipped lower than any other she'd ever worn before. The lower neckline hinted at the swell of her breasts, barely covered by the minimal corset, as was the newest fashion, or so she was told by the modiste. It would be considered scandalous in Sussex, but Diana had the suspicion that it was simply common in London.

She had a lot to learn, she knew. And fashion was the first lesson.

The fabric gathered just under her breasts, tucking in

and then fanning out in a graceful flow to her feet, covered by the most exquisite emerald slippers with silver threading. Never having worn anything nearly as fine, she was transfixed at the transformation of a dress and expertly styled hair.

"My lady? My lord wished to give this to you." The maid's words broke through Diana's examinations.

"Yes?" She turned to see the maid extend a simple white box. When Diana opened it, there lay a beautiful set of pearls, larger than the ones woven through her hair, but similar in color. There were also matching earrings to complete the set.

"Oh my," Diana whispered.

"Allow me." The maid took the box and withdrew the necklace, carefully draping it around Diana's neck. It completed the dress in a way that made her realize something was missing before, something crucial.

The earrings were like a delicate frosting on a cake, not necessary but delightful and decadent.

"You're very lovely, my lady."

Diana turned to the maid. "Thank you, so very much." After bobbing a quick curtsey, the maid took her leave, and Diana was alone with her thoughts.

Glancing to the clock, she noted that there was only a quarter of an hour before Brook would escort her to the ballroom. She took the opportunity to go to the window facing the front of the house. When she drew the curtain back, she noted the long line of carriages, all awaiting entrance to the courtyard. Several footmen helped ladies and gentlemen from their carriages, then moved along to the next one.

Was there anyone who hadn't accepted her and Brook's

invitation? She doubted it. Of course, Brook had said the curiosity of the ton would draw them all in.

Curiosity about her.

The anxiety returned, and she forced several deep breaths from her nose just when there was a knock at the door.

"Come in," she called, forcing a calm.

Brook opened the door, then froze as he stepped over the threshold. His eyes crinkled with a smile that soon was followed by his lips.

She waited for his approval, for him to say something, anything.

And in those stretches of silence, she realized just how important it was to her, to have his approval.

That was dangerous ground.

But certainly, as a friend, she could care about his opinion? But her heart whispered that it was something deeper. She silenced the inner voice.

"Diana." He whispered her name, then closed the door. "You're exactly as your name means, a goddess if I ever saw one."

A blush flowed through her, starting at her fingertips and ending up in her cheeks. It pleased her more than she was willing to admit. "Thank you."

"And your dress is lovely, nothing too scandalous. But I must say, if it weren't a little scandalous—only a little—people might question the marriage."

"Ah, your infamous reputation." She understood his implication.

"Only for finding the most beautiful women in England." He gave a slight bow. "And you, on that front, are certainly validating that rumor."

"Flattery." She gave a small wave of her hand, trying to lighten the mood with teasing.

"It will get you anywhere," he replied, offering his arm.

Diana took a deep breath and closed the distance. She rested her hand on his arm, drawing strength from him.

"I don't understand." Brook turned a confused expression toward her.

She met his gaze.

"You never once trembled when you were marrying me, a stranger, yet you're shaking like a leaf now. Where is my brave wife? The one who isn't afraid to be honest, the one who—"

"I'm here. I'm just . . . a little more reluctant to take on the ton. You . . . were less threatening."

"That, my dear, is a valid statement. I am far less frightening than the ton, but I will not leave your side. You're safe with me. On that you can depend." And his clear blue gaze conveyed the truth of his words.

Her heart calmed at his pledge, and with a pinch more courage than she'd had a few moments ago, she followed him down the hall and into the foyer.

The hum of voices floated up to them as they descended the stairs. Soon the hum of voices became a sea of silence as every eye turned to them. Diana could feel their scrutiny on her person, their eyes calculating, speculating, judging her worthiness or lack thereof.

It was single-handedly the most on-display moment of her existence, and she fervently hoped it was the last as well.

"You're taking their breath away," Brook whispered so quietly she almost missed the sweet words.

She glanced down to hide the fullness of her smile, and then when she was once more in command of herself, she met the collective gaze of the ton with more confidence than she thought was possible.

The fifteen seconds it took to descend the stairs felt like fifteen minutes, but soon she and Brook were on the ballroom floor and the hum of voices started up once more.

There was a flurry of introductions, a hundred names she'd never remember, and more than her share of sidelong glances from other women, but soon the music started, and Brook took her arm, leading her to the dance floor.

"It's only proper that we start out the evening. It is our party, after all," he murmured, then proceeded to dance to the cotillion. She exchanged partners, and was starting to enjoy herself. The music was lovely, the lights twinkled, and if she pretended hard enough, she could imagine that everyone was looking at someone else rather than her.

After the dance finished, Brook escorted her to the edge of the dance floor. "Would you care for a glass of wine? Some lemonade?"

"Yes, please. Lemonade," she replied, immediately desperate for the refreshment.

"I'll be only a moment." He lifted her wrist and kissed it, then disappeared into the crowd.

"Ah, Lady Barrington." A slightly familiar voice interrupted her thoughts. Turning, she met the gaze of Lord Walker and another gentleman with whom she wasn't acquainted.

"My lord." She curtseyed.

"Allow me to introduce my cousin's son, Sir Harrington."

"A pleasure." Diana offered her hand to the considerably younger gentleman. She guessed he was close to Brook in age, and stature.

Sir Harrington took her hand, kissing it politely. "You're even more lovely than Lord Walker mentioned."

She blushed at the compliment, but it wasn't one of pleasure, rather of anxiety. "Are you enjoying your evening?" she asked, like a good hostess.

"Even more now," Lord Harrington replied charmingly.

Lord Walker chuckled. "You're quite polished from when I saw you last, Lady Barrington." His eyes took on a narrowed glint.

"I'm sure," Diana replied, tightly. "But I'm sure you're far too much of a gentleman to imply that a woman is only as worthy as her clothing." It was as near an insult as she'd ever dare give a peer of the realm, but something felt off.

"Of course, he would never imply anything such as that," Sir Harrington replied.

"Anything as what?" Brook's voice was a welcome interruption into the conversation, and Diana took the opportunity to step back and allow her husband into the circle of discussion.

Why did she suddenly feel like a lamb amongst wolves? At least she wasn't alone; Brook would traverse the tricky ground for her, with her.

She wasn't left alone to defend herself, thank God.

And he wouldn't leave her.

He promised.

CHAPTER 13

———◆———

Brook tried to loosen the clench of his jaw. The moment he'd turned from the refreshment table, Diana had been surrounded in more ways than she'd readily recognized. Every eye was on her, calculating. And when Lord Walker had approached her, the old man had some sort of purpose in mind, Brook would bet his last pound on it. But it was the other gentleman with Lord Walker who caused Brook's fists to clench. He monitored his grip on the glass of lemonade as he tried to quickly dart through the crowd back to Diana. She was speaking to the gentlemen, and as she addressed Lord Walker the other gentleman's gaze roved over her suggestively, lingering on the dip of her neckline. Judging by his expression, he was appreciating the view far more than was appropriate.

Brook's blood had boiled, and a deep well of jealousy overflowed within him. He had stamped down his rather savage instincts and forced the charm for which he was renowned as he approached the small group.

Diana's posture had been stiff, and he was immediately

curious what they had said to create such a reaction. Just as he approached, the other gentleman mentioned something, and so Brook asked the question that would require the whole conversation to be repeated.

At the sound of his voice, he noted the way Diana relaxed slightly. It was out of the corner of his eye, but it was obvious—to him. How had he come to know her so well, in such a short time? It was disconcerting, delightful, and utterly distracting. He had to focus on the situation at hand, so he pushed the observation aside and directed all his attention to the gentlemen before him.

Lord Walker answered Brook's inquiry. "I was merely stating that your wife was quite . . . polished."

"I see. Actually, I'm sure everyone can see what a beauty she is. It's a rather unremarkable statement since it's overly apparent." Brook deliberately misunderstood the implication, opting not to insult the man directly. There were still some finalizations that needed to happen, and the last thing he needed was Lord Walker changing his mind, or making the process more difficult.

Lord Walker cleared his throat. "Allow me to introduce my cousin's son, Sir Harrington." He gestured to the other gentleman. Brook bowed, and then turned to Diana. "Your lemonade," he whispered, and intentionally brushed her hand as he handed the glass over.

An intimate smile teased her lips, and he was mesmerized.

"A pleasure to finally meet you. I've heard much about you from Lord Walker." Sir Harrington's voice interrupted Brook's appreciation of Diana's expression.

At this, Brook wondered just how much Lord Walker had shared, and why. "Ah, yes." He turned back to the man. "I'm happy you could come and celebrate with us tonight."

"Perhaps later we can discuss some details; there's been a change to the plans," Lord Walker said, his eyes taking on a shrewd glint.

Brook's chest tightened, but he feigned disinterest. "Change to what?"

"This is not the time or place." Lord Walker shrugged off the question.

"Yet you felt it necessary to bring it up," Brook replied coolly.

"I thought you should know, that is all."

Brook nodded. "A small detail change isn't worrisome; let us discuss it tomorrow, and enjoy ourselves tonight."

Lord Walker cast a meaningful glance to Sir Harrington. "The detail isn't as small as that."

Everything that Brook had worked for seemed to be unstable, shaking, and he wasn't sure how to navigate it. Lord Walker had agreed to the sale of the estate. The documents were drawn, the signatures given; all that was left was waiting for finalization. What could he possibly change at this point? Brook calmed himself with that knowledge.

He couldn't wait, though; he had to know. Certainly it was worth fifteen minutes of time to see this to an end? "Why don't we take a small break for brandy in my office, then?" Brook offered.

Lord Walker and Sir Harrington nodded, then followed him as he departed from the party.

His thoughts pounded through his head like his heels on the polished floor as they all adjourned into his study. He poured three snifters of brandy, and lifted a glass. *Let the deception be brought out into the light, or let it be put to rest*, he thought.

"Cheers."

Both gentlemen took sips, and then sat when Brook

gestured to the chairs. "What needs to be discussed? I was under the impression that all details were already worked out."

Lord Walker glanced to Sir Harrington, then leaned forward. "I have another buyer, who is willing to keep it in my family."

"And your honor and word mean nothing? Lord Walker, I have the documents, your signature; it's all but finished. If Sir Harrington wishes to purchase the estate, he might do so . . . but through me, if I wished to sell it. But I do not."

"There was a misunderstanding, and I'm trying to not interrupt your current plans, simply adjust them," Sir Harrington replied, then paused, leaning forward.

"What misunderstanding?" Brook asked, unclenching his jaw.

"I want the estate. I was under the impression it was already sold—"

"It is," Brook interrupted.

"Not yet," Lord Walker replied coolly. "I might not be able to completely halt the sale, since you have all the signed documents, but I'm sure I can keep it tied up in litigation for some time." he threatened.

"What do you want?" Brook asked, not even attempting to keep his teeth from clenching at the words.

"I want to purchase a percentage of the estate, and the right to pass it along to my family if you do not procure an heir."

"You do realize I'm going to have a family of my own," Brook stated, curious as to what plans were forming behind the scenes in the minds of Lord Walker and Sir Harrington.

"Let's not pretend, Lord Barrington. Your wife . . . You

certainly made it seem authentic, but no one goes to the English countryside and comes back married to . . . someone like her." Lord Walker folded his hands over his larger belly, as if resting his case.

"You don't believe in the authenticity of my marriage," Brook stated.

"Men like you don't marry. You might have signed the paper, bedded the wench, but you'll never have an heir worthy of my estate. Sir Harrington has two sons already," he said as if all this were a mere formality to the end he'd already planned for.

Brook bit back his anger. "So, not only are you insulting me, but my wife? Where is your honor, Lord Walker? You spout these ideas of family and heritage, but you are willing to discount any that don't fit into your ideals. I'll have you know that my *wife*"—he accented the word—"is very much a wife, and not a mistress, a courtesan, nothing as marginalized. She bears my name, my protection, and will bear my heirs. And if you wish to try and make these changes, then I trust you will have a large amount of time and lawyers dedicated to the venture, because you, my lord, will find my resolution unmovable," Brook replied with an icy tone. "Excuse me, I have a party to attend, and you no longer have a reason to stay and enjoy it." Brook stood, and motioned to the door.

"So you're resolved?"

"Entirely. And I'd appreciate if you'd never insult my wife again. I'll not be as kind the next time around."

Lord Walker met Sir Harrington's gaze, and both men stood and exited.

Brook waited till the door closed, then sunk in his chair, holding his hands over his face. "What a disaster," he murmured.

All the reasons he'd taken a wife in the beginning were for naught. He'd fight Lord Walker to maintain the sale of the estate, but it wasn't going to be easy. It was supposed to be a seamless transition.

A marriage of convenience.

A sale of property.

No distractions, no barriers to the final goal.

Yet it seemed that he was utterly distracted by his wife—which was unplanned. And fighting for what was his ultimate goal, Lord Walker's estate. What had seemed so clear, a plan so easily executed, was now in ruins and he was more entangled than he ever thought possible.

It was then that he admitted to the truth that he'd been trying to ignore.

He cared more for Diana than he'd ever planned.

He wanted her more than he'd ever expected.

And he was certain that she was not returning the attachment—especially because it was also at that moment that he realized he'd left her all alone.

When he'd promised to not leave her side.

Apparently it was a night of broken promises.

CHAPTER 14

———◆———

Diana's gaze kept straying to the door where Brook had left. He'd gone with the gentlemen without a backward glance, which hurt more than it should have. She knew her attachment to him was more than his to her, but that didn't stop her heart from feeling the truth of it. The moment he left, the whispers around her started.

At first, they were easy to ignore.

She sipped her lemonade, put on a brave smile, tried to remember the words Brook had spoken over her earlier.

Brave. She could be brave.

She turned to her side, meaning to make conversation with someone, but she met the cool gaze of a woman about her age, stopping her efforts in her tracks. She sipped from her glass again, thankful for the distraction.

But the lemonade only lasted so long, and the conversation was taking longer than she'd hoped. That could only mean that the "details" Lord Walker had mentioned were not merely details, but large changes.

Meaning, the business deal that had enticed Brook to marry her in the first place was potentially falling apart.

Was it all for naught now?

If so, what would she do?

What would *he* do?

Would he regret marrying her? Would he uphold his agreement to provide assistance to her family? Was it all crumbling now?

Her refreshment gone, she felt like an idiot holding her glass and waiting.

"Pardon me," a woman's voice called from behind her, and she turned to a lady slightly older than her. Her gown was threaded with silver, making it shimmer in the light. "Allow me to introduce myself; I'm Lady Ardell." The woman nodded gracefully.

"A pleasure," Diana replied. "I'm Lady Barrington, but I'm sure you're aware." She offered a smile at her little joke.

"Yes, it is your party after all," the woman replied, a little bit of cheek to her tone. "And where is your husband, Lady Barrington? It would seem your party is missing someone quite important." Lady Ardell spoke with a soft tone, but the expression in her eyes gave the words bite.

"He had some unexpected business to take care of," Diana replied coolly, but with a tone of respect; no need to make enemies already.

Though she was certain that the moment she walked out with Lord Barrington, she made many.

"I see," Lady Ardell replied, then nodded and turned to take her leave, pausing beside several other ladies. There were whispers, looks, and calculating glances that conveyed that Lady Ardell was communicating her recent conversation—though Diana was sure they could have easily overheard it. The speculation that followed the communication was humiliating, and without a backward glance Diana made her way over to the refreshment table. She procured another glass of lemonade.

She wasn't going to let them win.

No. She wasn't sure where Brook was, or what was going on, but for the moment, she was the hostess. She would rise to the occasion. So, with her head held high, she walked over to a collection of ladies and introduced herself.

And when she was finished with that conversation, she found another to be a part of.

The time passed.

And Diana almost forgot that she had been left behind.

That her husband had done the very thing he'd promised not to do, abandoning her to the tender mercies—or lack of mercy or anything tender—of the London Ton.

"Diana." He whispered her name, and gooseflesh rose up on her arms. Turning, she met his gaze. Unwilling to forgive so easily, no matter how his charming expression threatened to turn her insides to jelly, she nodded coolly. "My lord."

"Excuse me, ladies; I'm going to steal my wife away." He grasped her hand lightly and pulled her away amid whispers and a few sly smiles.

"How bad is it?" Diana asked, not wanting to prolong not knowing. Her future could very well hinge on the answer.

Brook studied her, and then led her to a small alcove. "You mean the business arrangement I've spoken about."

"Yes. The one that," she whispered softly, "required you to marry me."

Brook glanced away, and then heaved a long sigh.

Regret.

She could feel it in her bones, her heart clenched in her

chest, telling her the attachment she'd barely recognized had a deeper root than she'd admitted.

"Oh," she replied, taking a slow breath. She wouldn't cry; she wouldn't react. No. He wanted her brave; she would be brave—damn it all. But she wouldn't be brave for him; she would be brave for herself.

"I'm sorry." And she was. It was unfortunate.

For both of them.

"So am I," he replied. "It was a good plan." Diana nodded at the words, hazarding a glance at Brook, desperate to read his expression.

"It was. Too bad it wasn't as foolproof as I expected." He gave a self-deprecating laugh, without humor. "But I don't hold you responsible for anything; you have no need to worry. For this, I lay all the blame at Lord Walker's feet . . . and my own. I should have known it wasn't to be this simple." He sighed.

"I understand." Diana glanced down to her gloved fingers. "Let's just finish tonight with a brave face and then we'll figure out things tomorrow," she offered, hoping he would at least give her tonight. He was reconsidering everything, she was sure. It was a stab to the heart, and she felt breathless with the pain of it.

"Of course." He nodded, his expression slightly distracted, as if thinking over plans already.

Diana forced a smile, took his hand, and allowed him to lead her to the ballroom floor. The strains of a waltz started. Eyes turned to them, and when Brook made no motion to the dance floor Diana gave his arm a little squeeze.

After meeting her gaze with a curious expression, to his credit he caught on quickly and, with a charming smile, led them to start the waltz.

As he led them in the graceful movements, Diana closed her eyes, pretending.

Pretending that it was real.

Pretending it wasn't the last waltz.

Pretending that everything was going according to plan, and that this was the first night of many.

Not the first night of the end.

CHAPTER 15

———◆———

It was the first night since they'd been married that Brook didn't share a bed with his wife. Restless and preoccupied, he kissed her good night after the ball and led her to her private suite of rooms, rather than his own. She had accepted his kiss, but it was different. She was different.

But his mind was still reeling—the whole situation was too much to process—so he pushed back the observation and went to his study and poured another snifter of brandy, sure that the snifter would be one of many.

He made a plan, set aside a list of what to do in the morning, and when he couldn't think of any other necessary courses of action, he called his carriage to take him to White's.

The gentlemen's club was full this evening, and it was upon his arrival that he realized his fatal error.

In that moment, he confirmed the suspicions of everyone, and never before had he so deeply regretted living up to his name and reputation.

"I told Walker that you'd be in here later. Bored already,

Barrington?" Lord Whistler gave a mighty slap on Brook's back as he passed him.

"I told you his interest would last a week," someone added.

"It's been five days: I won the bet!" Another slapped the table, causing the glasses to tinkle.

Brook gave his head a shake. "No, you misunderstand."

"Sure we do." Lord Whistler winked.

"I wouldn't mind her warming my bed," another gentleman mumbled as Brook passed, causing him to pause.

"Pardon?" He turned to the gentleman, acid in his tone.

"He don't mean anything by it." His friend slapped his back.

"I doubt that," Brook replied icily.

"Ah, did I say he'd be here soon?" Lord Walker's voice penetrated the dull roar of the room.

Brook froze, then turned to the sound of the voice. Lord Walker and Sir Harrington were both lifting glasses in his honor.

"I don't see what you could possibly celebrate," Brook gave as a response to their clinking of glasses.

"Just the beginning of the end," Lord Walker replied.

"What do you mean by that?" Brook asked, taking a seat beside them.

"Just that you already are tired of the chit, the one you defended so valiantly earlier." Lord Walker raised his eyebrows. "An heir and family my ass."

"I did a little research on your wife, Lord Barrington." Sir Harrington nodded over his glass, then took a long sip. "Her father died, leaving the family of five daughters in financial straits. It was luck for both of you that she needed your money, and apparently the Devil's Bachelor was desperate enough for Lord Walker's property that you married the chit. How does it feel? Hmm? Knowing that you rushed into a marriage, probably paying off the family handsomely, only to have all you wanted to gain slipping through your fingers?" Sir Harrington arched his brows, then grinned when Brook didn't respond.

What could Brook say? Sir Harrington was correct . . . yet not. As much as Brook despised the man, he had a good question. How did he feel about it? Frustrated? Certainly. Regretful? No, not at all. The realization was sobering, and brought his current situation into sharper focus. Would he have changed the past and not married Diana? No. What had started as a marriage of convenience was now so much more. He'd gained a friend, a lover, and one day a mother for their children. Diana pushed him, was honest, and wasn't willing to let him be comfortable with his given identity but made him think of himself as more.

"You're missing one detail." Brook leaned forward, waiting till he had both gentlemen's attention. "Your observations are quite astute, but anyone could have uncovered those details. In fact, if you would have asked me, I could have told you. But as frustrating as this situation is, I don't regret any aspect of it. Nothing. My wife is far more of a valuable asset than your estate, and if I had to choose one, I'd choose her. But, since I do not"—he rose and leaned over the table—"I'll be meeting with my solicitor in the morning. I'm sure you'll be hearing from me . . . from us." Brook straightened up, and watched as Lord Walker sputtered.

"And I warned you to never insult my wife again, and you crossed that line." He straightened his jacket.

"You can't mean pistols at dawn," Sir Harrington replied with hesitant horror.

"No. Simply a promise," Brook replied in a calm tone. "That the moment you pass from this life, I will not hesitate to purchase every business venture, every estate not entailed, every scrap of property, and put my name on it, the name of *my* family, so that within a decade of your death, no one will remember you." He paused, letting the words sink in. "It will be as if you never were, and you, who were so proud of your estate, your family name, everything you built, will be mine."

Lord Walker turned an ashen shade of grey.

Sir Harrington's gaze shifted from Brook to Lord Walker and back.

"That will be all." Brook straightened his jacket, and took his leave of White's, listening to the whispers as the threat circulated the room. As he was riding back home in his carriage, he wondered just how many bets were placed on Brook making good on his threat. He didn't mind much, as it turned out his perspective had an elemental shift.

One person's opinion mattered.

And that was the one person who was the most unaware of her power.

That would change; he'd make sure of it. It was a step of faith, but if there was ever someone who deserved his trust, it was Diana.

As the carriage rolled to a stop in front of his house, fear gave way to a slight edge of irritation at fate's ironic joke. He should have known that this marriage of convenience was going to be bloody inconvenient. But it seems that love . . . if this was love . . . made his normally astute senses all jumbled.

It was late, but the need to speak with Diana was strong.

The compulsion to explore this new understanding was overwhelming. He entered the house quietly, and after he started up the stairs he halted and then changed direction to instead visit the library.

Rational thought reminded him that waking her wouldn't lead to a coherent conversation. As he approached the library, he noted a soft glow coming from the doorway. Quickening his pace, he paused at the door and noted the soft form of his wife, reclined on a sofa and reading the second book in the series she'd started the first night they were married. His heart pounded furiously at the sight of her. A thousand new emotions flowed through him, all stronger because of their newness. This had to be love, this breathless need for her, only her. He took a step inside, whispering her name. "Diana."

Jumping at the sound of her name, she almost dropped the book. "Brook." She sat up straight, regarding him. She tucked a loose strand of hair behind her ear; it was a nervous movement and Brook halted his progress.

"I thought you were . . . out." She cleared her throat, her gaze on her lap.

He took a step toward her. "I was."

"I see." She swallowed. "Where?" She glanced up at him then.

Her green eyes were unreadable in the candlelight, but he felt the weight of the question. "White's."

She nodded. When she didn't continue, he walked toward the sofa. Upon reaching it, he lifted her legs from their perch on the sofa and then laid them across his lap as he sat beside her. Gently, he traced up her legs with soft traces of his fingertips. Her breathing came in a soft gasp.

"Turns out, I didn't like spending the night away from

you." He spoke the words with a reverence, with a hope that they wouldn't be rejected.

When she didn't reply, he tickled gently behind her knee and met her gaze. She jerked slightly at his touch and then a smile broke through. "You did, hmm?" She tipped her head to the side, studying him.

"It comes as a surprise to you?" he asked, continuing to trace up her calf, then down to her ankle.

"I—that is, I wasn't sure how you'd feel after the disappointing meeting with Lord Walker," she answered, and then lowered her gaze, her fingers toying with the pages of the book.

"It turns out that while I care about the business with Lord Walker quite a bit . . . I care about you . . . more," he whispered, meeting her gaze.

"That's . . . unexpected," she replied softly.

At this, he chuckled. "Yes, most certainly unexpected."

"But not a bad surprise," she told him, "at least . . . not for me."

"Are you wondering how I feel about an attachment?" he asked, one hand reaching over to tip her chin up so that her lowered gaze would meet his.

"The question had crossed my mind," she answered.

"I think I'm quite lucky, actually." He gave a charming smile as he traced his thumb over her full lower lip, his lips hungry for a taste of it. But he restrained himself. "This wasn't supposed to happen. I don't know how . . . but I just know that it is. And I'm . . . glad." His brow furrowed with the truth of his statement.

"I was so afraid," she murmured, leaning into his hand cupping her jaw. "I thought you would regret me; I thought you already did. It nearly broke my heart."

"There's no regret." Brook couldn't resist kissing her any longer, so he leaned in, savoring the delightful sensation of her soft lips. "Diana." He spoke her name like a thankful prayer.

"No regrets, truly?" Diana asked, her green eyes gazing intently at his.

"Only that I waited this long to find you."

She gave a soft laugh. "Truly, I would expect the Devil's Bachelor to have better answers than something like that."

"Ah, but I'm the Devil's Bachelor no more." He kissed her deeply, searchingly, then nipped at her lower lip playfully. "But just because I'm not a bachelor doesn't mean I've given up my wicked ways."

"Is that so?" Diana asked. "I must say I'm not sorry."

"Hmmm." Brook nibbled the crease between where her lips met, tracing his hand up her calf and dipping under her dressing gown. Her skin prickled with goose bumps under his fingertips as he traced higher and higher till she gasped against his lips. "I suppose my wicked ways have advantages."

"For me. Only for me." She leaned back, her expression fierce, beautiful, and possessive.

It was a powerful emotion, to belong to another person, Brook decided. His body caught fire with the passion it ignited. "Only you. Only ever you," he whispered, then allowed his fingertips to trace her most sensitive spot.

She clenched against him, her breathing coming in short gasps. "But only ever me, all this . . . only mine."

He leaned down and traced his nose against her breast, her aroused tips peeking through her soft robe. "Mine."

"Yours," Diana murmured, her back arching.

Brook found her lips then, kissing her, his hands roaming her body, mapping it with a new appreciation. Want and need burned in him. He gave her one searing kiss, then tore himself from her embrace. Her green eyes were drunk with passion, and it was only the knowledge that he'd soon answer her silent demands for more that allowed him to make the quick trek to the library door to close and lock it.

No distractions, no interruptions. Just love, in every sense of the word.

CHAPTER 16

———◆———

Diana watched Brook approach from the door. With each slow step he tugged at a new piece of clothing. It wasn't long before his body glowed with the flickering candle-light, gloriously naked, yet it was his gaze that melted her from the inside out.

It was a new expression, one that brought to mind a thousand words, but none of them accurate enough to describe how it made her feel: beautiful, loved, special, wanted, needed, like she belonged. His soft touch gently moved the robe from one shoulder as he knelt on the couch beside her. His lips followed his hands, caressing the ex-posed flesh with a slow methodical kiss.

Her eyes closed, the sensations of his love washing over her. Though they had made love every night since their marriage, this was already different. Maybe it was the knowledge that it meant something more than a means to an end. Maybe it was because his attachment to her was known; maybe it was because she wasn't afraid to tell him of her own feelings. Whatever it was, her body ignited with a stronger burn, deeper, greedy for his touch, knowing it was for her, only her.

Brook's fingers traced feather-like caresses down her arms, removing her dressing gown. His lips followed the slow, sensual undressing as he pressed kiss after kiss to her feverish skin. As her robe slid from his hands, he didn't stop but lowered himself, kissing her belly still covered by her night rail. The sensation moved her, and her eyes closed against the love he poured over her with each kiss, each touch. His wicked, delicious hands traced lower, teasing the hem of her night rail with his fingers and a scandalous grin.

"I must say, unwrapping you is far more fun than any present at Christmastime," he teased, his hands sliding her robe up over her knees, higher till it pooled at her waist.

Diana leaned forward, pulling Brook's face forward. His hands paused and she met his lips with a searing kiss, tasting his flavor, caressing his tongue with her own, needing to feel all of him, so much more than his kiss. Needy, she broke the seal of their kiss and removed the last of her night rail. With a smile, she pulled at his shoulders, caressing up to his neck as he followed her command and covered her with his body. Arching into him, she met his lips, losing herself in the millions of sensations of his kiss, his body melting into hers, the feel of their rhythm as he entered her. Her hips arched, her heart pounded, and the world shrunk to just them. His heartbeat pounding against hers, his body becoming one with hers, it was almost too much, yet not enough.

"Do you like this?" Brook adjusted his position, going deeper than before.

Her body clenched around him as she barely gasped a, "Yes."

"I love the way your body responds. You're my personal fantasy, Diana," he murmured against her neck, nipping the flesh.

Diana could hardly breathe for the pleasure of it, her body singing with desire as she found her release, stealing her breath. Her back arched, pressing Brook deeper inside as her body pulsed. Brook groaned against her neck, his breathing hard as his body grew rigid with his own climax. Her sensitive skin prickled with the throb of his release, nearly sending her into another round of pleasure.

When she finally found her breath, she met the gaze of her husband, watching her with rapt attention. His gaze conveyed a thousand words as he mapped her face with a tender devotion. Never before had she felt as treasured, as safe or . . . loved.

"I think I love you, Diana." Brook whispered the words, testing them with his tone as he studied her reaction.

Diana reached up, her hand lacing through his dark hair and tugging softly. "Well, since you seem unsure, I think we only have one course of action," she replied, leaning up to kiss his lips, soft from her earlier attentions.

"I didn't mean—" Brook started, but Diana gave her head a slight shake as she grinned. "I know. But I do think, you know, to make sure, we need to just keeping working at this . . . forever."

At her words, Brook returned her grin. "You always do have the best ideas."

"I'll be sure to remind you of that, often."

"Of that I have no doubt," Brook teased, then dropped a sweet kiss on her nose. "And I don't mind. I'm sure it won't be the last brilliant idea you'll have."

"A husband who admits when his wife is right? How did I get so lucky?" Diana asked with a laugh.

"You didn't get lucky; I did. After all, I married you."

"That you did," Diana whispered. "A marriage of convenience." She gave a small laugh as she rolled her eyes. "That ended up being so much more."

"More than I expected, and certainly far more than I deserve. And I'll just have to spend my life accepting that."

"A hard fate, no doubt," Diana replied with a slight eye roll.

"I'm sure I'll manage." Brook's lips took on a wicked grin as his eyes wolfishly traced lower to her exposed breasts. "There are perks to my penance."

"Penance." Diana repeated the word dryly.

"I've been very wicked, you know," Brook reminded her, leaning down to lick her nipple.

Diana tried to think of a proper response but found she couldn't think past the pleasure, the ecstasy of his touch, of his words as they washed over her.

"No response?" Brook asked as he halted his teasing attentions.

Diana made the only reasonable reply. With a grin, she leaned up, captured his lips, and started to love him all over again.

Because their forever started now.

EPILOGUE

———◆———

Brook watched as his wife chased their younger son around the park beside her childhood home. Surrounded by her sisters and mother, Diana was always aglow with delight. Of course, the glow could also be due to the fact that their third child was due in a few months. For her confinement, she and Brook would adjourn to the countryside in Sussex so that she and their young ones could be with family. It also gave Brook a chance to catch up on his own estate business.

And over the past four years, they'd spent a good amount of time in the country, since Diana was everything her name implied: fertile. Of course, Brook didn't exactly slack in that department either, so it was only natural. As he watched his wife smile and tickle their son, Brook wondered if he could have ever imagined such happiness as he felt in those precious moments. From the Devil's Bachelor to the patriarch of quite the proper English family, it was an unexpected change but one for which he was eternally thankful.

Lord Walker had suffered an apoplexy a few months

after their disagreement, and all the litigation that had tied up the Caribbean estate was dismissed. Brook had taken ownership of the property, and then proceeded to purchase pieces of Walker's estate, making good on his promise of not so long ago. But rather than feeling resentment, Brook found it was a delightful thing to have such a large heritage for his own children to inherit.

Things had changed over the past four years, but one thing hadn't: his love for his wife.

As if sensing his attention on her, Diana glanced over to him and smiled. Patting their son on the head, she turned to come to where Brook watched. "Enjoying your day?" she asked, lacing her hand through his.

"Every moment," he replied, kissing her nose. "Are you tired?"

"Not enough to stop," she replied. "Are you ready to go home?"

"If that means I can have my own time to play with you, then yes," Brook whispered with a devilish grin.

Diana glanced heavenward as if pleading for help, then grinned as she leaned up and kissed his cheek. "Haven't given up your wicked ways yet, hmm?"

"Never," Brook replied, grinning unrepentantly.

"Good. See that you never do," Diana stated. "Give me five minutes." She winked, then slipped her hand away as she headed toward the house.

As Brook studied the house and Diana disappeared inside to say goodbye to her family, he thought back to the day he took a chance and made her an offer.

He had thought he knew what he was doing, but now it was certain that he hadn't a clue.

And he was thankful, because sometimes when you think you need something, you find out you were wrong.

And fate gives you what you actually need.

And he'd never needed anything more than he needed Diana.

Which turned out to be very convenient indeed.